Angelfire Series:
Promises in the Dark

by Karen Wiesner

Writers Exchange E-Publishing
http://www.writers-exchange.com/

Angelfire Series: Promises in the Dark
Copyright 2025 Karen Wiesner
Writers Exchange E-Publishing
PO Box 372
ATHERTON QLD 4883

Published by Writers Exchange E-Publishing
http://www.writers-exchange.com

Cover Artist: Odile Stamanne

The unauthorized reproduction or distribution of this copyrighted work is illegal. Criminal copyright infringement, including infringement without monetary gain, is investigated by the FBI and is punishable by up to 5 (five) years in federal prison and a fine of $250,000.

Names, characters and incidents depicted in this book are products of the author's imagination and are used fictitiously. Any resemblance to actual events, locales, organizations, or persons, living or dead, is entirely coincidental and beyond the intent of the author.

No part of this book may be reproduced or transmitted in any form or any means, electronic or mechanical, including photocopying, recording, or by any information storage and retrieval system, without permission from the publisher.

Chapter 1

At two a.m. on the dot, the head of security initiated last call in the usual pull-the-plug way that provided plenty of grumbling among Knuckleheads' rowdy crowd of biker patrons packed to the rafters. Sapphire Stephenson knew despite the "quiet" without music and television and the shutting down of the kitchen and last-round drinks, it would take a good two hours to get everyone out so the staff could begin closing procedures.

Almost as if she was targeting with a heat-seeking missile, she turned, scanned the low-lit bar and locked on to William Decker. While he was six foot four inches of pure, bronzed muscle--someone who would have stood out in any throng--that wasn't the reason she'd spotted him so easily. He'd deliberately put himself in her line of sight.

Across the space separating them, their eyes locked and Sapphire found herself unable to breathe. She'd been off the last two days, as he had been since their schedules were the same, and they hadn't seen each other since the close-down early Monday morning. *Two days of lecturing myself about this, and I'm right back where I started. I want him so badly, there's no way I'll be able to refuse when he reaches for me the second the doors are locked and we're finally alone--just like last time and the time before and...*

She swallowed in shame and desire, willing herself to break away from his intensely potent, dark eyes telling her the same thing they had since they'd both showed up at six p.m. for their shifts. *He's missed me as badly as I've missed him these past two days.* Sapphire felt choked by her derision to the understatement. *Missed?* She'd *ached* for him, *bled* for him, felt like she might die if she didn't see him soon, immediately. This went so far beyond *missing*. Her throat tightened. She could no longer deny she was in such trouble this time, it'd be a miracle if she could get herself out unscathed.

Ironic what had brought them together in the first place. Two months ago, same old same old, she'd had a big, hairy dude spend an entire shift coming on to her, gunning for what he believed he deserved after all his persistence. Usually, she could handle herself. And, for the times when situations inevitably got tough, she'd taken self-defense classes and kept herself in shape to be able to handle the overzealous creeps that came through the biker bar on a nightly basis. But against one with three-hundred pounds of passion that absolutely refused to be denied, she'd had little chance of escaping on her own. If not for Deck, one of Knucklehead's most loyal patrons, returning because he'd been worried about her, she would have been brutally raped by the a@#hole, too. Deck had said later he'd noticed the guy hovering around her all night, and it'd occurred to him just after he left that he hadn't seen her get in her car and drive away. So he'd turned around to check on her.

As his bartender for at least a decade, Sapphire knew best Deck had been blind-drunk that night, every night. Even still, he'd thought about her, worried, come back to make sure she was safe. He'd shown up in the nick of time, too. As soon as he was off his motorcycle, he'd shouted for her to get out of there, and Sapphire had found out later he'd not only beat her would-be rapist to within an inch of his life but he'd gone to the police and told them everything, describing her attacker in detail. The jerk had been picked up and arrested not long afterward on the basis of Deck's thorough testimony. Though she'd been reeling at what'd almost happened to her, she'd given a statement when the police showed up to talk to her, too.

The next night, when she'd come in to work her shift, she'd found out that her boss Duff, the owner of Knuckleheads, had hired Deck as his head of security. His shifts matched hers every night. Anticipating her insistence that she could handle herself, Duff had given her some story about the fact that Deck had been drifting since his career as the personal bodyguard of former-supermodel Roxanne Hart had ended and she'd cut him loose.

Point of fact, Duff hadn't been bulls@#g about Deck. While William Decker was a man of few words usually, when he was beyond-drunk, he talked. He talked to *Sapphire*. He'd been divulging his heartaches about Roxanne for years--specifically, his protectiveness toward her, maybe warranted by her self-defeating ways as well as the fact that her second bout with cancer was in remission. He talked about the guy Roxanne had been in love with, stupidly, most of her life, how Deck hated Jamie, didn't think this dude was worthy of her.

Without restraint when he was wasted out of his mind, Deck talked about his love for Roxanne, a love that would never die, even if she didn't and would never return his feelings and hitched herself for life to someone else, the way she would soon. She and Jamie Dubois had sent out their wedding invitations not long ago, and somehow Sapphire had warranted one probably because her cousin Cherish was a close friend of Roxanne's and the two of them had been trying to draw Sapphire into their tight-knit circle of friends for the past year.

More than once, Sapphire suspected Deck didn't remember confiding in her about his feelings for Roxanne. *Admitting to me what I don't believe he's ever admitted to* himself, *sober or drunk.*

After Sapphire's near-rape that first night back in the bar, Deck had sobered up, not touching so much as a drop of alcohol, the way most of the staff did as if they were here for the party instead of to work. He personally escorted all female staff to their vehicles at the end of a shift, and Sapphire, as night bar manager, was usually the last employee to leave. They'd been alone the night after Duff hired Deck, once the place was cleared out. She'd intended to tell him she was grateful for his intervention, for thinking about her for some unfathomable reason after he'd left. But he'd reached for her almost as if they'd planned it beforehand.

To this day, she didn't know what he'd intended. Up until that moment, she'd resisted the truth she hadn't wanted to face for years. Attraction had sparked between them long ago, as long as she could remember, maybe from their first meeting. Deck was the very picture of masculinity, of bad-boy mystery. Despite or maybe *because of* his infatuation with an unavailable woman, Sapphire would have had to be dead not to notice him as a man. But she'd been very careful not to let her own attraction become known to him or anyone else. She refused to be with any guy who drank the way Deck did. *And if he's obsessed with another woman... No. No way. I won't compete. I don't share. I don't have the confidence.*

His drinking was an issue that'd bothered her more and more since he sobered up and started working officially for Duff. She'd never met a man like Deck. He drank ten times what most people did yet he didn't "show" it the way other people did. Instead of becoming incapacitated or violent, hard drinking turned him inward and contradictorily seemed to make him *more* sober than the few times he actually was teetotaling. But she knew Deck sober and she knew him dead-drunk. He'd been sober for the past few months, since her rape. *And the protectiveness he's always shown the female staff and patrons, especially me, has been ruling him. That and...*

Though it'd been a long, draining shift and all she wanted to do was collapse, she couldn't seem to look away from him, fully aware what would happen as soon as everyone cleared out of here and the doors were locked behind them. His gaze was telling her in graphic detail that he'd spent every second of this damn long shift thinking about her and the intimate moments they'd spent alone together in the past two months, so hungry for each other their lovemaking had been shockingly swift each time. Almost before it started each time, the reckless act was over and all she could do was sit in the ashes of what had gone far beyond impulsive pleasure. With Deck, she was so easily aroused, both turned on and turned inside out, so contradictorily satisfied and ravenous each time they came together. What could ever be enough?

What does he think of me? I was almost raped that night he saved me. Yet the very next night, all he had to do was reach for me, I was kissing him and damnably out-of-my-mind eager for anything and everything he did to me, then, every single time since...

Her face burning, her body liquid under his scorching gaze, she forced herself to look away and get back to work. *What did he intend that night, that first night? All the ones since?* He *reached for me. Sure, when I kissed him, the rest just rocketed and he took over, but what did he initially intend? A hug?* Sapphire didn't know, couldn't guess, and the past weekend had been torment for her because she'd been in a tug of war with herself. Whatever was between her and Deck couldn't continue. She had a sixteen-year-old daughter she'd spent most of her life trying to be a good role model to. She'd failed often, but it'd been almost a decade since she'd stumbled into a bad romance simply because she ached for physical and emotional intimacy. The shadows of love had somehow convinced her these men had real feelings for her, too, that they weren't just enjoying what she gave freely without sparing a consideration about the future, about her heart when it ended. She hadn't brought home a man since Yasmine was five. Two years after that, she'd stopped getting involved with anyone, period. She'd decided secret trysts were as bad as the blatant ones she'd had when her daughter was too young to understand who the strangers in their apartment were.

What the hell am I doing now? Why can't I stop this? But Sapphire couldn't deny the answer to that. The past two days refused to allow her to hide from the truth. She was already half in love with Deck, despite not having the slightest clue how he felt about her...beyond obviously wanting what they shared together, that was.

Facing that she was in love didn't help, given that things had been so crazy between her and her daughter in the last year. She'd always told herself it wouldn't happen between the two of them. She and Yasmine had been impossibly close. But since her daughter turned fifteen, they fought all the time. They'd become more like mortal enemies than mother and daughter. *She's too much like me, like I was when I was her age. Independent. Rebellious. So sure I was right and the rest of the world was wrong--especially my own mom. But I got pregnant when I was fifteen. I can never forget that, even if I equally can't regret it. Given Yasmine's penchant for choosing all the wrong boyfriends, she could easily do the same sooner or later. She won't let me talk about sex, birth control. She absolutely refuses to let me be a mother to her.*

A knife twisted in Sapphire's heart as she washed glasses with single-minded focus on what she had to do as soon as the bar was closed. *God, do I need to be a good example to Yasmine, now more than ever. But...how can I give this up?* She'd known Deck for so long, more than a decade, yet she'd realized in the last couple days she didn't really know him at all. Not in the definable way she desperately needed right now to justify her feelings. *I'm not ready to give this up, give* him *up. Even if it's wrong, even if he doesn't feel anything for me beyond protectiveness and sexual desire...how can I* turn away from him? Why do I want what's happening here to be more? Can it be? Why does it have to feel so damn intense? I was sick, missing him these past two days. Why? Why should that have been the case? We don't have a relationship beyond coworkers and incredible, obsessive sex. Not anything romantic, tender. Bottom line, I'm hooked. I'm so hooked, I can't get myself to break away even when I don't have a choice about it.*

Last call was greeted grudgingly, but Deck was decisive and few dared challenge him. Sapphire could feel herself growing anxious as the bouncers escorted clients out, the wait staff cleaned up, and she and the barbacks reviewed receipts, distributed tips, closed out the register, melted the ice in the bin, cleaned the glassware, and put caps back on the bottles. Deck had an easier time of getting the staff out than she ever had, when they all seemed to want a drink or ten for the road after their shifts.

When the door was finally locked, the bar empty save for the two of them, she sensed Deck even before she turned to see him leaning against the wall next to the front door, looking at her with an expression she wanted to translate straight from his mouth. She could hardly catch her breath at the fierce arousal in his eyes. *What would he have done if I'd actually called him the times I picked up the phone to do just that these past two days? Was he thinking about me, too? Wanting to be together?*

She couldn't get herself to believe anything but that he would have met her anywhere, anytime if she had called him. *Why? And what would have I said? That what we have isn't enough for me? Or the opposite--that it's over and we can't continue a purely sexual relationship because...because I'm in love and I don't know what he feels for me...*

Sapphire tried desperately to draw in oxygen, but he was smiling, shy and sexy when he reached for her. "Hey, beautiful," he murmured in that sandpaper rumble that she sometimes felt right down inside her like a kick to her nerve ending.

God, he was handsome and intensely masculine--from his thick, closely-cropped dark hair and jet-black bedroom eyes--all the way down his trim, muscular body she couldn't imagine ever getting enough of with her eyes, her fingers, her own body.

Tears stung her eyes painfully. She wanted him to tell her something, *anything*, personal so badly, she could hardly stand it. The touch of his well-shaped, full mouth against hers--sweet and soft and so vital, she felt injected with a drug--sent her straight out of her head. She barely registered what she was doing or thinking or longing for. She only kissed him back, grateful that he still wanted her. She'd yearned for him, for this perfection of body on body, clawing for both during her days off. Without inhibition, she gave of herself, reveling in his stoned gazes, words, and groans.

What felt like only moments later, she was spiraling back to earth, lying naked beneath him on the sofa in the locked office. For a long time, they tried to catch their breath. The only sound was their heartbeats and panting.

Surprising her because it wasn't his modus operandi, he kissed her throat, her chin, the line of her jaw lingeringly. Under his breath, he muttered, "Don't rush off, babe."

She always did. *Like this is the scene of our crime.* She couldn't get away fast enough because she knew if she dawdled she wouldn't be able to get herself to leave him. She'd beg him to tell her he loved her, too. And because she usually cried all the way home, sometimes longer. Those tears wouldn't be denied for long. He'd always allowed her to flee. They'd wordlessly get dressed. He'd follow her out to her car to make sure she left his sight safe and sound. Before he put her in her car, he kissed her tenderly until she wanted to weep--and she barely made it until she was inside the driver's seat, pulling away, helplessly looking back at him standing firmly in place until she was gone. He always let her go without protest when she said, "I have to go."

Deck kissed her again before nuzzling her cheek with his nose, pressing his forehead to hers until their eyelashes all but merged with their eyes closed, their lips mere millimeters apart. Sapphire opened her mouth, a sob so close to the surface, only a miracle following desperate prayer kept it in check. Why was he being so gentle, like he didn't want this to end, didn't want her to leave him even for a few hours? He'd always let her go before. Maybe his eyes had been saying something else, but he hadn't voiced what she'd wanted to believe his gaze spoke louder than words: *Don't go. Don't leave me. Ever.*

Equally unexpected was the sentence coming out of her mouth when he drew back and she opened her eyes to see him looking down into her face. "What you must think of me."

He frowned, his thick brows furrowing above his sexy eyes. Why wouldn't he be confused? Her sentiment wasn't exactly appropriate after what they'd just done. "What do you mean?"

"This whole thing started..." Her face filled with lava-like heat. "...'cause some a@#hole almost raped me. You stopped him. And the next night, I... *This*..."

If possible, he seemed more bewildered, even a little concerned. "Your choice, baby. That's the point, isn't it?"

"*He* wasn't my choice," she said, as if that fact wasn't obvious--and just what Deck said: the point.

"I could see that from the first. You fought him. Did your damndest, too."

Sapphire held her breath, irrationally hoping he would follow the logic through to its conclusion. Miraculously, he did. "I assumed you chose what happened between us, Sapphire. You didn't fight. If you had…"

"I didn't. I couldn't. I don't want to. Not with you."

His hand cradled the side of her face and a shy, sexy grin lifted the corners of his mouth until she wanted to scream out loud that she loved him. "Then it's all good, babe," he said softly and kissed her, his mouth unhurried.

She wanted to say, "Don't make me love you more." Instead, she swallowed the lump in her throat at his unexpected after-sex affection that felt more like love than a bid for more of the same. "What about you, Deck?" she whispered. "What do you want?"

He smiled at her again, no subterfuge in his eyes. "Missed you, baby. Last two days were an eternity. Thought about you. So damn much, I didn't think I was gonna make it until we were alone tonight."

I wasn't alone, alone in my feelings. I wasn't…

Deck swore when the tears she could no longer dam up behind the protective wall she couldn't seem to shore up for long around him broke free in a flood. "What? What's this? What's going on, honey?"

"I don't know," she said, barely coherent and gasping, partially because he was so much bigger than her and suddenly his weight on her was suffocating.

Seeming to realize, he shifted so they were laying side by side, his arms around her so she couldn't have broken free even if she wanted to. "Tell me, Sapphire. Do you not want me to miss you?"

If you wanted an opening to end this, here it is. You've been down this road too many times to count. All this will come to is a bad ending, now or later. Might as well get it over with. Regret is all that's left now.

Sapphire realized she was out of control when she opened her mouth to say one thing and the opposite issued forth unbidden again. "I missed you. Days off... *Hell*. You probably don't wanna hear this."

He laughed in disbelief. "Lady, why *wouldn't* I wanna hear that?"

"'Cause..." She couldn't speak through the tears. She felt anger rise inside her at her own inability to stop.

"You just told me what I wanna hear, honey," he said, his smile tentative and unsure. "Don't change your mind now."

He'd said exactly what she wanted to hear, even if she shouldn't, but her overemotional state only intensified at this perfect balm. The way he held her, cradling her face and kissing her like he wanted to make everything better...*like he loves me... Why does he feel so right? Only him?*

She'd never known how to handle an excess of feelings like this, so she did what she knew. She kissed him, stroked him, but he surprised her with his reaction even then. He halted her seductive hand on him. "Did somebody hurt you, Sapphire? Tell me."

She swallowed, allowing him to hold her hand. "I'm not the type for one-night stands. You don't have to believe me…"

"Of course I believe you."

"Why 'of course'?"

"Baby, I've been coming to this joint for a long time. No man gets the time of day with you. You're willing to be friendly. Line in the sand. Nobody dares cross."

"You noticed?"

"I'm a lotta things, but I'm not blind."

Even before he'd officially started working for Duff, that had been his strength. He saw trouble in advance and he dispelled it. He was good at noticing everything around him, despite the crowded room. He was damn good at his job. "Deck…you…and I…are you just…?" She sucked air like grasping for courage. "…taking what you can get with me?"

Almost sheepishly, he admitted, "Yeah. Hell, yeah."

She reeled back. "You are?"

"I'm taking what you're giving. *Whatever* you're giving, as long as you're giving it, babe."

It wasn't exactly a declaration of love, nor was it the "player" response she'd anticipated because she'd heard it so many times before. "What's happening between us?" she asked, reaching up to wipe her cheeks.

"Hell if I know."

"You don't know?"

"Do you?" he returned.

"No." How could she hold his confusion against him?

"That mean we have to stop?" he asked point-blank.

She hadn't expected the question, let alone the obvious agony behind it, matching his expression.

"I'm... Deck, I'm a mother. I have a daughter. A teenage daughter. I can't be doing this. I have to be an example. A *good* one." *Who are you kidding? That ship has sailed.*

"So you wanna stop?"

The opening was there a second time. To end it. Do what she knew she needed to. She'd always chosen the wrong guys. Bouncers were the worst. They were corrupt, taking drugs from customers, keeping it for themselves, spending their whole shift drunk, banging every woman they could get while they were supposed to be working. She'd never known one of them to have morals. They cheated and lied right to everyone's faces. But the whole bar scene was made up of people like them. Maybe bouncers were the worst, but they were just part of the ensemble. *Until Deck. He's the head bouncer, but he's nothing like them.*

She found herself lifting her hands to stroke the carve-in-marble cheekbones, the thicker-on-top silken hair on his head, the muscled cords in his neck. *I don't want to go back. To being bartender and counselor to this big-tipping drunk. But even then he was my protector.*

"Damn that I can't read your mind, honey," he muttered almost savagely.

"Join the club."

Despite a ghost of a smile crossing his face, the question was out there, larger than life, screaming between them. *Do you wanna stop?*

"I don't want to have an affair. I...I don't know what's going on. But I don't want it to stop."

He grinned. "You're reading my mind."

"Yeah?" she asked.

"Yeah."

He sighed, shifting again so this time she was over him. His mouth was an inch away, close enough to make her crazy as their bodies settled together like pieces of a puzzle. Just like that, he was rock hard again. "I want you, Sapphire. Hell, that's about all I know these days. All I can think about is the way you kissed me that first time. And all the times afterward. You're so damn beautiful. So hot. Can't believe you even looked at a guy like me."

"You're not oblivious to your effect on the women around you," she insisted.

He shrugged them off. "You're not like them. Tell me what you want, babe. That's what I want."

Was he so willing? *How can I live without him? Without these caresses that get me through my dull, pointless life? Fill my every waking and dreaming thought? Even when he's not close to me, I'm thinking about him, whether he's at the back of my mind or at the front.* "Will you give me what I want, Deck?" she asked in a mere whisper.

"Anything."

He spoke without hesitation, without reluctance, with a kind of tormented passion that made her weak and needy. *He said he's taking what I'm giving--whatever I'm giving, as long as I'm giving it. But he didn't say that like he was playing me. He said it like he's loving me.*

When he kissed her again, Sapphire thought of love. She felt love. His mouth was tender, sweet. *He's not like so many other guys that drift into Knuckleheads. He's not smooth. He's awkward, if anything, especially around beautiful women. Around me...*

If the thought of ending this whatever-they-were-doing made her cry, the way he made love to her only solidified that urge. Instead of burning them both out in a blaze of glory, he kissed her, caressed her, put his imprint on every part of her body, savoring her as much as he seemed to be memorizing her. The things he whispered--urging her to lose herself in his erotic attention--freed her, made her burn, brought her to shattering culmination over and over. His kisses felt like a demarcation that she wanted more than anything in the world. *I already belong to you, the way I've never belonged to anyone else because this only comes from something mutual and right, something perfect. But is it love? What the hell is love? How should I know? But I know it's not about sneaking around, stealing something we shouldn't let ourselves give or take.*

When he finally gave in to his own gratification, he pulled her tightly down to him, groaning in her ear, "Come home with me, Sapphire. I want you in my bed. I wanna hold you all night...morning, whatever. I don't wanna let you go."

The back of her eyes felt hot again. Even as she thought, *Tell me you love me*, she knew he had. He just had, in a way she couldn't refute. When she pressed her face against him, closing her eyes tightly against the raging storm behind them, he held her even tighter, stealing her breath from her lungs, and said, "You have to go, don't you? Your daughter?"

She nodded even as she wanted him to try talking her out of

leaving him instead of going home with him where they could hold each other for all the hours they had off-shift.

They got dressed and he walked her to her car, kissing her lingeringly there, obviously not wanting to release her for anything in the world. Once she was behind her steering wheel, the window rolled down, he leaned in and said that maddening thing: "Whatever you want, honey."

He's taking what he can get with me, whatever I'll give him. Because the sex is so damn good between us, and there's no reason he shouldn't take what I'm giving him so freely? It was more than that for him. The last few hours proved that.

Maybe he loves me, too. Never mind that there were so many obstacles that needed to be considered if whatever-this-was extended into more than an undefined affair. She didn't want to think about that future--not yet. Not until he stopped insisting he'd give her "whatever you want, honey" and told her straight out what *he* wanted from *her*.

Chapter 2

What the hell did any of it mean? William Decker reeled mentally as Sapphire drove away. The last hour played itself back, shredding him again at her tears, the physical mind-blow of the sex, her unsatisfying allusions that didn't give him anywhere the amount of comfort and promise he hadn't realized until the past two, lonely-as-hell days that he'd been looking for from her. That Sapphire and Sapphire alone did this to him shouldn't have surprised him. Something about the woman had left him unhinged, exposed, without a prayer since he met her more than ten years ago.

The night she'd almost been raped, he'd realized so poignantly that he'd used his feelings for Rox to shut everyone else out. Black and white, he'd faced that night that he didn't want to keep holding the world at arms' length. Not with Sapphire anyhow. Maybe he should have run from her when he woke up after every drunken stupor and wondered if he'd said more than he should, a hell of a lot more--to Sapphire, his own personal shrink slash bartender.

He'd followed her home after beating the crap out of her attacker and then set the police on the bastard's trail. During those hours he kept secret watch over her inside her apartment building, he'd been bombarded to the point where he'd felt eaten alive by his need for her--to see her, touch her, make sure she was okay. He would have given anything just to catch a glimpse. And, hell, he'd told himself he'd be grateful if she gave him verbal confirmation she was intact, but even then it wouldn't have been nearly enough.

Duff had offered him the job of head of security as soon as Decker told him what'd happened, and he'd seen his way clear to watching Sapphire Stephenson like a hawk from then on. The money didn't hurt. Hell, he'd been aware he couldn't keep pissing his savings away on booze for a while. He had an incentive to make good on the idea of a change. He'd never cared much about having a career per se. He worked because he had to, because no damn way he'd ever let himself be a burden on anyone. That wasn't his way. The fact of the matter was, Duff and his wife loved Sapphire like a daughter and Duff had been trying to get Decker on board as an official, paid, head bouncer for years--mainly to watch over Sapphire, who drew attention as much because she was drop-dead gorgeous as because she was hard to get.

His first night on the job, the night after Sapphire's near rape, Decker found himself alone with her. About all he could remember now about the *before* was that he'd intended to tell her he was glad she was okay, glad her would-be rapist was behind bars. The words had flew from his mind, long gone, at the look in her eyes. He'd reached for her. She'd kissed him. That was all, all it took. After, he'd been floored, through and through.

He decided to give up the booze. That was the hell of the whole thing. He couldn't remember the last time he'd gone a single day without ending it face-down, skunk-drunk. With new incentive, he'd barely thought about Rox and the job he'd been paid for and would've done for free all those years as her bodyguard. She had Doobs, the sorry bastard who was finally treating her the way she deserved and they were getting married. She'd live, she'd beat cancer a second time, and Decker had had nothing for himself. Nothing but the booze, and a s@#load of it, at that. He'd used most of his savings to keep himself sauced. But that night when Sapphire had almost come to harm... *Hell, I knew she was inside me. I wasn't a mile from the bar before I realized I hadn't seen her get in her car and drive away. I couldn't get the thought out of my head. So I turned around. God, thank God I did.*

She's always been inside me. I knew it then. Now, I crave her like a damn drug. She's all I want, all I think about. I go to work, sober the way I haven't been for most of my life and not missing the juice one damn bit, just to see her, to see her after everybody else is gone. I'll take everything she gives me. I'd sell my soul for a glimpse of her, not that my soul is worth much.

S@#t, why'd I have to be right? He'd suspected for a while now that whatever they were doing wouldn't last much longer. She was coming to her senses, discovering he wasn't what she wanted...

Decker turned and walked to his motorcycle when Sapphire's car disappeared and there was nothing left for him to look after. If he was a stupid man, he'd let himself believe her tears meant she wanted what they had to last, not end, just like he did and didn't feel he had a right to push for. He wasn't in her league, but it hadn't stopped him from wanting every piece of her. The past two days were still too fresh. He might have been going through the DTs for how bad he'd missed her. Waking or sleeping, the memory of her low, husky voice, the scent of sesame oil she spread all over her body made him insane. He couldn't stop remembering the look in her sultry, indigo blue eyes. He'd forgotten how to sleep without dreaming of her, how to be awake without longing for her.

What the hell would she have done if he'd called her during their time off work, apart, told her the truth? He hadn't taken the risk because he'd rather have something than nothing with her, even if it wasn't everything he wanted.

"I missed you. Days off... Hell."

Decker braced himself against his Harley. The memory of those words had the same impact on him in recall as when she'd first said them tonight and made him so damn happy.

"I don't want to have an affair. I don't know what's going on. But I don't want it to stop."

She'd given him exactly what he wanted, yet... *Not enough. What* could *be enough with her?*

Deck raised his hand and the scent of her slammed into him, blowing him apart all over again. His whole body reacted viscerally. He felt like a damn fool because he'd been through this before. And it'd shattered him the first time so he was almost beyond recognition--even to himself. With Rox, he'd been vaguely aware he'd purposely set his heart on an unavailable woman, all because his life mottos were so ingrained, he acted on them without conscious thought. He couldn't be hurt by something he hadn't invested himself in and better to not love, to lose what he never had to begin with.

Sapphire... S@#t, I'm invested. Before our relationship changed a couple months ago, I was drunk. I was a drunk. That was pretty much my life. Getting soaked, being soaked, on my way to soaked. The few times I wasn't boozing, I worked on my house, my car, my bike. I haven't thought about doing any of that since I reached for Sapphire and she kissed me.

Hell, she's an angel. She's always been so far above anybody who passes through Knuckleheads. I can't have an angel. I'm the devil. It's a miracle I was allowed to touch her once, let alone the countless times in the past two months. Why does it have to be over? Not real? Not permanent? Without her, I'm languishing until she's there, in my sights, and I can see her again. Can function. I'm alive. Breathing. Happy. Worth something. I love...

Love. He didn't use that word to describe or define anything in his life. Love had meant too little. It was secondary, unimportant. Sure as hell couldn't consider what he felt for Sapphire as something as insignificant and mundane as love. She consumed him to the point where he was used up totally each time they were together and then she left him high and dry. Yet she renewed him, too. She gave him a purpose he'd never had before in his life.

He drove home, thinking about everything, wondering why she'd consider for one minute he'd think badly of *her* because some cretin had tried to take what he didn't deserve from her. Decker had no doubt she'd been treated badly all her life by men just like that one. She didn't trust anybody in Knuckleheads, not that she should. She wouldn't believe a man could be honest, true, loyal.

She's seen the opposite, too much. Why do I want to be different in her book? Why do I think I can be? That I wanna be more than anything?

The five-minute drive told him what he already knew. He wouldn't be able to sleep. He'd lay there wishing Sapphire was with him, letting him do all the things he'd done to her in Duff's office. There was no peace in this sanctuary he'd built for himself because he'd needed a place to crash when Rox gently told him to go home, get a life--often--all the years he worked for her and she wanted him to face the facts about them ever being together.

He pulled off his jacket, set his cell phone on the counter, wanting to call Sapphire but aware she'd probably do the noble thing next time they talked or saw each other. She thought the best thing was to pull herself out of this fire before she got burned, save herself so she didn't end up being a bad example to her kid. What right did he have to tell her he'd rather die than let her go because it'd be better that way?

"Will you give me what I want?"

Deck reached behind him and pulled down the bottle of whiskey inside the cupboard in front of him. He took a long swig, draining a third of the bottle in one go, barely feeling the kick, then thrust it back and shut the door. He drew in a deep breath, his gaze falling on the invitation in the next room on the coffee table. The rest of his mail from the past week was piled up there. Rox and Doobs' wedding invite was on top. He hadn't even opened it. Just carried it in with the mail one day and dropped the stack there. Though he'd hated the guy she loved, he had to admit that, in the past six months, Doobs--Jamie Dubois--had proved he was loyal to

Rox, truly loved her and would take care of her.

She's not my responsibility anymore. I don't want any part of that world anymore. I could have had her once or twice, too, but I always knew it'd be temporary, not worth the hell, heartache and regret I'd live with afterward. Story of my life. Evaluating the potential termination, anticipating a bad end every damn time.

He didn't want to accept that this time, but he already knew he wouldn't come out where he wanted to with Sapphire. Never mind that he'd been happy. Damn strange situation for him. The past couple months, he'd never felt like this before. He had Sapphire to look forward to after long shifts. Their time alone together couldn't be enough, but it was what he wanted. *Be glad. She ends it, I don't walk around like some damned deranged monkey anymore. But... Ahh, it's never mattered what I wanted before, least of all for myself. Why should it matter now?*

It shouldn't have mattered. But it did. Decker couldn't help wondering how much influence he had over the situation. Over Sapphire.

I don't want this to end. I'm not ready to let her go, and I'm not sure I'll ever be. Maybe in our hours apart she'll decide it's time to stop this. My only hope is that she wasn't sure. When we were together, she seemed uncertain that ending it was for the best. And I'm gonna do everything in my power to sway her toward the other side. If I don't...what the hell else is there for me? She's all I want. She feels like all I've ever wanted.

Chapter 3

On the drive to her apartment, Sapphire felt trapped in her own head and then suffocated as she let herself inside. As if the days without Deck hadn't been hard enough, now she found herself caught up in limbo that she'd brought about with her own inability to end it. Where were they now? Nothing had been resolved, yet she knew she couldn't continue this thing between them even if she couldn't let it go either.

After she hung her coat and purse on the tree then moved to lean against the archway leading into the living room to remove one shoe at a time, she was completely unprepared for what she stumbled on. Her daughter lay asleep on the sofa with the bad boy who'd been vexing Sapphire's existence since her little girl had started dating him. Yasmine had turned sixteen only a few months before, and this guy was twenty-one *at least*, despite what her daughter claimed with almost smug dismissal. While they were both fully dressed, the way they were tangled together couldn't have been more intimate if they had been naked.

Her head exploded, and Sapphire started screaming before she fully knew what she was saying. Both of them jumped, and Yasmine started her annoying pacification as she sat up, blinking away sleep. The tone of her voice as she said entirely too calmly, "Mom, you're overreacting. We fell asleep. End of story" made Sapphire even more frenzied.

She met Justice's sultry eyes and pointed the way to the door, saying in no uncertain terms, "Get out of my house and don't ever come back, you son of a bitch."

Just like Yasmine, his lack of concern in the face of her fury only fed the fire inside her. He leaned down to pull on his boots, in no particular hurry, until Sapphire threw his heavy jacket at him and went to yank open the front door.

Yasmine made a show of kissing him and saying she'd see him later. Justice's gaze flickered over Sapphire, skimming over her Knuckleheads tank top stretched over her full breasts as he meandering toward the door she held.

"Don't come back," Sapphire repeated.

"Whatever," he said like he could care less.

He thought she was a bitch--good, the reaction was better than his initial one. The first time Sapphire had met him, he'd spent an inordinate amount of time checking her out in a lewd, highly approving way that made her want to belt him in the mouth. That was right before he'd realized she was Yasmine's mother.

Before he'd even cleared the door, she slammed it shut with all her strength and locked it. Then she whirled on her daughter.

"God, you're such a presumptuous bitch," Yasmine said, picking up the empty soda cans on the glass coffee table and sweeping past her into the kitchen.

Sapphire was well-aware that setting herself against this relationship she knew for a fact wouldn't last was only creating more enmity between her and her daughter. But she'd known her share of guys like Justice with his leather jacket, too-long tousled hair, the heavy five-o'clock shadow. He was used to getting sex and getting it as often as he wanted from whoever he wanted. He wouldn't care that her daughter was barely sixteen (and had been fifteen when they started dating three months ago) and believed herself to be in love--justifying anything and everything in her young, romantic mind. That Yasmine was too beautiful for her own good with a body that grown women would kill for didn't help in the least.

Any more than it did me. All my life I got attention that I didn't hate. And I still do. Yasmine had Sapphire's waist-length, lion's mane of just-tumbled-out-of-bed, sable-brown hair. She had her midnight-blue, seductive eyes. She had the curvy yet lithe, deeply tanned body with mile-long legs, tiny waist and big chest. In almost contradiction, her face was the picture of sweet, innocent sensuality. She'd had "boyfriends" since she was old enough to know that boys were opposite of girls and easily manipulated into doing whatever she wanted them to. Unfortunately, her daughter also fell in love too easily, with all the wrong guys, and inevitably the relationships came to a bad end, leaving her depressed to the point of suicide.

I raised her better than my mother raised me. I wanted

everything to be different for her. I wanted to show her she could make something of herself. Hell, I didn't want her to get pregnant and end up forced into a life she didn't want with a jerk who was just using her and felt pressured to "do the right thing" at first but quickly regretted his only act of decency, just like Justice will in the same situation.

"We talked about this, Yasmine. He's not allowed here when I'm not home." Sapphire followed her daughter into the cramped kitchen, watching her toss the cans into the recycling bin.

"Oh, Mom, we just fell asleep. It happens. It's not the end of the world. You're overreacting the way you always do."

"And, if I go through the trash, I'm not going to find a condom or two?"

Yasmine leveled a glare at her that contradictorily managed to be both bored and hateful. "You're such a hypocrite, Mom." With that, she stalked out of the room and, a moment later, Sapphire heard the lock on her bedroom door click.

Sapphire closed her eyes against the poison her daughter had leveled straight into her heart with unerring accuracy. Shuddering, she yanked out a chair at the kitchen table and sat bent over her knees. *I am the very definition of a hypocrite. But all these years I worked so hard to set a good example for my daughter...do I get no credit for that?*

Sighing, she acknowledged that maybe she didn't deserve any. She hadn't been a saint in all this time. She hadn't had any kind of romantic relationship in almost ten years, hadn't brought anyone to the house, but there'd been rare times that she'd given in to her physical needs--at a guy's place, in the bar with Deck. She hadn't wanted Yasmine to know about those embarrassing weaknesses, that she'd craved sex and intimacy, affection even if it wasn't love.

But I wanted *to be loved. Though I refused to bring anyone home with me ever again, I couldn't deny I still had needs. I held out until they gave me the words I wanted. Maybe it'd taken them a couple nights of wooing, of waking up to the fact that I wouldn't give out until they gave me words of love. Small price for them to pay. Stupid. The times I got the words 'I love you', I knew almost before the sweat dried that I'd been told what I wanted to hear just so they could get me into bed. Somehow I felt like I wasn't a bad example even then. Idiot. I was still justifying the sex with love that wasn't real.*

With Deck, I don't know what the hell I'm dealing with. I've never felt anything like this, and I've never known a man like him.

She was lying to herself again. The past two days proved that she did know what she was dealing with. She knew straight out she was in love with this guy in a way that was so much bigger and stronger and strangling than anything she'd been in before. In the past two days, while Yasmine had been doing a lot of babysitting, she'd been alone and couldn't hide from herself what she was going through. She'd felt like she might die without Deck, without him touching her, looking at her, making her whole with his mere presence. *I've never thought I'd go insane for needing a man, not even when I was a teenager and stupid beyond belief. God, I wish he was here now. Wish I was with him, in his bed, in his arms…*

She forced herself to her feet, going to retrieve the wad of tips she'd brought in today, more than $250, and put it in the tip jar in the cupboard where Yasmine could take what she needed. Not that her daughter needed too much these days. Her babysitting jobs had provided her a growing nest-egg since she was twelve. She'd had enough to buy her own used but decent car after she got her license a few months ago, enough to fill her closet with a wardrobe of clothes and shoes and jewelry that was unequalled. Despite all her extravagance, Yasmine had done the unthinkable and followed Sapphire's advice when she started babysitting by setting aside half of everything she made in a savings account slated for college.

Closing the cupboard door, Sapphire's gaze landed on the trash. She could have checked it for condoms, just as she'd insisted she could, but she didn't want to. She didn't want to know. *I am a hypocrite. My own daughter can see it better than anyone. An hour ago, I was doing exactly what I accused her of doing with Justice--sinfully. How can I tell her she's wrong to make love with someone she believes she's in love with when...?* She groaned, her eyes burning, her head and heart whirling with too much emotion.

Though she'd all but lost her sense of smell years ago, she knew the stink of the bar was on her and she took a shower as soon as she got home most mornings. Before long, her feelings overwhelmed her again under the unrelenting spray. Feelings for Yasmine, who'd been her whole life since she'd been born, and now they could never see eye to eye. For Deck because her longing for him was a noose around her neck. For her own failures, always the same ones, over and over like a broken record.

When she pulled her blanket over her and closed her eyes, her eyes swollen from tears, she imagined the tender way Deck had held her on the sofa in Duff's office. For a moment, she almost experienced tangible comfort at the memory. But the same recollection told her she had to end the relationship and soon. Like a mantra she'd lived by for ten years, she recited her own truth in her head, *I have to be an example for Yasmine. She needs that, even if she thinks she doesn't, and even if I'm not a great example because I've failed to live up to my own vows.*

Sapphire swallowed. *How does she even know I'm a hypocrite? I haven't brought a man here in so long, ever since she was five years old and asked who the guy in my bed was in that totally innocent, not concerned way that slapped me in the face and led me to take a hard look at my life and my responsibility to her. I've never been so ashamed. I knew I had to change, to stop needing validation and the love that I only get in the form of sex. I never wanted Yasmine to see me the way I saw my Mom when she had the nerve to lecture me about boyfriends and sex.*

Sleep claimed her hard and ruthlessly, so she woke hours later with a headache, her face and eyes feeling like glue had dried over them. After she got up and pulled on ragged shorts and a comfortable old t-shirt torn at the shoulder, she splashed cold water over the hot skin of her cheeks and under-eyes. Then she put on makeup and fixed her hair, listening and guessing in the silence that Yasmine had left hours ago--to babysit, see friends, or to see *him*. She verified the situation once she went out and saw that her daughter's keys were gone from their hook.

Although she didn't feel particularly hungry herself, she started dinner, since Yasmine would probably come home later and want something. As she worked, enjoying the methodical task because it felt like she was doing something proactive, she thought about calling her cousin Cherish when she was done, confiding in her and her alone the situation with Deck. Somehow she thought Cherish would understand what she was going through. Cherish had fallen in love with the brother of a colleague and close friend. She'd done this in the space of time it took most people to brush their teeth, and Sapphire had to admit she'd been hard on her about the rush. Cherish had barely known the guy and she'd willingly given everything she was to him overnight. *I was so hard on her. I wanted to protect her. I advised her to take it slow, get to know him.* But Cherish and Ty were married now, and Sapphire had never seen her cousin look so happy. *I was wrong. I didn't take my own advice. I jumped in head-first with Deck.*

Not sure she was ready to share this with anyone, not even her cousin and best friend, Sapphire poured herself a cup of the strong-enough-to-grow-hair-on-the-chest black coffee and took it out to the tiny, second-floor balcony that was a joker's idea of a patio. There wasn't room for a single chair. She stood in the tiny space. The day was warm and full of sunshine that hurt her sore eyes. She leaned over the railing, for a long minute seeing nothing of her surroundings--her view of the parking lot wasn't really worth focusing on anyway. But abruptly she saw a cherry red Harley Sportster, not something that was generally parked in the building lot. Half-sitting on the motorcycle was Deck. He seemed to be waiting for her to notice him.

Straightening in shock, she called down, "What are you doing here, Deck?"

He stood fully, looking a little guilty, so she had to wonder just how long he'd been here, whether he'd intended to just stand out in the lot or actually try to see her. He'd obviously changed clothes so he'd been home long enough to do that, probably showered, too.

Lord, I'm so weak. The worst thing I can do is be with him, be alone with him. But I've never been so glad to see anyone in my life. He looks like heaven. So damn sexy...

Once more, her mouth was saying the opposite of what she was thinking. "Do you wanna come up?"

Two minutes later, he was following her into her apartment and she was grudgingly, finitely aware that her daughter could be home at any time now. How the hell would she explain this?

"How long have you been here?" she asked him, turning to face him after she put her cup on the kitchen table.

His gaze shifted to the shoulder of the ripped t-shirt that fell down her arm. "'while," he muttered thickly, longing in his eyes once he turned them loose on her. "Couldn't stop thinking about you, babe."

She could hardly inhale for the tightness in her chest. Could he tell how much she'd been crying since they parted? "Why?"

He reached forward, grazing his fingers over her bared shoulder. Her breasts reacted to his proximity instantly, swelling, tightening.

"You didn't seem okay. You don't now."

His hand continued up the side of her neck and cradled her face. Sapphire couldn't resist another second. She knew for a fact that he wanted to have her nearer, and she felt like she was torturing herself, needing him to hold her. The sob building in her throat escaped, sounding strangled, as he dragged her against him and held her so tight, she couldn't deny she felt whole again, as if she belonged here, pressed against his heavily thudding heart. Even as he became gloriously aroused, she couldn't escape the sense of rightness, being with him again. Days might as well have gone by since their separation.

Her mouth was spluttering out the reverse of what was in her mind. "I have to be an example for my daughter. I can't keep doing this, Deck. I know you can't understand this. There's no reason you should."

"I was afraid you were gonna say that."

"Then why did you come here?" She lifted her chin so she could look up into his face.

He leaned down, drawing her tear-stained face closer to his with his hand on her jaw. He laughed but there was nothing like mirth in the raw, helpless sound. "Talk you out of it?" He suggested it like he wasn't even sure himself.

Sapphire swallowed. "Why? Because if you don't, you won't be able to 'get what you can' from me anymore?"

He sighed. "Something like that. Babe, I'm well aware I'm outta your league and I'm no better than all the losers who pass through Knuckleheads. I don't have any promises to make you. I don't have a f@#in' clue what I'm doing here. I just…"

Never before had she wanted to understand a person's tormented expression so badly. She wanted desperately to believe she was seeing love in Deck's face. Love for her.

He shook his head. "I don't wanna let you go, Sapphire. That's all. I'm away from you for a second, and I want you so damn bad I can't breathe. Can't sleep. Can't eat. I don't give a f@#k about anything but the time I spend with you."

She closed her eyes. "I know. I'm the same." She lowered her head and pressed her face against his shirt, breathing in the clean scent. She wanted to hold on to him so tightly, he could never let her go. *How can I trust myself? I've never been right about any of this. I assume too much. I need the words, but the words have always been lies.*

Laying her palms flat against his rock hard waist, she offered, "For the record, I don't consider it a matter of worth. You're a good guy, Deck. The best in a place like Knuckleheads."

"Maybe. But only in comparison."

"No. In fact."

She caught his small smile when she dared look him in the eye.

"Glad you think so, honey."

"I've made mistakes. Too many. I've spent the past ten years trying not to make another. But I've failed."

"Ten years is a hell of a long time to be alone, baby."

"For you, too. I know you're…you're not like the other bouncers. Never caught you banging some dumb twit too drunk to remember *it* or *you* in the morning. But I know you've been propositioned. Often. You deflect the attention."

"Not interested. In them. But you… Honey, I understand you don't wanna make another mistake. What am I if not a mistake?"

"It's not a reflection on you. It's me. I…I got pregnant when I was fifteen. And now I have a sixteen-year-old daughter."

Deck raised an eyebrow that wasn't surprised. "Get the feeling you've been paying for that since you conceived."

"Who else?" She'd made the mistake of thinking she was invincible. That she could act and never have to face any consequences. Ironically, the outcome had been the best thing that'd ever happened to her. Yasmine was her life.

"You ever brought anybody home, where your daughter is?" he asked.

"Yes. But not since she was five. But…I haven't been perfect. I feel things. I want things. I need them. I tell myself I'm in love. I tell myself they love me."

"Hooking up is normal for you?"

Instantly, she went rigid, feeling incendiary heat fill her face. "No!"

She would have pulled back, but she realized by his expression, by the words he'd chosen and his tone, that he was trying to prove her goodness--as if he already believed the best about her. She halted when he put a finger on her lips. "You're preaching to the choir, honey. You said it yourself. It's not normal for you to hook up, get what you need to get off. And I'm not hooking up with you, babe. I promise you I'm not."

"You said you were taking what you can get."

He laughed. "Ah, Sapphire, what else do sinners do when an angel appears and offers heaven? I want everything you're giving. But I don't hook up either. It's not my style. But I'm not perfect either. You're right that I get propositioned. A lot. Just like you do at work. I don't hook up. You don't. You're not just some lay. But, no joke, babe, even if this *was* just sex, it'd be exceptional. Worth fighting to keep going."

Sapphire drew in a shaky inhale. "It's not just sex for you?" she asked hopefully.

"Ain't gonna lie. I'm strung out on you, baby, on everything about you. But that's only part of the buzz. I feel like I'm living for you. You're the only thing that matters to me anymore."

She tried to breathe, tried to think, tried to speak. He'd said almost everything she'd ever wanted and feared in the same paragraph. Unfortunately, he backtracked a second later. "Look, whatever you want here, Sapphire. I didn't come here to hand you some obligation. If you wanna quit me--"

Quitting Deck--it felt like sticking her head into a guillotine. "You'd be okay if I did?"

"F@#k no. Nothing would be worth nothing, ya know? But it's your choice."

God, he frustrated her. "Deck..." His name bled out of her, even as she reached for him, pulling his mouth down to hers. He clutched her to him, kissing her hard and deep, a sense of relief in the gesture, but more. So much more. She felt in his kiss exactly what she could have if she allowed this to continue. He would fill her, hard and deep and so full, she might never be empty again.

As their mouths worked, his hands slid up to cradle her butt, slipping beneath the worn denim she wore without anything beneath. He groaned out loud, bring his fingers to her center, and she went weak, liquid, as his body hardened against her again.

Clarity stabbed into her mind a second before she would have let go completely, and she gasped, "My daughter..."

His hands reluctantly stilled. "I know. Okay."

"Okay...? What does that mean?"

"Whatever you want it to mean."

Sapphire's teeth clenched. "Dammit, Deck, I wanna hear what *you* want from me."

"Anything. Anything that means I'm a part of your life. She's part of your life. She means the world to you. So, if I can have you in whatever way you'll allow, she's part of my life, too. She'll mean the world to me. What matters to you matters to me."

She couldn't help staring at him in disbelief. No man had ever said anything like it to her before. It was a promise without precedence that assured a future.

Her arms around his neck, she held his face against hers. "I'm scared, Deck." *I'm already so far in love with you, but I can't see the bottom. It's so dark. You're giving me just enough light for one step ahead at a time.*

"Don't be. I'd never let anybody hurt you. Not even me."

She remembered the look on his face the night he rescued her from that rapist. She believed him without a single doubt.

Chapter 4

The expression of hope on her face gave Decker all the encouragement he needed. He kissed her the way he'd wanted to since she all but killed him by leaving him hours ago. Something he scoffed at as pure unadulterated joy but wanted so badly gave him the freedom to ease her against the wall nearby, slide his hands around her warm, familiar curves, fitting her against his hard, unrelenting lines.

Damn, he loved her body. She was tall for a woman, tiny at the waist, but her breasts were amazingly full and ripe, her hips softly rounded. He'd spent more years than he could remember wanting to touch this gorgeous woman.

Knowing he couldn't go too far, not here and not now, he ended by tucking his fingers beneath the fall of her sexy-as-hell hair, against her graceful neck. The thick strands felt like satin against his fingers, and he pressed himself against her again, feeling her body respond. Tight, soft. *Caramel. Sticky and sweet... Ah, dammit.* He couldn't keep his hands from inching down over the silken column on her throat. She broke away from his mouth, panting, lifting her neck to give him free access. His eyes gobbled up the skin exposed by her torn t-shirt, one beautiful, bare breast, rock hard from inadvertent stimulation.

He hadn't come here for this. Truth be told, he hadn't been able to talk himself out of coming, even if just to be close to her, whether he could see her or not. He hadn't anticipated getting this far, being in her apartment, holding her again. She hadn't given him anything like a promise for a future together, but he already knew he was taking her response that way. He couldn't help himself.

Sapphire's hands slid over his wide shoulders, coming back in a triangle to his chest, stroking him almost unconsciously the same way he wanted to stroke her, making him painfully aroused as he imagined taking her in his mouth the way he had hours ago. *Strawberries. She always reminds me of strawberries. But she tastes like spicy, hot sesame oil...*

"Yasmine's not here. She probably won't be back until she thinks I've left for work at five. We had a fight. She never comes back until I'm gone when we've fought."

Decker closed his eyes, battling himself until he knew for sure he could move in. "Sure she won't show up?"

"Yes."

The word was little more than a gasp. Maybe she was going against her own vows, but he couldn't doubt she was giving him permission. He slid the t-shirt over her head without preface, his mouth and fingers latching on to her breasts. Her gasp told him exactly what he wanted to hear. *She wants me as bad as I want her. I couldn't be happier.* "I respect the hell out of you, lady. That's the truth," he murmured as he laved her just the way he knew she liked.

"Do you?" She looked amused by his choice of words, but her eyes slid closed, her fingers slipping into his hair, guiding him as she gasped and he sensed her excitement building to the critical point. One hand easily passed beneath the waist of her jean shorts and he was drawing her moans from her almost effortlessly with his consummate strokes. From their first time together, he'd seemed to be able to bring her to this place easily. Exhilaration competed inside him with humility at his power over her. She did the same to him.

He held her when her legs gave out with her shudders that left her weak. He kissed her mouth tenderly. "I don't wanna do anything you're gonna regret later. I don't have any regrets with you. I never will. Whatever we do or don't do together."

"You actually believe that, don't you?" she asked without energy.

"'hundred percent, baby." *Even if it means I don't get mine here…*

Her smile was emotional. "You're not like any man I've known, Deck. Not just bouncers. *Any* man. That must be why."

"Why what?" He couldn't help focusing on her wet, lush mouth, wanting it open under his again. The memory of her saying her daughter would be gone for more than two hours was torture.

"Why I feel this way about you," she offered on a gasp that sounded like a sob. Her eyes were sparkling like the gems she was named after. "I honestly don't know how to have a legitimate relationship. I wanna get to know you. Outside the bar. Outside...the incredible sex."

He raised an eyebrow. "You know more about this relationship stuff than I do. I'm going on instinct."

"Instinct?"

"Sounds less wimpy than 'following my heart', doesn't it?"

Instead of laughing with him, her gaze went totally hazy, maybe even romantic. *Damn, I could die wanting her about now. And I ain't got one ounce of self-control. Not when I wanna prove to her that I'm worth her effort, her hope, her desire.*

Like a lamb, he didn't utter a word or protest when she took his hand and led him into her bedroom, locking the door behind them. Maybe he could have kept being noble, but the second she shed her little short shorts with not a blessed thing under them, he didn't have the willpower of a push-over kid. He was on fire, beyond reason or objection. He knew if he didn't touch her, didn't kiss her and love her the way they both needed, he'd burst right out of his skin. He'd never been more excited in his life, and he unapologetically took all the liberties he'd been denied on that pitifully, cramped couch in Duff's office. Just like he suspected she would, she gave herself to him the way he'd only dreamed of in the last couple months. She was both aggressive and vulnerable, giving as good as she got, not seeing anything as taboo between them.

"Don't cut me loose, babe," he gasped when she lowered herself onto his chest, panting raggedly, as decimated as he was by their loving. "Whatever you do, don't do that."

She brushed her face against his like a cat seeking stroking.

Everything inside him tensed, anticipating she was about to say something that would hurt him bad enough to bleed. *Not now, babe. Don't say it now, when I'm never gonna get the taste of you outta my mouth, your scent out of my nose, this passion for you out of my veins. It's replaced all the blood in my body, and it's all that's keeping me alive now.*

"I'm not...*it's* not about that. But I don't think we should...at work. After work. Anymore."

For a second, hope flared. "But you don't mean it's over? You just mean, not there?"

For a second, her eyes could have been a neon sign broadcasting her feelings for him. "I don't want it to be over. I want to do this right, Deck. I know that's not what you want. But I need to get to know you, you to get to know me. I need to--"

Justify the sex. He didn't doubt she meant that without the words. "Okay. Get to know each other. Date?" The word wasn't the most familiar to him. He knew it, but he had little if any experience with the reality. He didn't date. He never had. Like Sapphire said, his relationships were all short-term. Short enough that, more often than not, he didn't know something as basic as a name before he'd tripped the woman's fuse, gotten what he needed, end of story.

"Yes. Whatever that means."

"Okay. Works for me. But I'm guessing you mean spending time together without sex?"

Just like that, her face and neck and even part of her chest went deep-red with obvious shame. He didn't want her to feel it. Not with him. "I'm just asking, babe. I think we both needed...that." *We didn't exactly pledge promise rings, but as close as people like us* are gonna get. And we both needed the unfettered, down-and-dirty sex once we made it mutual. I needed to know she belongs to me. I want her to want me enough to long for the same.

Hell, this is as new as it gets for me.

"I love what we do, Deck," she murmured softy. "You know I'd be lying if I claimed I didn't. I'm like the Fourth of July with you. But I can't just do this stuff like I did when I was a teenager. I have responsibilities now."

She didn't add, *"Don't take advantage of how easily you can get me off."* He heard the unspoken words anyway, and the uninhibited look on her face, the heat in her eyes as he'd pleasured her came back to him, making him go hard again. She had to know it was his regular state of being while he was around her for any amount of time. Didn't matter that they'd already satisfied each other once. That'd never be enough. "I understand. I respect you. I'll try to keep myself in check. Can't blame a guy for fallin' off the wagon sometimes though."

"I'm not saying we can't kiss…touch…"

Her tone was positively breathy. He knew exactly where both led. From the minute he'd reached for her, she'd kissed him two months ago, neither of them could stop at a kiss or a touch. Half the time, he was in a daze, half-insane, and didn't come to his senses until it was over. He suspected she'd gone through the same in all this time. Still, he murmured, "Drowning man's happy with a life preserver."

When she scooted down and laid her head on his chest, he had to mentally restrain himself from moving his hands where they wanted to go on her amazing body, claiming all of her for his own.

Somehow, he was hungrier than before, given that he might not have her again for whatever duration of time she stipulated.

"Aren't you going to ask how long?" she asked a moment later, clearly surprised, as if she'd been anticipating him asking that since he agreed to her rules.

While he would have been lying if he'd told her he hadn't been thinking about it, he didn't bother mentioning it. He slid his hand to the back of her neck, behind the heavy waterfall of hair. "I'm just happy to know we'll have something. The rest'll figure itself out."

She lifted her head once more, her expression worried. "Are you sure you're okay with this? You won't get...bored?"

Looking up into her beautiful face, her body draped over his, exactly where he wanted it a hundred percent of the time from now on, he wanted to promise her the moon and every star in the sky besides.

Huskily, because he felt like his heart was in a vice, he told her only a fraction of what was tangling up inside him, so knotted he wasn't sure he'd ever sort it out. "Known you for longer than a decade, babe. Bored's the one thing I've *never* been where you're concerned."

Chapter 5

She heard Deck suck in his breath as her hand, her fingers cradled to stroke him and she realized she'd gotten carried away in her half-asleep state when he muttered, "You're not making this no sex-thing very easy, babe."

She was doing the opposite of no-sex, and she found the willpower to get herself to stop was so elusive as to be nonexistent. She didn't want to get out of bed, didn't want to get dressed, didn't want this to be the last time they were together like this for the foreseeable future. Like it or not, sex and love were so entwined for her, she'd realized from puberty that she'd face trouble. Everything Deck said and did made her want to love him, to make love to him and show him how much she loved him. She wanted to drive him out of his head with pleasure. And she very nearly had.

"Trust me, I don't mind," he offered in a barely-there, strangled tone. "That..." She hadn't realized he'd been watching her mouth on his chest while her strokes had brought him to the edge of insanity. "You feel so damn good."

He did, too. They'd been relegated to Duff's miserable sofa for months. There'd been no freedom to touch, move, explore. How often had she thought of just this? Her own bed, his, doing anything and everything they wanted to each other? "I'm sorry. I'm a hypocrite."

He drew her up, groaning his disappointment when their hips collided, nestled, so close to the heaven she'd woke up craving. Their faces pressed together, cheek to cheek. She could feel the effort it took for him not to take her body, already well-prepared to receive him, instead of soothing her, refusing to let her believe for a second he thought of her with the same lack of respect she thought of herself.

"When I got home from work this morning, I found my daughter on the couch with her boyfriend who's much older than the eighteen she claims. They were dressed, just sleeping, but…" She shook her head, inhaling and exhaling too fast for the gesture to be relieving. "I was fifteen when I got pregnant, and the guy who did it was hardly my first. How can I tell my daughter anything she does is wrong, knowing that?"

"So you and me…this is the same as relationships you've had with creeps before you got pregnant, after, when your daughter was a little girl and you brought 'em home?"

She sighed. "In setup, no. It's not, Deck. But it feels different."

"Why?" he asked in a voice that didn't allow her to hedge or deflect. He wanted an answer.

Sapphire swallowed, shaking her head in surprise at his

pursuit of the subject. "*I feel different, and you...you're telling me some of what I want to hear, the way they all did just to get what they wanted. Once they got a couple throw-downs with me...well, those words proved to be false when they disappeared. But you...you're not telling me *everything* I want to hear. Damn you. You're only telling me enough to make me want more." Her body was straining toward his, searching for fulfillment she was only too aware he must be aching for about now.

He lifted his hand to her chin as if to prevent her from looking away, should she be considering doing that. "What do you wanna hear, babe?"

"I don't know," she lied, and she knew without a doubt he was equally aware she was lying to both of them.

She'd never seen his thickly-fringed, dark eyes look this unflinching as they held her gaze. "You wanna hear I love you, Sapphire? I honestly don't know what the hell love is and if I knew, it was never good. You don't wanna know what 'love's' been in my life. It's been pain. F@#ed up. Let's just leave it at that. It ain't unicorns and fairies skipping through the clouds hand-in-hand and fartin' magic dust over everything."

She stared at him with her mouth open in shock at the funny, gross, and deeply disturbing, cynical thing he'd said. Despite saying "leave it at that", she sensed the agony he didn't want to discuss behind his cynicism. She'd known of its existence for years, since he'd started drinking so much, he actually confided in her when he was bombed out of his head. She couldn't imagine he comprehended what he was saying then, let alone remembered any of it once his darkest emotions were out in the open between them.

"If love is being utterly consumed with wanting another person, living just to see her, feel her, get her to look your way with softness, hoping to hell for anything she'll give you 'cause it's all that's gonna get you through another s@#t day… If love is praying to God she's not gonna break your heart in two by ending it--today, tomorrow, any other f@#in' day 'cause if she's not in your life, if you're not seeing her, then you're dead, or might as well be and should just dig the damn grave and be done with it…"

Sapphire stopped breathing, almost terrified at the level of desperation he was speaking incomprehensibly with. She understood that in his lifetime he'd experienced clawing, tearing, ruthless need--he'd felt it for Roxanne Hart. Was it possible for him to feel it for someone else?

For me?

"If all that's what love is, then yeah, I love you, Sapphire. I'm f@#in' outta my head with it where you're concerned."

The dam burst with her sob, and she hugged him so hard, she all but saw her life pass before her eyes. She'd never been so happy, so scared because nothing had ever, ever gone right for her in this department, and she couldn't imagine how it could work out this time. But she wanted to believe it could, more than anything. Though the words were on the tip of her tongue and she wanted to give him her verbal love, too, something stopped her before she could, some scar of reminder. At the same time, she kissed him and gave herself to him the way she wanted to every day for the rest of her life.

Just this, just today. Then I'll do the right thing.

Deck turned them over and she couldn't protest in the least.

She rose to meet him, not surprised at how insanely she wanted him inside her. Feeling wild, she guided him, and he entered her slowly, waiting to see her reaction, groaning when she accepted him readily and met his next deep thrust. Suddenly, she didn't give a damn about her no-sex rule, that she didn't have the slightest clue how either of them could be strong enough to enforce it later. She only knew she needed this, needed him, and he needed their love, too. She'd heard him talk about the shadows of loveless life he'd endured, the kind of torture he'd put up with as if he deserved it for self-imagined crimes.

"I want to be good for you, Deck," she whispered as they strove together, holding tightly to words they'd spoken, words that were driving them, hearts and minds and bodies. Their fulfillment was mutual, taken as one, cries guttural and mingled, arms wrapped around each other, absorbing the force of each other's shudders with their own flesh. "I want to make you happier than you've ever been in your life."

"Check it off the list, babe. You did that when you didn't pitch me overboard today."

"And took away 'what you can get'? Well, kind of."

He chuckled and the sexy rawness of the sound sent her spiraling higher into the stratosphere they'd reached together. She ground herself against him, where he was still inside, driving her toward the pinnacle again. She clutched him fiercely, unable to breathe and not caring if she ever did again. She didn't want to think about separating herself from him, physically or in any other way, but he gave her what she knew she'd ask for later even in the aftermath of deep, life-changing love. "I won't keep pushing you for this, Sapphire, even if keeping my hands off you feels like a death sentence. Damned if I don't try when I can't take it anymore…but 's long as I'm in your cage, I'm happy with the accommodations."

"Am I in a cage, too?" she asked softly, shivering slightly at such a barbaric image when things had been so loving and sweet a moment ago.

"Aren't we all, one way or another? We start building it from the day we're born. Whether we're willing to stay in it or not, alone or with somebody else…that's the question, the answer and purpose, our happy and our grief."

Unable to stop herself, she flinched at the sentiments expressed and he instinctively tightened his arms around her. *I've known him a long time, he's told me things--probably more things than he's ever told another person, has even let himself admit in his own head. But I've barely skimmed the surface of this man. He's damaged, maybe more than I am by my experiences. Can I heal him? Can our love? Will he allow either to? Or will he ultimately become harder, more jaded and scarred? And what do I know about healing anyone anyway?*

Sapphire didn't know what love was any more than Deck did. She'd had little experience with it, beyond the broken and bleeding kind, where the only thing left was to pick through the ashes and piece together armor from shattered bones and badly repaired scars. She didn't know where to start with loving and healing him. Even as she anticipated failure, she couldn't turn away. He'd created a possibility inside her--the possibility that the love they made together could be different, better, good.

Worth the risk.

Chapter 6

"Are you hungry? I made dinner. It won't take long to warm it up."

He nodded, watching her get up and start dressing for work without moving himself. "Wish we didn't have to go to work." All he wanted to do was be with her, even if he could only look at her like this. *Wasted our days off. We could've been together every second. Next time and all the ones after, for damn sure.*

"I wish that every night of my life," Sapphire said almost as if she wasn't thinking.

"You hate your job, don't you?"

She shrugged. "It was all I was ever good at."

"Doubt that."

"It's true. I don't have any work experience. I didn't do well in school. I found a tavern owner willing to teach me the ropes at bartending. That's what I've been doing ever since. But, yeah, I hate it. I hate that it feels wrong to do it. I'm serving alcohol to a bunch of people who already have no self-worth and sure as hell won't get it by drinking this s@#t. I thought about going back to school and trying to learn a skill so I can get a better job, but the fact is I make more money as a bartender. You can't beat the tips. I'd rather save for Yasmine, so she can go to college. You went to college for a while, didn't you?"

He laughed at the memory. "A year. Wasn't my thing." He'd gone because there hadn't been a reason not to. He'd gotten good grades, qualified for a few scholarships, grants, and he didn't have the slightest idea what he wanted to do with his life after high school. The jobs he'd had up to that point were dead-end. He'd done them just to ensure he'd have a future when he got out of foster care. He'd met Roxanne his first year at Columbia. She got discovered as a fashion model and pursued a career as a rock star-- all while she was getting a music degree. In his second semester, Decker realized he didn't care a damn about higher education and sure didn't care to pay off countless debts in that regard. He dropped out after completing his first year. When Rox offered him a job as her personal bodyguard, he'd taken it and realized he was actually good at something enough to make a living off it. But he'd never doubted Rox paid him ten times what he deserved, in part because she didn't give a damn about money herself. He told himself she wanted him to be a part of her life. Even if his services were in demand all the time he was protecting her, he was bound to her by more than a job.

He got up and dressed in two seconds flat while Sapphire brushed her hair. As soon as he could, he put his arms around her from the back and hugged her. "You sure I should stay for dinner?

Your daughter won't show up unexpectedly?"

She shook her head, embracing him with her arms over his. "I told you, we just had a fight. She always stays away until I'm at work after one of our blow-ups. Come on. I'll feed you."

Decker couldn't help grinning. He'd never had anyone to take care of him, and the idea that Sapphire wanted to made him feel like a little kid with the toy of the century.

"Sit down," she said once they reached the kitchen. "Coffee?"

"Sure."

She poured some from the pot into a big, shiny black mug that probably held three full cups of liquid. "Black, right?"

Since he'd started working for Duff, he'd been drinking strong black coffee during his shift. "Thanks."

While he sipped the stiff brew, he watched her move around the tidy kitchen, a little surprised because a hot beauty like Sapphire Stephenson shouldn't have looked so at home performing domestic duties. Yet she did. *There is something motherly about her. I see it in the way she treats the customers. I always assumed it was deliberate--kept the SOBs from getting the wrong idea about her. But I think now it's who she is. She's a caretaker. She feels like she's giving those bruisers poison with every drink. No wonder she hates her job.*

"Need any help?"

"Nope. I've got it."

While she set the table, warming up the food on the stove instead of in the microwave, which was about the only way he knew how to cook, he got up with his coffee and looked around the apartment. It was a nice place, nicer for how neat she kept it and her own little touches, and he realized those were exactly what his own house was missing. He'd bought the fixer-upper years ago mostly to give himself something to when Rox didn't need him. He'd spent the last twenty years renovating it. No matter how much work he did inside and out, something about the house always felt unfinished to him. He didn't mind much because it was just a place to crash for him. But he knew what was missing now, after all this time. *A woman's touch. Sapphire's.*

Decker glanced back at her from the living room archway, feeling soft in a foreign way as he watched her ease in handling the tasks she'd set herself. *What I wouldn't give to have her in my house. My bed. Permanently.* The extreme thought bothered him because he'd never had any like it before.

Over the table, the ceiling lamp flickered and then one of the bulbs burned out with a loud pop. Sapphire glanced up at it, then turned toward a cupboard and got out a new bulb. Grabbing a step-stool from near the fridge, she unfolded it.

"Let me get it," Decker offered.

She was already climbing up the steps to the lamp. "I'm using to fixing everything around here. Superintendent is lazy. He takes a few weeks just to get up here to look at anything. I've taught myself how to do everything. I've even done some plumbing on my own." She handed him the spent bulb and screwed in the fresh one.

The respect he already held for her multiplied, but he'd sensed she was more than capable of handling herself in every situation, and to do it with the kind of calm finesse he admired. Despite that, he couldn't help thinking he wanted to take care of her. He wanted to do the so-called manly tasks in her life so she wouldn't have to do everything herself.

As she went back to what she was doing, Decker felt a strange kind of expansion inside him as his experience stretched in a direction that was more than a little unfamiliar to a bachelor who'd never so much as had a long-term lover.

His gaze fell on the fridge, covered with little notes and knickknacks, but mostly with photographs. He knew in an instant the girl in the pictures was her daughter. "She looks just like you," he said, pulling off one of the two of them together. Neither of them looked wildly happy. Obviously someone had forced them to "say cheese" when they weren't getting along.

Sapphire smiled slightly, looking over his arm at the print he held. "You should see pictures of me at her age. We could be twins. Other than the obvious age difference."

"Obvious, hell. You look more like her sister."

She laughed, and he stated emphatically, "That's not the first time someone's said that to you."

"No. I guess not. I'm sure old age will hit me suddenly when I turn forty, like it did my mom. This is ready."

Decker pushed the photograph back up under the magnet, then went to sit down. "Looks like a feast, babe. Thanks."

"Do you want anything else to drink?"

He shook his head. "This is more than I usually have." He dug into the pork chop right away, not surprised that it was better than anything he'd ever tasted before, moist and flavorful, the rice and vegetables served with it obviously fresh, from scratch, the hard way.

"The rice is spicy--"

"Just how I like it. This is incredible. Never met anybody who was a good cook."

She smiled, looking pleased. "I'm guessing you don't cook yourself."

"If you call opening a can, pouring it into a bowl and nuking it in the microwave for a couple minutes 'cooking', sure."

She laughed. "You own a house, though, don't you? What do you do with the kitchen if you don't cook in it?"

Decker raised an eyebrow. "Pass through it on the way to the living room?" he suggested. While she laughed again, he added, "I use the fridge. That's about it."

"I bet it's nice. You renovated it yourself, didn't you?"

"From the ground up, pretty much, yeah. You ever wanna break in the kitchen, you've got an open invitation. You'd be the first."

Her expression was disturbed when she asked, "The first?"

"I've never had any visitors there."

"What? Not even one?"

"Nah."

"But…your friends?"

He shook his head. "Don't got a lotta friends. Duff and Bev. With him in a wheelchair, it's easier to get together at their place."

"What about Roxanne?"

He snorted. "She knows where I live. Never been there. That's not how it worked. She called. I jumped. Never any reason to change it up. Where'd you learn to cook?"

Her expression told him she'd noticed his abrupt halt to the conversation, and he wanted to take it back or insist there was no reason to talk about something that didn't matter in the least anymore. He just couldn't get himself to do it. Instead, he focused on enjoying the meal she'd cooked.

"My mom. Sort of. She wasn't the greatest or most diverse cook, but everything she made was edible. She taught me mostly because she wanted to pass the torch to me so she wouldn't have to do all the cooking. By the time I was twelve, I was doing pretty much all the cooking in the house."

"Was it just the two of you?"

She nodded. "My parents divorced before I was born. I suspect my Mom got pregnant with me, and she did confirm that a few years ago. The split was bad. She didn't want anything to do with him, and she refused to even put his name on the birth certificate. She gave me her maiden name. She burned everything associated with him, wouldn't talk about him at all, and took me to where her family was in Atlantic City. I grew up with her men coming and going through the apartment, obviously sleeping with her. She never tried to hide it. She worked hard. I don't fault her on that count. She worked two jobs, so when she got time off, she got bombed. A good night off included smoking, drinking and getting laid. I knew that about her all my life. I was on my own a lot. And I followed in her footsteps. Smoked, drank, and got involved with bad boys that were far too old for me. Just like her, I chose all the wrong ones."

"Your daughter's old man?" Decker guessed. He'd had the feeling her story would be something like this.

"Cougar was the worst. He was twenty-two when I was fifteen, and, when I got pregnant... Let's just say my mom was a total bitch, just like my daughter thinks I am. She was married by this time. Finally found one bad guy willing to reform, so she could quit her job and be taken care of like some soft princess. So…I got pregnant. Coug up and decided we should get married, and my mom became the ultimate champion for his cause, even when being tied down to one woman with a daughter on the way proved to be the worst thing for a guy like him."

Decker's jaw tightened, bracing for the impact he knew was coming.

"By the time Yasmine was born, I'd fallen in love with her, and Coug had gone completely the other way. He was cheating all the time, drinking, not doing anything to help me raise or pay for our life together. When he was really drunk, he got violent. Even mildly drunk, he was abusive and…I could never win. I wasn't strong enough. He was in that state almost all the time. Mom watched Yasmine during the day and I got a job as a bartender. But Coug used to come into the bar every night I worked, and he was so jealous if anyone so much as looked at me."

"If?"

She conceded the point with the inclination of her head, adding, "I lost the weight after having Yasmine almost right away."

"He took his jealousy out on you, didn't he?"

"Me and anybody who stepped into his territory. After a year, I couldn't take it anymore. I was afraid he'd hurt Yasmine, too. He hadn't dared up to that point, but I couldn't trust him. I asked my mom to help me divorce him, but she thought I should make the best of it, claimed Coug was trying hard to do right. I guess I knew then escaping him wouldn't be easy."

"Couldn't do right by you but didn't want anybody else to have you either?"

"Yes. Exactly. And, even after he consented to the divorce, he started coming around my mom's house, threatening her, so her husband was afraid for her, so he asked me to leave and take Yasmine anywhere that wouldn't bring my mom to harm. I didn't have any money or anywhere to go. My step-father told me how to find my real father, and I ran there with Yasmine. He lived in Albany. I took his last name. He tried to help, but Coug found us barely a year later. I don't know how. Maybe he threatened my mom and her husband told him just to get him off her. Mostly, my real dad didn't want to get involved in the whole thing, even after or maybe because Coug punished me--the worst he'd ever done-- when he found us. My dad didn't want anything to do with me after that, so he did the same thing my step-father had. He told me I had a cousin, my mom's sister's daughter, and I met Cherish after I fled Albany in the middle of the night to get away from Coug. She let us stay with her for a while, but I knew it wouldn't be long before he found out about her, and I didn't want her to get hurt, so I had to leave. I moved around a lot for the next five years or so, got jobs where I could. Eventually, I came to Staten Island, Duff gave me the job, and he was protective of me, so that helped. I'd learned how to defend myself. But I was always ready to run if I needed to."

Decker had sensed her situation was something like this, that a bastard or ten had happened to put her on the defense. She'd stopped relying on anyone else to take care of her or her daughter. His hands were clenched so tight, hearing all this, the knuckles were dead-white. The memory of seeing that SOB But I was always ready to run if I needed to. "trying to rape her flooded over him like an exothermic reaction. His only goal had been to destroy the one who'd dared to touch her without permission. "Where is the bastard now?" he asked, not willing to stand for her living in fear for a single second more. He would personally see to it that her ex- would pay for every single last threatening word he'd spoken to make her fear him, every wrong touch on her delicate skin.

"Dead."

"Dead?" he choked. "You're sure about that?"

"Five years ago, Cherish found his obituary. I'd showed her a picture and told her his name so she'd be on her guard if he ever showed up. But he was killed in a motorcycle accident--on Staten Island. I don't know how long he was there, if he knew where we were, though I doubt he did because he would have come after me in a heartbeat." She took a deep breath. "I didn't wish him dead, other than the times he hurt me and acted like I belonged to him personally, but I was glad when I found out he was. I couldn't help it. For the first time since I was fifteen, I was free."

"He got better than he deserved. Saves me the trouble," Decker muttered viciously.

Sapphire laughed, but there was something else, something dark, in her expression, prompting him to ask, "What?"

"I suppose when I was her age I was just like my daughter is now. I talked about my dad all the time and acted like he was some saint compared to my mom. Now I know better."

Perspective. She's not saying it, but I can guess that her daughter must talk about her dad a lot, acting like she wishes the SOB was taking care of her instead of her mom. Decker had little personal experience, but he'd heard teenagers were nothing if not insensitive. Sapphire's daughter had cut her deeply, and not just with the normal teenage rebellion stuff.

"My daughter is a good person, Deck. Don't judge her by our relationship. She's a mature, responsible, kind teenager. I'm really proud of her. She takes care of herself and everyone around her the way I always taught her to."

He pushed away the plate he'd cleared, then moved around to sit in the chair next to her. "You got a lot going on, honey."

She turned to him, then leaned toward him until he put his arm around her. "Are you sorry you're getting yourself into this with me? The further it goes on, the more you'll realize I'm a basket-case. Especially lately."

He drew her chin toward him so she was looking at him. "I don't have any regrets. I told you I won't. I've spent the past ten years wanting to know what makes you tick, lady. I don't judge you or your daughter. I know you raised her right, the best you could, especially on your own. You won't give yourself any credit for it, not when she's this age. But she is a teenager. Sure doesn't make it easy on a parent but, with or without a cause, it's how they work in this age group. And it don't matter if you're sixteen or sixty--you're always gonna believe you know *more* and *better* than your own parents."

Her smile was soft. "True. I know you're right."

Decker leaned in and kissed her, trying to tell her how he was feeling, after she'd confided in him about her past, in the gesture. "You're one hell of a woman, Sapphire. You know that, don't you?"

Her expression was wry. "Most days I'm not so sure."

"Well, get used to hearing it often 'cause I won't let you get away with believing anything but the truth. No one's gonna utter a bad word about you in my hearing, especially you."

He kissed her again, and she sighed, her eyes sparkling with unshed tears when he eased back. She averted her touched gaze to her half-full plate. "What about you, Deck? Did you have Mike and Carol Brady for parents?" She laughed, obviously knowing he hadn't had anything of the kind when she added, "Not?"

Reaching across the table, he snagged his mug and gulped the cool coffee. "Far from," he offered because she was looking at him expectantly while she chewed. "Don't have a clue which drug dealer provided the sperm, but my old lady's an addict. Always has been, always will be. I was taken away from her right after I was born. Raised by foster families who didn't give a s@#t about anything but the next paycheck my presence brought 'em. My real mom's in and out of my life, mostly to make herself feel better and to try to con me into paying for her bad habits. I won't. Never stops her from wheedling for it, of course. Not much more to tell."

The sympathy in her eyes reminded him too much of Rox and all her compassion, something he'd never wanted from her and turned away from every damn time she offered it. A little stunned, Decker's mind felt boggled when he realized he wanted tenderness from Sapphire, craved it almost as bad as he did her beautiful body.

"I'm sorry, baby," she murmured.

Sapphire had laid her life story out for him. No doubt about it, her mom hadn't been a prize, but she'd stuck around, made some effort, half-assed as it was. Compared to his old lady, Sapphire could easily win Mother of the Year. Even without the unfair comparison, she loved her daughter and everything she did was to protect and teach her the right way, a better way, than she'd experienced growing up. She'd never believe good of herself, given the current state of affairs with her daughter, but Decker saw the best in her. He'd seen it before she told him. Yasmine had been *wanted*. The difference that made in a person's life... *S@#t. I'd like to convince myself I'm over my old lady's flake on me, but I'll never be. I came into this f@#d-up life unwanted. Not a whole hell of a lot has changed in the thirty-five years since either.*

"When did you last see her?" Sapphire asked.

He shrugged. "Couple months ago. She tends to show up like clockwork in that way. Miracle she hasn't ODed. Permanently." Feeling numb, he drained the rest of his coffee. "What about you? You see your parents?"

"Honestly? No. Most days, I don't hold anything against them. But the fact is, I don't have much common with them. They've never showed much interest in having a relationship with me, with Yasmine. Can't be bothered to leave their comfortable homes to visit me or their granddaughter. But I talk to my mother sporadically."

She ended on a bitter note that told him what she wasn't saying in so many words: If her daughter wasn't embraced fully by everyone in her life, Sapphire had no use for that person. *I better listen up. She's willing to include me in her life as long as I include Yasmine in mine. Whatever that means. Frankly, I don't have a clue what it does mean, but for Sapphire there's nothing I wouldn't do. We'll figure it out.*

She looked up at the clock on the wall, sighed deeply upon

seeing how little time they had left, and went to work on finishing her dinner. This job, their shift, left little time to do anything outside of it. Having a private life was all but impossible, but if they'd been working different shifts in the same place it would have been so much worse. He'd never cared about his hours, the "fullness" of his life until Sapphire kissed him and made him want a life with her. Almost unconsciously, he spoke his thoughts out loud, "If we'd done this last Monday, we could've spent our days off together."

"I know. I wish we had, too."

"You were all I could think about. But I suppose days off are really the only time you spend with your daughter."

"Are you kidding?" she scoffed. "She'd rather die than spend time with her mother. She always has something else, something better, to do. I don't remember the last time we did anything together. Every time I suggest anything, she refuses." Instead of sounding angry, she came off as utterly defeated.

Decker ached at the loneliness he understood she felt nearly all the time. No wonder her vow to not get involved in any kind of romantic relationship had crumbled. Her life was her job, a job she hated. She wanted and needed more. He wanted more for her. She deserved everything life had to offer.

"I spent the time wishing I was with you," she told him. "I say 'wishing' if you can call miserable, clawing agony anything so harmless."

He stroked his hand over her arm obsessively. He couldn't get enough of her silky skin. "What about the next time we get our days off?" Every week, they both took off Monday (after the bar closed between 2 and 4 a.m.), all day Tuesday, until 6 p.m. on Wednesday. Duff had been adamant about hiring Decker to specifically watch over Sapphire. The rest of the female staff was a priority as well, of course, and the bouncers were required to see them to their vehicles safely after every shift. Decker had drilled that into his team until they couldn't doubt that any slacking would mean their termination and possibly worse if he heard they were hitting on the waitresses after hours. But Sapphire was the daughter Duff and Bev had never had. She was the one that got Decker's personal attention.

Sapphire pushed her plate away and turned to lean against his arm. "I want that more than anything, Deck. God, do I. I don't have a clue what I'm doing. You don't have any restrictions on your life. You don't have to set an example for anyone. I don't want to deprive you of what you can have with any other woman--"

"You're the only one I want. Whatever you want, lady, I want. Whatever you don't, I'll live without. But I wanna see you during our time off. I wanna spend every second you'll give me together."

"I wish I could go to bed with you, sleep in your arms." She sighed, clutching at the front of his shirt. "I know this doesn't make any sense."

He closed his eyes against the image he'd had fixed in his mind for the past two months: Sleeping in his bed with Sapphire in his arms. That image and his wish--if-you-could-call-miserable-clawing-agony-anything-so-harmless--had kept him from getting more than a couple hours of sleep every day. "Makes perfect sense."

"How? It doesn't make sense even to me."

Putting his arm around her, Decker cradled her head against his chest, stroking her hair. "Even if your daughter calls you a hypocrite, you wanna know you're not, that you're doing what you believe is right in your own life, setting the example she needs."

She lifted her head to look up at him. "You do understand."

"I do, babe. Trust me, I do. But I don't think it's wrong for us to be together, any way we wanna be."

"Because we're adults?"

Maybe she didn't roll her eyes, but he heard the gesture in her tone.

"As if that makes everything moral and upright."

Decker stroked the line of her jaw, noticing a small scar in her arched left eyebrow. *From that bastard ex-husband of hers?* "We are adults. It doesn't make everything right. But we're not kids who don't have a clue what they're getting themselves in for. I'm old enough to know sex means responsibility. So are you. But that's not the point. That's not what's driving you. I get that."

"What is the point?" she asked, sounding anguished, maybe because she really didn't believe he understood why she was being so cautious with their relationship.

"This isn't just sex. Not to me. Not to you. We're not having an affair that's only gonna last as long as if feels good. Can't imagine it won't always be hotter than hell between us. But I'm not drifting in and out of anything here. I'm in it. As long as you want me, I'm yours, babe."

"I'm yours, too. I want to be with you indefinitely. But it's not so easy to convince myself it's okay to have sex without marriage when I'm telling my daughter she's not allowed to do the same."

Sex without marriage? *Not without* love? *Did she deliberately avoid that word?* Decker knew she was skittish about love. He didn't blame her. He was himself. But he wanted the words from her. Dammit, he wanted them badly enough to turn his whole life upside down and topsy-turvy. He'd never wanted those words from anyone else, not even Rox, because she'd said them often, too often, and coming from her they hadn't meant what he wanted them to. If Sapphire said them… *She'd mean 'em, the way I want 'em to, maybe for the first time in my life.*

"When Yasmine calls me a hypocrite now, she's right. I am. Just because I'm an adult and what we're doing isn't a one-night-stand doesn't make it moral."

He nodded. "I respect that. I respect you. You're in control here. Whatever you want. As long as I know we're together, I'm your man."

She wrapped her long, slim fingers around his wrist. Mutually, they laced their fingers together. She was shaking her head as if she couldn't comprehend her own confused mind. He kissed the back of her hand, then pressed their linked hands against his heart while he leaned in and kissed her mouth slowly, savoring what he could get. She sighed again, her eyes hungry but resigned when she pulled back. She started to stand up, reaching for the dirty dishes. "I can't imagine what you're getting out of this, Deck."

He snagged her back, this time pulling her down on his lap and closing her in the circle of his arms. "Thought I was getting you. Your heart, a place in your life, your hands touching me any way you want, any time. Your eyes telling me I'm not alone in feeling this."

In the intensity of her gaze, he saw she'd guessed exactly what he was referring to. The past two months, sharing pained glances at each other across the noisy bar, when they couldn't do anything until all those people were blessedly gone gone long gone, touching each other in passing in ways that no one else had probably noticed had healed him like nothing else could, giving him hope to look forward to the very second the premises were vacated and they could finally be alone...

Decker brought her face closer, her incredible mouth to within a fraction of his. "If I can kiss you when nobody's looking..."

He kissed her, his hands around her jaw, maneuvering for a deeper taste. She gave freely, helplessly. It'd been like this between them from the very first time. His appetite for her grew instead of lessening over time.

"It won't be enough," she managed as though reading his mind, her eyes closed tightly. Her tone was as heavy as his arousal.

"No. But it'll be what I need to survive."

"I want to do more than survive. I want you to have more, too." She lifted her chin as he kissed the soft, fragrant skin on her neck, the curve of her ear. When he caught the lobe gently between his teeth, she sucked in her breath, her arms tightening around his neck. Every instinct inside him told him she wouldn't refuse him if he slipped his hands under her Knuckleheads tank top, to the lacy but functional bra he'd discovered the fun way she wore to work. He heard, saw, smelled how excited she was, knew how to unhook the silly garment in the back, exactly how to tease her ultra-responsive breasts to make her unable to refuse him anything.

But he didn't do any of it. He stroked her throat, nuzzling her, holding himself in check the way a drowning man kept his head, barely, above water.

"So, when you're ready--" he whispered, against her ear again, and she shivered, letting out a moan. Without words, he accepted that she was imagining, tempting step-by-tempting step, just how he would have seduced her if she hadn't asked him not to already.

Their mouths came together again, and he swore in his head. Five minutes--about all they had before they had to leave for work--of bliss would be all it would have taken for both of them. Though they didn't take what they easily could have and he conceded that what they were doing would be hellish torture sooner or later, he'd already acknowledged he was so far in it with her there was no escape. He didn't want one. Even agony with Sapphire was a form of ecstasy.

Chapter 7

Sapphire had always counted on her shifts moving so fast, she sometimes felt like she blinked and the hours were over. Tonight, she couldn't stop looking for Deck, wanting to catch his gaze, share a mutual look, wanting exactly what they'd shared together after work for the past couple months. *Now we don't even have that to look forward to...but will I be able to get myself to forbid it when the time comes? What restraints have we had thus far? None. We didn't have the words of love to match the physical act. Now we won't have the physical act, just the words. How stupid is that?*

"You're such a hypocrite, Mom." Her daughter's cruelly stealthy words came back to her over and over, reminding her why she'd drawn a line for her and Deck, a line she didn't have a clue how to get herself to stay behind. But a half hour after the last employee was gone, they reached for each other, both muttering how much they'd missed the other, and they kissed the second the door was locked. Somehow, they were both still dressed a minute later. She realized why, too. Deck hadn't "taken what he could get". She knew without a doubt he wanted her to be able to respect herself, not to be a hypocrite for her daughter, not to regret anything between them.

He's not playing games, she marveled as he held her tight enough to make her want to burst into tears. He was willing to give her exactly what she needed. She'd always been aware of how different he was from the other men she'd known, the lowlifes that came through the bar looking for nothing more than a good time, a transitory fix. During her shift, she'd thought about the ten years he'd been coming in, drinking so much, lesser men would have been on the floor hours before. She'd heard dark pieces of his life, but now that he'd told her more, about his mother and a string of uncaring foster parents, she realized she'd been right in assuming he was a man who'd been badly hurt in his life. *But maybe he's not so much a survivor as someone who's learned how to avoid pain altogether.*

More than once during the endless hours of their shift, she'd marveled that he'd said he wanted to be with her, wanted to get to know the private parts of her that almost no one else was aware existed. He was getting involved the way he claimed he never had before, and she believed him. She'd also wondered endlessly what he could possibly believe he was getting out of all this--especially since she'd put an end to their intimate relations.

She'd played his words over and over in her head until she'd all but memorized them and they flooded her with molten heat and precious tears each time they replayed. *"You wanna hear I love you,*

Sapphire? I honestly don't know what the hell love is and if I knew, it was never good. You don't wanna know what 'love's' been in my life. It's been pain. F@#ed up. Let's just leave it at that. It ain't unicorns and fairies skipping through the clouds hand-in-hand and fartin' magic dust over everything. If love is being utterly consumed with wanting another person, living just to see her, feel her, get her to look your way with softness, hoping to hell for anything she'll give you 'cause it's all that's gonna get you through another s@#t day... If love is praying to God she's not gonna break your heart in two by ending it--today, tomorrow, any other f@#in' day 'cause if she's not in your life, if you're not seeing her, then you're dead, or might as well be and should just dig the damn grave and be done with it... If all that's what love is, then yeah, I love you, Sapphire. I'm f@#in' outta my head with it where you're concerned."

Why didn't I return the words? she berated herself as they held each other in the shockingly quiet bar. She pressed her face against his chest. *I've done that before. Spoken the words too soon, regretted it as soon as he decided he'd gotten the "love" he was after. That last time I got involved in any way, I promised myself I wouldn't have sex* until after *he said the words. I wouldn't get involved until he spoke them, and I wouldn't return them if he didn't say them first. But Deck gave me the words, we've had sex, and here I am still holding back.*

Sapphire clutched him a little tighter because she understood he was holding himself in tight check. *It'll hurt worse with him...if this goes wrong, and what are the odds it won't? I've been in love before, or thought I was, and I never doubted it'd end. Every time. I knew it would, Just didn't know when. Why does this time feel different? Like I can't just pick up where I left off on my own once the grand fairytale shatters and I have no choice but to go on with my life alone?*

"I should go," she murmured, not wanting to leave his arms, aware that the longer they denied themselves and each other, the hungrier they would become. Damn that his huge, muscular body felt so good against hers.

"I'm not ready to let you go," he said quietly, for the first time not releasing her instantly when she said she needed to leave.

She looked up at him. The agony in his eyes made her flinch. He was gazing down at her as if separating from her now would physically kill him. *Just like it might kill me. Why does it have to be like this? Why can't anything ever work out so there's no pain?*

Feeling like a wicked witch for persisting, she gathered her things, he walked her out to her car and gave her a last, lingering kiss. Getting herself to drive away from him when tears strangled her eyes, her throat was a form of hell. Viciously she fought her reckless desire to turn around, jump out of her car and run into his waiting arms. She wanted to tell him she loved him so badly, never wanted to be separated from him for a single second.

Sapphire manually inhaled, exhaled, realizing as if for the first time that she understood her daughter so well right now, she might never have insightful perspective like this again. Yasmine believed herself to be in love with Justice, a creep who was only trying to get what he wanted with a beautiful girl. But Yasmine believed he loved her and loving someone led to wanting to be with that person sexually. *And here I am, telling her to break her own heart and stay away from the person who means the most to her. No wonder we're at each other's throats all the time. She's at odds with me because I haven't been at all sympathetic to her feelings. But how could I be? I know Justice has a single goal here. I've been with bastards like him all my life, ones who tell me what I wanna hear so they can fulfill their own selfish desires. Unfortunately, I never see them for what they are until it's too late. Don't I have an obligation to share the benefit of my experience with my daughter, who's too young and naïve to comprehend any of this? She doesn't want to hear she's not the love of Justice's life, the difference that will reform him. She certainly doesn't want to face she's just a tool for him to use.*

I'd die if I found out that's all I am to Deck...

Maybe sympathy wouldn't solve all her and Yasmine's problems, but, even if only a tenuous bridge could be constructed between them on that basis, it was worth pursuing. She'd missed her daughter, the one she could talk to and laugh with and be there for. In the last year, they barely talked, never spent time together, and laughter was its own joke. They were strangers who lived in the same apartment on conflicting schedules.

When she got home, she hung up her purse and coat, took off her shoes. Wary of what she might be walking into--*God, please, not a repeat of yesterday, or worse*--she looked and listened. The apartment was silent. She saw Yasmine's keys on their hook. She went to her daughter's bedroom door, pressing her fingers lightly to the wood. *Small blessing. She's home in bed, asleep. I'll take it after yesterday.*

Following a quick shower, Sapphire slipped into her own bed, all but suffocated by the memories of Deck here, all the things they'd said and done together. As she closed her eyes against tears, she wondered what he was doing, if he was missing her as badly as she missed him.

Against her will, she slept, requiring the rest badly. Barely a handful of hours later, the scent of strong coffee woke her and she got up, navigating to the kitchen blurry-eyed. She saw Yasmine pouring herself a cup. She was dressed in one of her fashionable outfits with adorable shoes, just the right touch of jewelry and makeup, looking so beautiful and wary Sapphire wanted to apologize effusively even when she didn't believe she'd done anything wrong.

She got herself coffee and they sat together at the table, hardly looking at each other. Once she'd had more than a few bracing swallows of the hot coffee, she started, "Look, honey, I realize I haven't been very understanding of your feelings since you started dating *him*--"

"He has a name. It's Justice. And he's not an amalgamation of every mistake *you've* ever made, Mom."

"He's too old for you. Don't tell me he's eighteen again. We both know he's not." Sapphire bit down on the instinctive retaliations that filled her mind, urging her to continue, and those would have been voiced without delay in the past. Her newfound perspective insisted, *You don't build bridges by burning them.* "But I want to talk to you about something else."

Yasmine said nothing for a long minute, but she was at least looking at her now--albeit with an accessing glare that mingled her perpetual boredom into the mix. "If you're going to tell me I can't see Justice anymore..."

"He's not what I want to talk to you about."

As reluctant as a snake wary of leaving the shelter of warm

rocks, Yasmine just barely nodded her permission to go ahead.

The words Sapphire had decided to speak out loud didn't come easily. Sooner or later, she had to tell her daughter about Deck...without telling her too much. "I don't know how to tell you this. But...I'm...I've been...seeing someone. It's...well, it's..." She buried her mouth in the rim of her cup without taking a drink. "...serious."

Was there a flicker of interest? Sapphire decided she'd imagined that.

"Someone from work?" Yasmine asked.

Where do these teenagers get these cool tones that give nothing away? Is she being sarcastic? Surprised? Disgusted? Happy? How would I ever know?

"Not...well, not the way you'd think. I've known him for about ten years. He's Roxanne Hart's former bodyguard."

"That Decker guy?"

Sapphire gaped at her daughter in astonishment. "You've met him?"

"No. Not in person. Aunt Cherish mentioned him. I don't even remember why. When. Probably talking about Roxanne or something. In connection with her."

Nodding, Sapphire drank more coffee. A very distant memory came to her--Cherish had told her that Roxanne decided to play matchmaker out of the blue--intended to fix Deck up with Cherish. Her cousin had found him attractive, off course, but nothing had come of it. Cherish hadn't felt a connection with him, had felt mild fear of how big and muscular he was, and she'd spoken in no uncertain terms about how Deck hadn't been on-board with

Roxanne's matchmaking. Not at all.

Thank God.

"I actually sensed something was up for the past couple months, Mom," Yasmine said in a haughty, unconcerned tone. "I thought you said you'd never get involved with someone from the bar?"

Just like that, Sapphire sensed the accusation arcing from her daughter like a laser beam. With Yasmine alone, Sapphire didn't automatically jump into defense mode when cornered. Instead, she became whiny, started making excuses. She cringed even as she started explaining in a desperate way. "It's complicated. He's not like the biker dudes who come into the bar. He's nothing like the other bouncers, bartenders, barbacks... He's a good guy. If you met him, you'd see that." Sapphire winced at the echo of her defensiveness. Each word felt weighed--and wrong.

Yasmine let out a bored sigh. "If you're going to tell me you're sleeping with him, Mom, I'm not a little kid. I get it. Do you want my permission or something?" Scorn bled through the shrugged-shoulder attitude.

The implications burned holes in Sapphire's confidence. Heat flooded her cheeks. "I won't lie to you, Yasmine. I haven't been a saint, but, for the past ten years, I've tried to set an example for you. I didn't bring anyone home..." *Who are you kidding? You've failed. You know. She knows it. There's no point in justifying myself like I'm without sin.* "Go ahead and call me a hypocrite, but I want you to know that I don't believe it's okay for me to sleep around just because I'm adult, not even if it's a serious relationship."

Yasmine laughed. "Why? Because you know it won't last?

You've always said bar relationships are doomed to failure and stupid to get involved in."

"They are. And this isn't one." She swallowed, feeling guilty and dirty from past mistakes. This wasn't the same.

"How is it not the same old, same old you've insisted were bad in the past? Does he work there? Is he associated with the bar?" Yasmine rolled her eyes. "Look, Mom, I could care less if you're screwing him or anyone else under whatever flimsy guise seems appropriate to you."

The disdain leveled at her was as shattering as a rock through stained glass. Her daughter was sitting across from her a few feet away, judging her and assuming... *The truth. She'll never believe I'm in love, he's in love, that love endorses whatever we want together. I don't even believe that myself anymore. Besides, how strong will I be in denying Deck and myself anything we long for together? In a day or two, I'll crack. I'd be lying if I tried to act self-righteous about that.*

So much for building a bridge. We're even farther apart than before. Only now she feels outright disgust and contempt for me. Meekly, Sapphire offered, unable to look up from her cup, "My point in telling you about this was...is...that I understand what it's like to be in love, to want to be with someone in every way because you're in love. But sex implies responsibility--"

"Mom, are you telling me or yourself that?"

There was no way out from under the down-to-the-core, scrutinizing microscope. *Her* morals and values *were* in question. *I've failed, and I can't win here. I can't get her to want to build some kind of relationship with me. That ship has sailed and it's never coming back.*

Yasmine shook her head, blatant disdain written all over her face. "Your point in telling me was to show me why I can't keep seeing Justice--because *you* think sex is wrong between us. Don't bother. You can't tell me what to do."

"I'm your mother," Sapphire insisted, her ire rising at her daughter's shocking disrespect.

"Yeah, what does that mean? I have my own car. My own money. My own life. My own hours. How do you think you'll stop me from seeing him, short of chaining me up in my room while you're at work? You know you can't stop me, so don't even try. And I *don't* want to meet this guy you're screwing. We both know it won't last. If you end up…I don't know…unfathomably *marrying* him, fine. I'll meet him. Otherwise…"

Sapphire was so dumfounded, she couldn't process anything after her daughter left the room and locked herself in her bedroom. Her cell phone rang, and she got up on auto-pilot. In her room, she sat on the edge of her bed and picked up the phone from the nightstand.

"I wanna see you," Deck said without preface.

The anxious sound of his voice brought forth tears she couldn't fight a second longer. She gasped, clenching her teeth in an attempt to prevent the sob swelling inside her from rising to the surface.

"Sapphire?"

She couldn't talk even then, and he said in a tone that almost seemed like he understood what was happening, "Baby, are you okay?"

"Yasmine…fight…" she choked out.

Even as he sounded slightly relieved that what was going on wasn't something worse, he murmured, "Hell. She's there, I'm guessing?"

"Yes."

"What'd you fight about?"

She managed another single word on a gulp. "Us."

"Us, as in you and me? You told her?"

From across the hall, Yasmine's door opened and Sapphire wished fervently she'd closed her own. She didn't want her daughter to see her cry. *Not that she cares*, she realized when Yasmine didn't bother glancing her way. She was carrying her phone and purse. A moment later, Sapphire heard the jingle of keys being taken down from the hook and then the front door slammed behind her.

"She's...gone," she told Deck, gasping as she tried to get words past the sobs tearing out of her throat. "She believes...we're having an affair that'll...end... Doesn't believe..." She shook her head. "Doesn't want to meet you... So what's the point? Of anything?"

"Wow," he breathed.

"She's...not wrong."

"The hell she's not. Can I come up?"

"What?" Sapphire demanded in shock. "You're here?" She shouldn't have been surprised, but she wondered if Yasmine would see him, recognize, assume the worst.

"Parked a block away just in case. She won't see me." His tone became softer, gentler. "Couldn't sleep I missed you so bad."

"Come up." She didn't have a single doubt she'd cave in, throw off her vows like so much chaff. She was too weak right now. She needed him too much to care about anything else.

Chapter 8

Decker knew the second Sapphire opened the door and threw herself at him that there was something almost as bad seeing her almost raped. Seeing her devastated, crying, not a hope in the world was by worse than he could have imagined. He pushed the door closed behind him and held her hard, cringing because the sounds of her sobs made him feel so helpless. He remembered reckless nights with Rox, when she'd been so damn suicidal, he'd known if he left her for a second, she'd take her life. Not sleeping, not eating, not taking a g@#m s@#t because he didn't dare. He'd understood what being completely powerless was then. He couldn't influence anything. All he could ever do was hold back the knife until she got too tired to wield it.

He moved them into the living room, sat on the couch and drew Sapphire over him so he could hold her, stroke her hair and tell her they'd convince her daughter somehow. He offered her tissues from the box on the coffee table nearby. She used most of them, tossing the dirty ones wherever they landed. He had the feeling that wasn't something she usually tolerated. Finally, she was breathing almost normally, not sounding choked, and she managed, "God, this can't be pleasant for you."

"Stop it," he scolded. "I'm with you. Tell me what happened."

She told him everything, breaking out in fresh tears, and he read between the lines about how mortified she'd felt by her teenager's assessment of her life, her morals. Yet in the end, she defended the kid who couldn't know her mother at all to come up with such crazy opinions of her. "Don't judge her, Deck. How can I expect her to respect me? I haven't been a saint. I work in a rough, biker bar. I'm not exactly contributing positively to society. I'm facilitating intoxication...and sin. I'm a human alcoholic beverage dispenser. The only reason I took the damn job is 'cause it's all I'm good at and the tips are so good, in a single night or two, I can sometimes pay my rent for a full month."

"You had to take care of yourself and your little girl. That's noble, baby."

She scoffed, reaching for the last tissue.

"What, you don't think that's noble? My mother didn't give a f@#k whether I lived or died. She didn't even try to take care of me. She let the authorities take me away from her, put me in homes that didn't care any more than she did about me. She wanted her next fix. They wanted the money for putting up with me. You're a damn good mother, Sapphire. You're completely unselfish and that you can actually feel guilty for anything you've done because you're lonely--well, who the hell wouldn't be?--only proves what a good mom you are. Your daughter doesn't have any idea how good she's got it with you."

"Maybe in comparison," she conceded softly.

"No. In fact. There's not one damn scenario that doesn't point to you being a good mother."

She sighed, cuddling against his chest. "I'm glad you think so."

"Who would know better, babe?"

She flinched at his words instead of drawing comfort or smiling, what he'd hoped to coax from her. She hugged him as she murmured, "I'm sorry you had to go through all that, honey."

"So am I. But I'm right about all this, and you know it."

She snuggled deeper against him. "Thank you. For being here. For enduring yet another meltdown."

"You need me. Where else would I be?"

Lifting her head, she looked at him for a long minute, and then she leaned forward and kissed him. Instantly, he wasn't thinking about anything but the hours he'd been without her, filling the ones stretched out in front of him with her, with them. With memories they could make together.

"Why didn't you sleep?" she asked, nuzzling against his lips with her own as if she didn't have the physical strength to continue what he didn't want to stop.

"If you're not right next to me, I don't wanna sleep anymore," he murmured the point-blank truth.

"You have to sleep sometime."

"Did you sleep?"

"A little. But I'm overtired at this point. Exhausted. I feel like all I do anymore is work. There isn't enough time to really sleep, have something like a life outside that damn bar. And I'm so emotional lately, even if I wanna sleep, my mind won't let me for long." She rolled away, getting to her feet and reaching for his hand. "Come on, let's get some sleep."

Decker couldn't protest when she led him into her bedroom, locking the door behind them. When they were wrapped in each other's arms, maybe not naked but at least close enough that he felt the comfort of her body, she said, "Thank you for caring for me, Deck. I wish I could give you everything you want."

"You are," he assured her. "You do."

"No, I'm not. But I want to."

"And that's enough for me."

She sighed, her smile already half-asleep. "You're such a good guy."

The words gave him almost as much gratification as sex would have. "Go to sleep, babe."

She snuggled against him, saying with what sounded like the last of her reserves, "Don't judge my daughter. You're only hearing my side. I want you two to get along."

"I'm not judging. I understand the way it is with teenagers. Maybe not personally, but I've heard. She's rebelling. A bad parent gives in on everything to keep the peace and tries to be friends no matter what the cost. You're a good enough parent to stand up to her when she needs it. You judge yourself too harshly."

"I'm glad you think so. How is it you're not taken? You're so good."

Marveling slightly that anyone could mean those words when saying them to him, he murmured under this breath, "Never wanted to be taken before."

"Not even by Roxanne Hart?"

The reminder that he'd divulged private things to Sapphire when he was drunk on his ass sobered him and made him wonder if that would come back for him to regret the way he hadn't to this point. "She was a friend. That's all she ever was. No 'in love' about it. She felt sorry for me. I always knew it."

"Felt *sorry* for you?" Sapphire repeated in disbelief.

"'Cause she knew she'd never love me back, not the way I wanted. It was one-sided all the way. Stupid. A waste. Especially when I look back on it all now."

Sapphire shook her head. "I can't imagine. I mean, I can't imagine how she couldn't love you. You're so amazing. On looks alone…but you're so much more than that."

Warmth flooded inside him. He ended up grinning like an idiot that she could find *him* attractive, given how hot she was. "You never seemed interested before two months ago."

"Good. I'm just good at hiding those things, but with you it was harder to hide."

"Damn good."

"I'm good at hiding it until I'm not good at hiding anything anymore."

That about sums it up. Decker chuckled. For the last ten years, she'd given him every indication she wasn't interested in him--at all, physically or any other way. Not that there hadn't been times she'd looked at him in a way that made him wonder if she found him attractive, even against her will. Like she said, after the first time they had sex, he'd known she'd been hiding a lot. There was no going back from that. "Lady, you're so damn beautiful, it's no wonder guys get ideas. You don't wear the Knuckleheads uniform like anybody else."

"Uniform. I'd hardly call a tank top a uniform."

"Maybe not. But you'd make a gunny sack look sexy as hell."

"I'd say the same about you."

Because he couldn't deny himself, he let his hands slid up and down her sleek waist, her torso. He encountered her incredibly full breasts on the way up but he didn't ease fully around to the front. *Kill to have her again, but I promised myself I wouldn't take advantage, especially when she's vulnerable, willing, like she is now. She needs to believe she's doing the right thing for her daughter, and she is, whether or not we make love. But she needs the boundary line. So she's gonna have it. If it kills* me. He'd be dead if he didn't at least entertain the idea of skirting the edge of that boundary line she'd set. He suspected she wanted him to.

"What am I supposed to call you now?" she asked in a husky tone, betraying her crumbling willpower. "William?"

He laughed. "Nobody but the old lady and Rox call me that. I don't care what you call me."

"So having someone call you 'William' isn't special?"

He snorted. "Far from it." But he knew what she was getting at, what the wary look in her eyes was. "Baby, don't do that. Don't get jealous of Rox. There's not a damn reason to. She's getting married soon, and there was never anything between us. Not like there is between us."

Though Sapphire seemed apologetic and uncertain, she told him, "She sent me a wedding invitation. I assume that means her cancer is in remission. Didn't she tell all her friends she wouldn't marry Jamie Dubois until she was in remission and would look good in a wedding dress?"

"Yeah."

The first time she'd gone through the disease, Rox had done it alone, unwilling to let anyone help her, so much as hold her hand. When the same damn cancer came back barely a year later, she'd prepared her whole life so she'd be assured of dying alone. Decker would probably never forget that day, two and a half years ago, that she'd told him to go away and leave her alone. She'd been cruel on purpose. But by that point he'd already guessed she was at least partially motivated by her returning cancer and she planned to surrender to the disease without putting up a fight. Hadn't been hard to guess she was trying to save him from himself. She'd always been aware how he felt about her, what he wanted, and she'd loved him as a friend. She hadn't wanted to hurt him even as she made it clear that she couldn't return his feelings because she was in love with Jamie Dubois and nothing and no one would ever change that.

All along, she'd been inaccessible to him, and that'd made it easier for him. How often had he questioned why he deserved to be loved by anyone at all, most of all her? His own mother couldn't love him. Rox couldn't, beyond friendship. *Somehow, with Sapphire, it doesn't matter whether or not I deserve it. I want her to love me anyway. I'll take anything she's willing to give me as long as she lets me hang around her.* "She's gone. She's not part of my life. You are."

"So you're not attending her wedding?"

He grunted. *Hell no.* "Didn't plan to." *Not that she'll accept that easily.* She'd been leaving voicemails of the ilk, "Be there, end of story." She wouldn't hear of a reason why he couldn't or wouldn't come to what she considered the biggest event of her life. She was used to getting her way with him.

"She'll be disappointed."

"You going?" Decker asked.

Sapphire sighed. "I don't know. I'd have to take off work. She's my cousin Cherish's friend. I was actually surprised to get an invitation at all. I barely looked at it. When is the wedding?"

He'd opened it when he got home from work after four. He wasn't even sure why he'd gone that far. He told himself he had to at least open it before it landed in the trash. "Two weeks from now. Saturday. I don't see a reason to go."

She eased deeper into his embrace, her fatigue stealing over her with more sway. "I wish we could make love," she whispered with her eyes closed.

His body reacted to the words like they were the very deed. Though he couldn't hide his arousal from her, he made sure she knew where they stood. "So do I. But I've got you just where I want you. I'm the happiest man alive."

"I'm crazy about you, Deck. I really am."

He swallowed at the serene look on her face, her thickly-fringed eyelashes laying on her silken cheeks with her eyes closed, feeling his chest expand on words that were maybe spoken out of utter exhaustion. He didn't care. He was still taking whatever he could get from this angel.

Chapter 9

Sapphire hadn't been kidding herself. Sleeping with Deck, even in the platonic sense, would lead to exactly what she'd vowed to avoid. Despite sleep making her brain foggy, her body took over, rushing ahead from the memories of their previous lovemaking. Deck shifted, the flame blazed, the friction of their bodies through clothes sweet agony as the blood in her veins became hot lava. Her hips began to move of their own accord, seeking the hardness of his body with sharp teeth of his zipper open and what strained out from it easy prey, the wall of his chest covered with ribbed cotton abrading her swollen breasts. His fingers touched her lips, she drew one inside, mindlessly working it until they were both panting. She found fulfillment so fast, she knew she couldn't deny him the same, especially when she heard him groan out loud in pure male gratification while she cried out passionately at how good she felt.

Purposefully, she slipped her hand down his rock hard stomach toward his arousal. "Let's make love," she whispered, opening her eyes a slit.

He shook his head, his eyes closed tightly in obvious pain, his hand grasping hers to keep her from touching him the way she ached to. "Just hold still, baby."

"I don't want to torture you," she insisted, drifting closer. "We're not teenagers--"

"We're adults. Does that make it right?"

She recognized her own words and flushed. "No. But you don't believe we're doing anything wrong."

"I don't. But you do, honey." He pulled her against him hard, and his mouth touched her ear. Huskily, he muttered, "Besides, I like watchin' you--"

Sapphire gasped, her entire being filling with fire at the word he whispered so low, she longed for the intimacy they'd shared without restraint until recently. She couldn't deny that she liked watching him reach the same place, that she wouldn't do anything to bring him to that point and do it with wild ardor.

Here I am, in the same position Yasmine might have been in with her too-old boyfriend just a day ago. The only difference was that she and Deck were in her bed, that they were older. *Smarter? More responsible? More respectable? Not likely.* The cold water made her shiver with self-disgust.

Turning, she looked at the clock, grimacing at how late it was. In a few hours, they'd be back in the damn bar. Same old grind. "Do you want to shower?" she asked, shame making her feel chilled to the bone despite the hot air in the apartment. She hated sleeping with the air conditioner on.

He laughed in disbelief. "If you mean together, babe, I can't promise I could be a gentleman. I'm barely making it now. One kiss, and I'll be a teenager with no other recourse all over again."

"You had that kind of life as a teenager?" she asked, curious about what kind of teenager he'd been. She could easily imagine he'd been just as much of a heartthrob then.

"Yeah. But even then, getting off for the sake of getting off wasn't worth much."

"Most young guys think getting laid is everything."

"At first. But I always felt empty after, wanted to escape, like everything was pretend. Better to be alone."

Sapphire sat up him so she could look down into his face. His gaze shifted to the loose top that did nothing to hide her continued needs. His eyes flickered with fire. "Are you saying you haven't had relationships--sexual or otherwise--since you were a teenager?" she asked.

"You could say that, for the most part anyway. I fell off the wagon a couple times over the years, but not often. You said it'd been a decade since you last had any kind of relationship. It was the same thing for me--until that night I reached for you and you kissed me. Since then, I can't stop thinking about you. I want you so damn bad, you're all that matters to me. Never been like that for me, with anybody else. I don't know when I realized it, but this ain't about relief. Everything reminds me of you, makes me feel like I'm addicted and I can't get enough of you. The sight of you, the smell, the taste, the touch. I'm gone. The more I get of you, the more I want."

She'd seen his behavior in the bar even before he started working for Duff. Women propositioned him left and right. He'd never seemed interested. She'd assumed he'd gone elsewhere for his "relief". Now he was saying he found sex for the sake of relief empty and not worth the heartache that came afterward.

What a sad, lonely existence he's had. We're so alike in that. God, do I want to make a difference in his life. I want to be good for him, transform him so he considers what we share the best part of his life. I don't want him to ever regret any part of what we've shared.

"You're good with customers, Sapphire. I've noticed that all the years I've been coming to Knuckleheads. You were good with me. But I've never felt anything like sympathy for them. Maybe I don't seem much different from them, but *you're* different. You're different than anyone else in that place."

"So are you."

"I want you to see me that way."

"I do. I have from the beginning."

His smile was so humble, it was barely there on his rugged face. She reached down and touched it tenderly. Beneath her fingertips, his face was covered with thick, bristly five-o'clock shadow but his lips were soft and firm. "I think we've both had the kinds of lives where it's hard to see anything good, even in ourselves."

He sighed, his hands stroking her shoulders, her neck, coming up to cradle her face. "I wish I could take you away from that place, baby. Away from your life. The bar. You feel about Duff and Bev the same way I do, but if neither of us ever had to go back there, I wouldn't cry."

"You're right. And I wish you could take me away. But I have to take care of my daughter." Sapphire had a sudden memory of her daughter telling her like it was: *"I have my own car. My own money. My own life. My own hours. How do you think you'll stop me from seeing him, short of chaining me up in my room while you're at work? You know you can't stop me. So don't even try."*

"I know you do. You're an angel in a hellhole."

His expression was so loving, she almost burst into tears at the brittle memory of her daughter's lack of sympathy. *But how can I blame her? I've been just as unsympathetic toward her love of a guy who's only going to bring her down. She has no reason to believe Deck would never do that to me.*

"Are you sure you don't want to make love?" she asked softly, feeling vulnerable and needy for the physical love that convinced her she'd never be lonely again with him.

He laughed, shaking his head. "Babe, I want that more than my next breath. But we're not gonna do that. Not until you're really ready and won't feel like you're compromising your self-respect."

"I'm not sure I'll ever feel that way. But I don't want you to miss out on anything, especially since I haven't."

"Memories'll get me through. Or torture me. Whatever." He chuckled. "Either way, I'm good."

She leaned down and kissed him, wanting to tell him she loved him for his nobility, his concern for her self-respect, for the good man he was. "I'll make you dinner," she whispered.

He lingered over the kiss for a little longer, and she couldn't help wondering yet again, *What is he getting out of this? Why put himself through torture when he could have anyone else at any time?*

Does he really love me this much?

The way he looked at her answered the question and made her want permanent intimacy with him again that much more.

Chapter 10

The week went by like slow but somehow pleasurable torment for Decker. All he was looking forward to every minute was being alone with Sapphire, even when they weren't physically together, and those hours made him feel alive, worthwhile, as if he had purpose for the first time since Rox had cut him loose. He'd never been happier. *Never been happy before, period.* The thought of their two days off became more and more of a beacon for him. Before he and Sapphire had gotten involved two months ago, he'd gone almost a decade without so much as one episode of sheer-relief sex. Now he didn't know how he'd get through the "weekend" with Sapphire without reaching for her. The few times he was alone, his need for her was almost unbearable.

Not gonna get easier, knowing her daughter'll be babysitting the whole time Sapphire is off work. Yasmine had been babysitting nearly all the time the past week. She was Darlene and Jace

Radcliffe's regular babysitter since they'd moved to Staten Island in March. The Radcliffes were close friends of Rox. They were expecting their third kid any day now. After a lot of false labors, they'd asked Yasmine to stay with them overnight for the whole week so she could be on call when the event really happened.

"She'll probably be there the whole time I'm off. She's already packed her bags and she's heading over there now," Sapphire had told him when they got to the bar for their shift Sunday night. Decker had followed her into Duff's office and she'd closed the door, though he knew she'd only gone in to stuff her purse in her locker.

Decker reached for her and pulled her around into his arms. "Come to my house."

He anticipated a fight and kissed her, hoping to soften her toward his cause. Unexpectedly, she gave in easily. "Okay."

"Okay?" He didn't have a single doubt how this would go once their shift was over and they were alone. Restraint or nobility would crumble to dust after a week. He'd tried hard to be a gentleman because he knew Sapphire needed that in order to prove something to herself. As far as he was concerned, she was under no obligation. She was a good person, good woman, good mother. Nothing she did could change that in his eyes.

The fact that she seemed to realize she couldn't resist him either, not for a second longer than it took to get to his house, bothered him throughout the shift. He couldn't even explain why. But he didn't surprise himself in the least when they were inside the front door of his Colonial brick and vinyl two-story, and she reached for him. He'd never wanted anyone or anything so badly in his life. Nothing could stop him. "I want you in my bed," he said, dangerously aroused.

"I want you."

Those were the magic words, and all his fantasies came true in the next few hours as they loved, slept in drugged snatches, and he finally woke with her naked in his arms late that afternoon. Decker felt almost choked by the softness crowding into his throat and chest, looking at her, sleeping like an angel, her sexy hair mussed, her eyelashes like a fur coat against her satin skin. *This is everything I ever wanted. She's all I want, all I care about, my whole life. Nothing else matters but her.*

Even as the bitterness of his past was reflected in desires that felt familiar yet altered, he couldn't help remembering the more than twenty years he'd been Roxanne Hart's *lap*dog, as well as her *watch*dog. He'd lived for the times she'd summoned him. But those same disappointing heartaches had bled the life out of him. He'd felt dead most of the time, alive only when she needed him, when his focus had been on protecting her, saving her sometimes from herself, keeping her from her self-destructive course.

For the past week, she'd been leaving voicemails on his phone, demanding why he hadn't RSVPed to her wedding invitation. He'd even gotten one from Dubois', saying Rox had told him to call and make sure he knew they both wanted them there, that it was important to Rox to have the people she loved most there with them on their wedding day. Decker had no desire to admit the truth to either of them. He didn't want to go. Their "most important event ever" was the last place he wanted to be. How could they not understand? He was done with the person he'd been back then.

Sure, yeah, he was relieved as hell she was alive, she'd outlive maybe all of 'em, and she'd beat cancer a second time. If pressed, he might even say he was glad she was happy. *Bottom line, I don't wanna be friends, sure as s@#t don't wanna make nice and act like the situation's normal or healthy.* He didn't care to explain why it was anything but to him. He plain didn't want to go backward. For the first time in his life, he was happy and he had everything he could ever want. Why couldn't the rest of the world just go the hell away and leave him alone?

But I don't have everything I want, do I? I don't have Sapphire the way I want her. Our relationship is on her terms, just like it always was with Rox. And, just like then, this fool lapdog would rather have the scraps than nothing.

When Sapphire stirred against him, he murmured, "Wish we never had to leave here."

She smiled without fully opening her eyes. "Me, too. You feel so good."

Her naked body against his didn't allow him to hide his instant response to her words, and she laughed and opened her eyes. "This is so crazy. I don't know what I'm doing anymore. But I'm happy. Here." She sighed, snuggling against him. "I wish I could reconcile all these complications, but I can't. Right now, I don't care."

"You gonna feel guilty about this when we have to go back to work?" She had to realize as well as he did that they both needed this. The fact was, her relationship with her daughter hadn't improved during the week they'd restrained themselves. They'd both sacrificed what brought them joy for an example that didn't seem to make a bit of difference to her teenager. Yasmine assumed the worst of her mother without fail, or maybe Sapphire was the one making the assumptions.

"Probably," she admitted.

"You think she'll give you credit if we go back to no sex in a few days?"

Sapphire sighed, all the contentedness she'd woken up with extinguished. "No. It's moot anyway now, isn't it? I'm not cut out to be a nun when I'm in…a relationship."

When you're in love? Decker wasn't surprised she had trouble reconciling the complications in her life. She couldn't win, no matter what she did. And, regardless of her own actions, right or wrong, she'd think the worst of herself. That she wanted to give her daughter what she needed, even if the teenager acted like she didn't care one way or the other, only proved her goodness. But Sapphire would never see it that way.

I wanna give her whatever she wants or needs, but I don't think she knows herself. "We could move into together," he suggested.

Her beautiful eyes opened wide in shock. "How will *that* help?"

Her reaction made him grunt a laugh at his foolishness in suggesting it. "Know it'd help me. I don't sleep anymore unless you're with me. I don't wanna sleep without you."

"Oh, Deck."

When she tucked her face against him, hiding the shame he saw no need for, he lifted her chin so she had to be straight with him. "How long we gonna do this, babe? 'Til she moves out of your apartment when she graduates high school? Will it be right between us then?"

"You're mad," she realized, not even sounding defensive.

"No. I just don't know how long I can live with only half of you--or whatever you can give me."

Moving like she was a rusty cog or something, she turned so she was on her back. She drew the covers up around her neck. "Do you not want to do this anymore?" Her glance back at him was worried.

He curled his body so he was completely surrounding her again. "I want you. That's all I want, Sapphire. But I can't have you."

She looked like she wanted to argue with him, but the reality of their situation was too blatant. She was trying to give her daughter what she thought she needed. Doing that meant Decker couldn't have her the way he wanted to.

When she tried to turn away again, her expression as she hid herself one of misery, he dragged her back to him, her back to his front, holding her tighter when he realized she was crying. Instantly, he waffled in pursuing this topic. He put his head against hers. "It doesn't matter, baby. I'm happy. I'm with you now. That's all I need. I don't have any right to make demands on you."

"Why would you even say that?" she choked. "Of course you have a right."

"Why would I? I'm nobody's prize."

"You're a model citizen, Deck. Don't even go there. You're law-abiding, you don't even drink anymore--and that's the biggest shock of all. I can't believe how you quit overnight."

"Guess you'd know best how much I can put down in a few hours."

She turned her neck so she could look back at him, inhaling

and exhaling as she seemed to be trying to get her emotions under control. "I sometimes wondered how you were able to stand. But you didn't have the signs most people do when they're drunk on their asses."

Decker laughed. "Must've been 'cause I was conceived that way, pickled in the s*t instead of embryonic fluid."

"How did you quit, Deck? I mean, my gosh, to go from how many bottles of the hard stuff and countless beers to *nothing*? Didn't you experience anything like withdrawal? How could you not? It's like you're not human."

He shrugged her awe off, uncomfortable for a reason he didn't want to define. "Guess I found something else to do."

"What?"

"Want you?" He grinned, not really joking. "'sides, Duff doesn't like it when the staff drinks on the job."

She snorted. "Doesn't stop most of them, especially the bouncers."

"No, it don't."

"So did you join AA? Did you get a sponsor? It's not possible to quit cold turkey. I've never see anyone else stop like that without help."

He shook his head.

She turned onto her back and looked at him for a long time. He could almost see the gears in her head turning while she tried to work out his secret. She must have decided he would fall back into his habits sooner rather than later because she pleaded, "Maybe you *should* join, Deck--as a preventative measure. I mean, most people can't do it themselves for the long haul. That's the whole point of having a sponsor."

"You seem to know a lot about it," he commented, wishing they could talk about anything else. Or do something a hell of a lot more interesting than talking.

"I'm a member of AA. There was a time in my life when I was afraid I'd become an alcoholic, and I couldn't risk it. Not with a young daughter."

"After you moved to Staten Island and started bartending at Knuckleheads?"

"Yeah. I joined and got a sponsor just in case things got out of control. I didn't want Yasmine to have an alcoholic for a mother like I did."

"*When* did you drink a lot?" Decker asked pointedly, unable to imagine her being a drunk. She just wasn't the type. She was in control nearly all the time. At work, outside work, he'd never seen her touch the s@#t.

"When I was a teenager, before I got pregnant. After that...like I said, it was a preventative measure--just in case I ever found myself drinking more than I should."

Decker shook his head, reeling at what he was hearing. "Let me get this straight: You're a member of AA but you've never actually been an alcoholic?"

"Is that really so weird?" she had the nerve to ask and to look completely unsure why he was surprised.

"F@#k yes! Who does that? Seriously, babe, who does that?"

She offered an embarrassed smile. "Okay. Maybe it is strange. But I grew up with a mother who drank like a fish. Even on nights when she had to work the next morning, she usually passed out from too much booze. She had a hangover pretty much every morning of her life. That doesn't even get into her blow-out weekends. She left her bottles lying around the house wherever, not locked up. I was drinking her leftovers since I was twelve, and I gravitated toward a crowd of older kids who drank and smoked all the time. True, they all consumed ten times as much as I did. And alcohol was Coug's biggest problem. He didn't have any self-control when he was wasted, which was most of the time, especially after we got married. I knew where it could lead for me, and I didn't want to get to that point."

"Wow," was all Decker could mutter.

"What?"

"Nothing. You're amazing."

She still seemed embarrassed, but she said in a steely voice, "So are you, to quit the way you did. But you should join, Deck, to have a backup when you need it."

"Nah. I haven't needed anything. Haven't felt much urge to drink since I quit."

"Doesn't mean you won't at some point."

He nodded. "Look, I get it. You don't wanna be with a bastard who could turn into your abusive SOB ex-. If I have trouble, I'll go with you when you attend a meeting. How about that?"

"I actually haven't been going to many lately,"

"Two months?" he guessed. *Since we got together.*

"Something like that."

"You're the only drug I need, baby."

She curled herself toward him, sounding sleepy again. "I don't want to be anyone's drug."

"You know what I mean."

"I have to call Yasmine. Or go home."

"Will she wonder where you are? She stayed overnight at Jace and Darlene's, didn't she?"

"Yes. Just before our shift was wrapping up at two she called to say Darlene had another false alarm. "

"Do we still have our time together?" he wanted to know the bottom line.

"I should go home--"

Decker dragged her against his hardening body, cradling his hands around her heart-shaped rear end. "Not yet. I'm not ready to let you go, sweet thing."

She sighed pleasurably when he kissed her and found her softest spot at the same time. Without fight, she murmured, "Okay."

Chapter 11

Sapphire woke alone in Deck's king size bed, wondering where he was. Slipping from the warmth of the covers, saturated with the scent of him, she saw his tank top on the floor. She pulled it over her nudity as she went to the adjoining bathroom. On the marble-like double sinks, she found an unopened toothbrush that she knew had to be for her. She had a vague memory of him saying--after she'd agreed at the beginning of their shift to go home with him-- that he'd "stocked the house" just in case she ever wanted to come over.

It's odd how comfortable I feel here. I never feel comfortable anywhere except at home, where Yasmine can find me and I can usually find her at some point during the day.

After she brushed her teeth, she saw another in the stand fastened to the wall beneath the mirror. Feeling a little giddy at the intimacy, she dropped her brush into the slot next to Deck's. Her hair was pretty wild, but she wasn't entirely sure where her purse was. They'd rushed inside his house, to the bedroom. She remembered little in-between that wasn't about lovemaking and sleep.

Easing the tank top further over her hips, she went to search for him. She almost reached the living room when she heard voices and halted in the hall. She instantly recognized that the person Deck was talking to at the open front door belonged to a female, her tone low and husky. *Roxanne Hart*, she realized with a start when the woman demanded, "Are we even friends anymore, William? You never answer my phone calls, or even the voicemails."

"Busy," he said simply.

Sapphire wondered about his tone. It wasn't cowering, pleading, meek. It was more like... *Dismissive. Like he doesn't want to talk to her, wants her to go away and not ask him these questions.*

"If we're friends, why aren't you coming to my wedding? Why aren't you happy for me?"

The hurt in Roxanne's voice became what Sapphire had expected Deck's to be--pleading, upset, desperate. When he swore viciously, Sapphire tensed, insecurity piercing her reason. What did he feel for this woman? He insisted he was over her, but people didn't generally avoid things that no longer bothered them. They avoided the things that still had the power to affect them.

"What the hell do you want me to say, Rox? What do you want me to do? I'm f@#n' thrilled you're gonna live. Okay? But *friends*? Baby, you're marrying him. I accept that. I've moved on."

"Baby, you're marrying him..." *Does Roxanne find his words as illogical as I do? As telling?*

"Moved on? Have you really? Nobody sees or hears from you anymore. I don't know whether you're alive or dead."

"What does that prove? You run with a different crowd. You always have. 'sides, you don't need to worry about me. I'm not your problem anymore."

Why is his voice so hard? Like he's pretending he doesn't care on the outside while inside he's being torn to shreds.

"You were never my problem, William. I thought we were friends. Isn't that what you were always saying? Do you no longer believe that?" Roxanne sounded like she was in tears now.

Deck's voice softened as he comforted her, saying, "Don't, Rox. We're friends. Okay? G@#t, we're friends. Don't cry anymore."

He's not over this woman. He can't be. No one says things like he has, acts the way he is, if they're unmoved. This thing between us, how can I believe anything except that it's what's gotten him to "move on" from Roxanne? Move on, but he's not healed. He's not over her. Maybe he wants to be, but it's obvious he's not. He can't even deny the truth to her for long.

Before she could get herself to fully consider what she was doing, Sapphire rushed back to his bedroom and closed the door, only aware of the sound of the light slam after it was too late. Not really know what she was doing, she started piling her own clothes over his tank top, freaking out as the words "I have to get out of here" went around and around her brain, growing more and more anxious. She couldn't think about anything else. She wasn't sure how she'd get herself to talk to him. She just knew she needed time to analyze what she'd overheard, whether anything between them had been real or simply rebound behavior.

What the hell had she been thinking, getting involved with a guy she'd known first-hand for a decade was badly damaged, maybe beyond help?

"Hey," Deck said after he opened the bedroom door and saw her trying to jam her shoes on. She couldn't doubt she probably resembled a toddler who didn't yet know how to tie her own laces. He swore between clenched teeth as he came toward her. "You heard that?" he said plainly, not a question, kneeling before her.

I'm hopelessly in love with a man who'll never be able to love me the way I need him to. All this has been one big lie. I think I knew that deep down, but I didn't want it to be true. Now I know his words to me were an illusion he constructed to convince himself he was over Roxanne Hart.

"You're overreacting, Sapphire. Calm down. Look at me, dammit."

"I have to go."

"You're making too much out of what you heard. Saw."

"Am I?" she asked, sounding as strained and crazed as she felt. "It sounded to me like you're not over whatever it was you felt for her all those years. And she said you're the one who kept insisting you were friends. What was this? Am I your transition to help you get over her, even when you know it's not possible--?"

Just like that, she was crying again, as if she'd never stopped since the last time. Lately, emotional overload seemed to be her normal state of being.

When she jumped up and tried to run out, he grabbed her and held her so hard, she had no doubt she'd have bruises wherever his fingers had tightened over her flesh. Semantic memories kicked in, and the training she'd undertaken to defend herself surfaced. "Let me go!"

Deck let her go and backed up without a pause, looking stunned at her reaction. "Look, I won't hold you, but I'm not gonna let you believe a lie. You're wrong about my feelings for her. Dead wrong. I can't prove anything to you, dammit. I don't know how. But I don't love her. I'm with you, Sapphire."

"You're with me but you *want*--"

"I love you. But you're not gonna believe that, are you?" He swore again, this time so she winced at the viciousness in his crude words. "Maybe it doesn't matter to you anyway. You never claimed you love me. Don't think I didn't notice, babe."

As if he'd slapped her in the face, Sapphire gasped, killing her fight-or-flight instinct cold. She'd never felt so exposed. *Sorry. Because I hurt him when I withheld what he needed from me. But if I say those words now...God, it'll hurt so much worse if this is over.*

She wrapped her arms around herself, shivering despite the warmth of the house. "Deck, I need to think. I have to think. Give me..."

"Whatever."

His cold dismissal, followed by him walking out of the room, turned the knife inside her heart, twisting and plunging it deeper. Though she hated leaving everything like this, she had to for her own sake. She'd made too many mistakes when she was desperate. She had to be sure what was right or wrong before she made any decisions.

She somehow found her purse and drove home, not surprised

to find the apartment dark and empty. Yasmine was still taking care of Darlene and Jace's children. The hollowness of the familiar rooms she and her precious daughter had made a home in, settling down for the first time in their lives once they moved here, made her feel fragile, like she was holding onto her sanity by a bare thread.

Her hand drew her cell phone out of her purse, but the thought of calling Cherish filled her with mortification. *Am I seriously embarrassed? Because I feel like me and Roxanne Hart were in some competition for Deck's affections, and I lost without a single point in my favor? I can't compete. How could I ever compete with someone like her? She was a supermodel, a rock star, so beautiful and talented, and what I am? Nothing. A lowlife bartender with no other skills or assets with a daughter who all but hates me and maybe has every reason to.*

God, I am my mother, exactly what I promised myself I'd never be.

Though she had to concede she'd normally be weeping bitterly, she felt almost numb from the overload of emotions she couldn't handle. She huddled in the corner of the sofa with her legs tucked up close to her chest. Heart sick and exhausted, she thought about her mother, her upbringing, years that were wasted and superficial.

Instead of blaming her mother the way she always had by default, this time she compared herself to her. Just as she and Yasmine were always at odds these days, she and her mother had forever been on opposite ends, no sympathy or understanding for the other between them. Even as the old arguments to justify herself against her mother rose up, she shot them down as she saw how alike she was. Her mother had been a terrible example for her, drinking like a fish and falling in and out of love with men who weren't worth the time she spent f@#g them without bothering to be secretive.

I may not drink myself, but I work in a place where I encourage alcoholism and the drowning of sorrows in inebriation. My relationships are nothing my daughter can respect. No matter how hard I try, my own needs always come first. And I seem to need love, affection, validation, and sex too badly to ignore my overpowering urges. How can my daughter do anything but disrespect and pass me off as a hypocrite?

Just like I always did with my mom.

Though Sapphire had the feeling it would be a mistake, she pulled her cell phone toward her and called up her mother's phone number from her contact list. She didn't consider that it was evening, maybe late for some until it was ringing. But her mother answered, saying, "You're calling late."

Now that she'd heard her mother's voice, she had no clue what to say. She retained so few memories of confiding in this woman *(just like Yasmine has all but stopped telling me anything).*

"Sapphire, are you there?" her mother asked when she didn't speak.

"Yes."

"Is everything all right?"

"Mom...what was it like? After you left Dad?"

The pause that followed was long and excruciatingly uncomfortable. She didn't think her mother would answer, assumed she'd hang up in another second. Yet she eventually asked, "What do you mean? You were a baby. How am I supposed to remember that far back?"

The impatient dismissal was so familiar. *She never made it easy to talk to her, so I rarely tried. Am I like that with Yasmine? Is that part of the reason she's so distant with me? Rarely bothers anymore?* "You remember, Mom. I know you remember."

"What's to remember? I had a newborn I had to provide for. Alone. So I did."

"You worked two jobs when I was older."

"I had to. It wasn't easy to make ends meet. A maid doesn't make a huge salary. You needed so many things. Clothes and food and..."

"You got wasted every time you had a night off. You dragged some lowlife home with you every weekend." The words were out before Sapphire could consider the wisdom of speaking them out loud.

"I earned a little R and R. I worked damn hard. I did it for you." Her mother's vocal pitch had entered that dangerous, defensive, challenging one that always brought Sapphire's ire up.

"Are you actually claiming you did all that for me?"

"Well, didn't I?"

For the first time, Sapphire realized she would say the same thing to her own daughter. But she didn't drift into bad relationships for her daughter, no matter how hard she tried to justify her loneliness to herself. Instead, she wondered constantly why she worked hard, did everything for her child, yet didn't deserve love--just like her mother would and was claiming now.

"Why did you marry Dan?" Sapphire asked. "Why him?" *When there were so many others? So, so many.*

"He wanted to take care of me," her mother said simply. "He was the only one who ever did. He stayed. No matter what, no matter how we fought, how often we broke up, he always came back and said he loved me too much to let me go for good."

"That's how you knew he loved you?"

"I couldn't doubt it anymore. What was the point of doubting it anyway, when I wanted the same things he did?" Her mother sighed deeply, sounding just like Yasmine. "Why are we talking about all this, Sapphire? It's ancient history. Is something going on?"

"No," she lied, not for a second considering her mother her priest. "I've just been thinking about things a lot lately."

"Because Yasmine is in her terrible tweens? She's fifteen now, isn't she?"

The fact that her mother guessed Yasmine's age, or pretty close, didn't convince her to believe her mother was trying to do better in connecting with them. All it really meant was Yasmine had been doing that in-your-face thing she'd done since she was child when she wasn't getting the attention she felt she deserved from someone in particular. In this case, her grandmother. She'd probably been calling Sapphire's mother often, subtly reminding her of things she should have known, like her birthday and age, as she would if she was a better grandmother. Sapphire didn't doubt that her father got the same kind of phone calls from her daughter.

"That's when your irascibleness started."

"*My* irascibleness?" Sapphire instantly wanted to shoot down the insinuation that *she'd* been the cause of even one of their problems. She'd always believed she'd reacted to the crappy circumstances her mother thrust her into with her own bad example and immoral habits. *Maybe it wasn't just her. Maybe I wasn't easy to live with. Maybe I wanted to blame her for everything so I wouldn't have to feel guilty.* "Mom, I feel like I don't even know my daughter anymore. She's so far away. She seems to..." The look of disgust and disdain on Yasmine's face when she'd said that nasty thing about meeting the guy she was "screwing" only if she ended up, inconceivably, marrying him came back to her and drowned her in concrete heaviness.

"Hate you?" her mother guessed without an ounce of pity.

I never hid my feelings for Mom's actions. I wanted her to know it--wanted her to never doubt how she'd failed me.

"Just desserts, I'd say, my girl."

Knowing she deserved the unfeeling remark, Sapphire asked, "I don't know how to be a good example for her, Mom. I don't know how to balance being a role model with...life. Loneliness."

Her mother barked out a laugh, proving to Sapphire that she would never, ever be on her side about anything. "And you called me, thinking *I* might know how? I could do no right in your eyes. I was always the sinner. You were always your own saint. After a while, I figured there was no point in trying because nothing I did made you happy."

Sapphire unclenched her teeth. "So you made yourself happy? To hell with me?" *I can't do that. I have to be better. I can't give up. I want Yasmine to respect me, to see me as a good mother and not the poorest example available.*

"You always acted like you were above it all. Wonder-Woman with her to-hell-with-men invisible plane! But women are designed to want and need love and physical affection from men. It's just the way it is, baby. It's our purpose, and we can't be happy if we deny that or act like it's archaic and somehow belittles us as a gender. You can fight your own loneliness just to preserve your self-righteous reasons. You can act like you're any different from the rest of us weak females. But you can't run away and hide your head in the sand forever, my girl. You'll get it sooner or later, and I'm suspecting maybe you're realizing the truth now. And Yasmine will in her time, too. Until then, you can scorn and sneer and tell yourself you're holier than the rest of us--"

"I never thought that, Mom," Sapphire insisted. "You don't know me at all if you think I believed something like that."

"Oh, really? That's why you spent all your time trying to shame me? Enjoy your retribution, Miss Goody Two Shoes. Maybe now you can be a little more humble with the rest of us mere mortals."

Even as Sapphire slipped back into believing her mother was cruel and too hard on her long enough to say, "I have to go" and hang up, she couldn't stop thinking about the things she'd said. There was nothing else to conclude but that her mother thought she was as much of a hypocrite as her daughter did. *Am I? Do I just not want to admit the reality of the situation to myself?*

Ravenous hunger made her stomach growl loudly in the quiet room. She ignored it in favor of huddling in the dark *(running away and hiding my head in the sand?)*. She jolted when her phone rang and she looked down at the screen on the cushion before her. *Deck.*

God, I can't talk to him now.

Even as she forced herself up and into the shower, leaving behind her phone, then got into bed wearing only Deck's tank top, where she could feel sorry for herself, she thought about her mother's words about her husband. "*He wanted to take care of me. He was the only one who ever did. He stayed. No matter what, no matter how we fought, how often we broke up, he always came back and said he loved me too much to let me go for good. I couldn't doubt it anymore. What was the point of doubting it anyway, when I wanted the same things he did?*"

Deck wanted to take care of me. He said he did. He said he wanted to take me away from everything, my whole empty life, the bar with its pointlessness. And I didn't give him what he needed--took away the lovemaking because I needed to step back from that for my own self-respect. Whenever I couldn't stand my own need, I reneged on that though. Couldn't give him the words of love he needed, the full commitment he said he wanted with me because saying 'I love you' and my own submission to a commitment might turn on me when the romance went sour as it was bound to.

As she'd been asking herself all along, she wondered what he'd gotten out of any part of their short relationship. Little or nothing, nothing lasting anyway. *Some really good memories of the hottest sex ever.* It was almost as if she'd subconsciously engineered it that way.

Disgusted with herself, she wondered why being hypocritical was so second-nature for her while honesty was utterly foreign. *Do I even know how to be honest? With myself? With anyone else? What is the honest truth here?*

Sapphire closed her eyes and hugged her blanket tighter against her, the images behind her eyes making tears sting ruthlessly. *I love Deck. I want to be with him constantly. Permanently. I want to be the love of his life. I want to truly know him, give him everything he needs to heal and forget Roxanne Hart. I don't want to deny him or me any part of love. But I want my daughter to respect me. I want to make choices in my life that won't make her hate me and see me as weak and stupid. I don't know how to do any of that because if I do one, I fail at the other. There's no way to win. My life has become nothing more than a no-win situation. The only happiness I've had in so long are the moments I'm with Deck, when we're together the way we both want. I'm not sure it's smart, but I don't know if I can let go of that.*

Is it already too late? Is it over now because I was too stupid to see the best thing that's ever happened to me?

Chapter 12

For a long time, Decker blamed Roxanne for her piss-poor timing in deciding to confront him about his silence today, on his day off. He wished she'd never come, wished he'd had the determination to just tell her to go on with her life, be happy, leave him the hell alone permanently. He needed to move on, and that meant they went their separate ways--dead separate. He never wanted to see her face again. *F@#k friendship.*

Ultimately, the fault was his own though. He should have been honest with her. She never would have come here, ruined his short time alone with Sapphire, if he hadn't been such a bloody coward. *I should've told her once and for all I don't wanna go to her g@#m wedding. I wanna get on with my life, and I can't do that if she's any part of it. I don't want any reminders of how stupid I was to feel anything I did for her.*

Standing at his kitchen cupboard, he dialed Sapphire again.

Instead of waiting for it to go to voicemail, he hung up, reached back onto the shelf and brought out the bottle. Somehow the long draught gave him clarity for an instant. Sapphire believed the reason he couldn't tell Roxanne the truth was because he'd have to admit, to himself and therefore to everyone else, that he wasn't over her.

Am I?

His teeth clenched as his mind brought back the sound of a door slamming from the back of the house while Roxanne had tried to make him answer for himself. She'd shut up in a hurry, even foregoing her tears, when she'd demanded in shocked curiosity, "You're not alone, are you? I saw the car parked in your driveway--" She'd turned back toward it, then faced him again, saying, "Something familiar about it..."

"Dammit, Rox, I can't do this now."

He'd shut the door in her face. His first thought had been Sapphire--she must have been close by, overheard everything, and he'd known she'd assume the worst. Over and over, he wondered why she cared so damn much that he might be in love with another woman if she didn't love him in the first place. Maybe she cared, but it wasn't love for her. Ironically, it was the closest thing he'd ever experienced.

Be glad it lasted as long as it did. Did you expect it to work out? That she'd be walking around with Valentine hearts in her eyes for you for the rest of her life? S@#t. His own mother couldn't love him. He'd spent most of his life believing he'd be alone, man against the world, forever.

Get used to it.

Instead, he'd gotten used to Sapphire, fallen in love with the idea of her being here in his house, in his life. in his bed. *What did we even have together? We were either f@#n' or refraining--because she needed that. Not exactly the love affair of the century.*

He felt dead now.

Hours later, he'd tried to call her a dozen times over the time and he finally went down to the basement, got another case for his cupboard, taking one bottle for himself that wouldn't make it onto the shelf. He didn't care to distract himself with TV or anything else. Didn't want to eat. Didn't even care if he stunk to high heaven after another empty bottle littered the living room floor.

Beyond drunk, he was on the other side of the circle, closing in on sober again, when he thought, *I should've asked her to marry me. Would've solved every damn last problem. If we were married, we could be together all the time. She wouldn't feel like we're doing anything wrong. Her daughter could respect her. Most of all, Sapphire could respect herself. And maybe she could love me the way I wanna love her. To hell with the rest of the world. All I want is her. Now all that's left are memories of the only happiness I've ever experienced in this godforsaken life. If I wasn't so stupid, I would've thought about marriage right away. Would've gotten into the far back of her cage so she couldn't push me out easily. What I wouldn't do to have another chance.*

If it was over, as he was almost sure it was, he concluded he didn't have any reason left. For anything.

Chapter 13

Sapphire forced herself to get up and start a meal that could be heated up later, just in case Yasmine came home. She showed up at almost noon. Trying not to remember how they used to greet each other, with hugs and kisses, joy at being together again, she asked dully, "Are you hungry? I made something."

Sounding almost uncertain, her gaze analyzing her, Yasmine said, "Sure." She set aside her things and helped Sapphire set the table for the two of them.

"How's Darlene?" Sapphire asked as soon as they both filled their plates.

"Another false labor last night. She's miserable. They want me to stay with them indefinitely when I go back. It should be any day now, but if I just stay they have less to worry about. I ran out of clothes. I'm going to pack more, just in case. I don't have much time."

"Can they really afford to pay you so much?" Sapphire wondered. Darlene and Jace had moved into a house on Staten Island a few months before. After being crammed into a small apartment in the city for so long, their new home was huge, with four bedrooms and lots of space for their kids to get into trouble. They even had a backyard to run around in.

"I don't want them to pay me overtime. Just the usual they pay every day. I insisted and, after objecting a thousand times, they finally agreed."

Sapphire couldn't help looking across the table at her daughter with warmth and admiration. Darlene and Jace loved Yasmine like she was a daughter to them. She was a kind, sweet, generous person who loved their children as if they were her own siblings. They couldn't ask for a better babysitter. "You're a good person, sweetheart. I'm proud of you," she said softly, feeling the burn of tears she didn't have the energy to cry.

Fully expecting Yasmine to sneer at her, to say she didn't need her pride, Sapphire tried to put up her armor but found all her defenses were stripped bare. After so many hours of misery, crying until she had no tears left, she couldn't manage anything by way of pretending.

"Something's wrong," Yasmine said finally after looking at her for so long, Sapphire had gone past uncomfortable to feeling utterly exposed and vulnerable. "What happened? You've obviously been crying. Did you break up with that guy?"

Impossibly, her eyes filled again. A million times she'd wanted to call Deck, answer his back-to-back messages. The fact of the matter was, she hadn't felt capable of being sensible. She couldn't talk to him for that reason. She missed and loved him so much, she had no doubt she'd agree to anything as long as he stayed with her. *I need to act out a clear mind in which I've considered all my options before carefully deciding what's right for me. But I've never done that before except when I divorced Coug and ran with my daughter.*

"Feel free to say 'I told you so'," Sapphire invited listlessly.

"No thanks," Yasmine said, but, despite her decline, there was no warmth in her tone. "You're obviously sad. Did you love him that much?"

Maybe a lie would be smarter, but she spoke the truth in a pained whisper, "Yes."

Now her daughter's expression opened a little in astonishment. For a moment, she almost seemed sympathetic. "Why is it over then?"

"I'm not sure he's capable of love." *What am I doing? I can't talk to my daughter about this.* Yet Sapphire couldn't shake the feeling that they'd somehow switched roles. She was now the pining schoolgirl while her daughter was the sage mother she'd rarely been herself.

"What makes you say that?"

"I saw him with Roxanne Hart. I *heard* him, actually. I think he's still in love with her. I don't think he'll ever get over her."

Yasmine sat back, looking relieved. *Relieved!* She shook her head. "Well, who wouldn't be, Mom? You've met her, haven't you? She's one of Aunt Cherish's best friends."

Sapphire frowned in confusion. "I've met her. I barely know her. What does that have to do with anything?"

"Mom, she's beautiful. Inside and out. She's someone everyone loves, not just all the men who fall at her feet because she was a supermodel."

A gasp of shock that her daughter could be so cruel by pointing out she could never compete with Roxanne Hart rattled out of her chest. As if she didn't already know well enough that she couldn't compete in any department with the love of Deck's life.

"I didn't mean it that way, Mom. Honestly. All I'm saying is that they were together for like twenty years. Maybe they weren't *together* together, but they were friends. They were close. If he was in love with her all that time, well, it's not easy to get over something like that. Even if he has accepted he'll never have her the way he wanted to all that time, it would *have* to affect him deeply, so he wouldn't recover overnight. Now she's getting married to the love of her life. It's bound to have repercussions emotionally. But what you don't seem to realize is that none of this means he *doesn't* love you as much as you love him."

"It doesn't?" Sapphire asked, not sure how to interpret her daughter's wisdom, let alone embrace it herself.

"If you're concluding that because he still has unresolved issues over *her* he can't love *you*, then you're probably wrong. You're reacting jealously. What did he do after you broke up with him?"

"I didn't actually break up with him. I..."

"Fled the scene?" Yasmine guessed expectantly. "Hid in our apartment like it's a dark cave no one can find you in?"

Sapphire swallowed, feeling like this was a judgment on her usual modus operandi. "He kept calling." *He kept calling despite the fact that he pointed out I never told him I loved him and then he said*

"Whatever" as if none of it mattered--to him personally. Obviously it did because he called me within an hour after I left and about a hundred times since."

"So do you think you're wrong? That you assumed one love negated the other?"

Wanting to refute the possibly on principle, Sapphire recalled how Deck's love had felt real, more real than anything she'd ever experienced. *It felt like true love.* "I don't know."

"Well, think about it. Personally, I know how you are. I don't doubt for a second that you jumped to conclusions. The wrong ones. Maybe you shouldn't give up so easily. If you love him this much and you think he might love you, even if he's still reacting to disappointment over a situation he had no say in, maybe it's worth pursuing."

Sapphire didn't know what to say, what to do. She watched her daughter eat, picking at her own meal, hungry without the energy to care about filling the void.

"I really should get back, Mom," Yasmine said when she stood and put her dishes in the sink. "Thanks for dinner. Sorry I can't help you clean up."

"That's okay."

After her daughter rushed to her room to shower and pack fresh clothes, Sapphire sat thinking about all she'd said. Funny her mother's "advice" on the phone earlier had done nothing but make Sapphire want to rebel and scoff that they were nothing alike and her mother didn't know anything about anything. She remembered Deck saying, whether a person was sixteen or sixty, she always believed she knew *more* and *better* than her parents. *I always know better than my mother, and Yasmine always knows better than I do. It's the way it works. How is it Deck, who's never had children and barely knows what it's like to have parents, realized this when I never saw my own behavior as rebellion against my parents, a cycle that works its way through every generation without fail and all through life?*

Her cell phone rang, and she rose to look at it on the counter. Her cousin Cherish's picture came up on the screen. She'd thought about calling her more than once so she answered, thinking maybe it would do her some good to hear a bunch of different sides. *But am I ready to admit I fell in love, maybe stupidly, to another soul? Bad enough I confided, partially in my mother, and in Yasmine. My daughter!*

Sapphire all but planned not to confess anything but Cherish didn't give her the option when she answered immediately with, "You're seeing William Decker."

"Wha--? How did...?"

"Roxanne said she went to his house to ask if he was coming to her wedding since he hasn't been calling her back. She saw your car there. She didn't recognize it at first but later realized it was yours. Now tell me everything. Were you trying to hide this? How long has it been going on?"

God, I gave her such a hard time when she was just getting involved with Ty--said all those clichéd things about her jumping in with her eyes closed, advising her not to rush things when she was madly in love with the guy almost on sight. And here I am, doing the same things I accused her of and just as adamantly not wanting to talk about--or be talked out *of--any of it.* Deep down, she was *convinced nothing would change her mind about him, even when she knew herself her heart was moving too fast.* "Cherish...things are complicated right now--"

"I bet. Just tell me how long. How serious."

"Maybe I should remind you how close-mouthed you were when you started seeing Ty Foxx."

"I wasn't close-mouthed," Cherish defended. "I just knew how you'd react if you know how much I loved him, what we were doing."

Quietly, Sapphire pointed out, "You were brutally raped by two men when you were only a teenager. That scarred you most of your life. The thought of you jumping into something with a guy that was at least as dangerous as those criminals--"

"Ty *isn't* dangerous."

"He was messed up by his past, by bad experiences."

"Aren't we all?"

"Yes. Some worse than others," Sapphire agreed.

"You especially. And William Decker? He has issues, too, a lot of baggage."

"He does."

"Roxanne says his mother was an addict and he basically had no caring family structure for most of his life."

Not surprising he fell in love with Roxanne probably the second he met her, maybe even from afar, on the campus they were both going to school. She's a caretaker, I've heard--the motherly sort. Maybe that's the opposite of what most people might believe when it comes to supermodels and rock stars, but all her friends see her that way. Deck needed...needs...that more than anyone. He's had no softness his whole life outside of what she gave him in friendship and human compassion.

What can I possibly offer him? I don't know if I'm motherly--not to anyone except my own daughter, and maybe Cherish because she was hurt so badly by men.

Sapphire's heart answered her question so quickly, she almost felt winded by the fly-by. *I can love him, the way he's always needed and never had. I do love him that way. I can give him everything he wants and needs. But does he really want that from me? Truly? Or is he just settling because he can't have it from the woman he's longed for most of his life?*

"I don't know him well, Sapphire, but Roxanne believes he's one of the best men in the world. He's a good man, maybe even worthy of you," Cherish said in a non-confrontational voice.

"I know he is."

"But..."

"Can we talk about this some other time?"

Cherish sighed, clearly put out by her unwillingness to divulge, but she said, "Fine. But don't make me wait too long."

"Okay. Thanks."

Sapphire hung up, hearing the shower go off. She sat down and ate a few cooling bites, already aware she was talking herself into calling Deck. Maybe she didn't like her reason--she loved him and loved how he loved her too much to give up already--but Yasmine was right. She'd made assumptions that were unfair, as unfair as she'd been in taking what he was offering without giving him what he needed in return.

Swallowing the lump in her throat, she dialed his number,

tensing as it rang, three, four times, then his voicemail kicked in. She frowned, surprised because he'd called so many times, she would have thought he'd pick up on the first ring. Instead of leaving a message, she hung back, staring at the phone, trying to think where he might have gone that he wouldn't answer. Had he gone to work? Did Duff ask him to work on his night off? Had he done it on his own, paid or not, just to be doing something? But he'd still answer his phone if he was there. So what was going on?

Yasmine came out, her waist-length, thick hair partially blow-dried. She only wore a little makeup but she didn't need it anyway. She always looked adorable. Setting down her suitcase, she said, "Did you call him?"

"I...tried." She rushed to add, "Cherish called."

"Good. You should tell her everything. You need to talk to someone, Mom. You're terrible about that."

"What?" Sapphire asked in shock at the unexpected slam.

"You like to hide in your misery. You can't keep doing that. People care about you. Let them."

"You?" The meek question was out before she could consider, and then she could only cringe as her daughter stared at her in shock. She rushed to say, "Even if we're always at odds, Yasmine, I love you. And I know it sounds stupid and clichéd and hypocritical, but I want to be the best mother I can to you. I want to do the right things. I don't want to see you get hurt the way I did so often when I was your age."

"I'm *not* making mistakes, Mom. I'm living my life. I know right from wrong, and I live by those values. You and I just don't agree on what those things are. No biggee. But you should do the same. Live your life instead of making yourself miserable. I'm not judging you, whatever you think." Yasmine leaned down and kissed the top of her head. "Love you, too. I don't know when I'll be back again. I'll call you when I can."

After her daughter was gone, Sapphire concluded that the teenager was smarter and wiser than she tended to give her credit for. *And maybe I'm not the worst mother in the world.* If Yasmine loved her and was just doing the rebellion thing that all kids, regardless of their ages, did, then their volatile relationship was to be expected. All in all, it was better than most, even if Sapphire missed the loving closeness they seemed to have lost almost completely.

She got up, cleaned the kitchen, then went to dress and fix her face and hair. As an afterthought, she packed a small bag, hoping for the best even though she had no idea what to expect. She drove to Deck's house. After parking her car on the street, too unsure to occupy the driveway this time, she saw his motorcycle in the garage, but when she knocked, more than once, there was no response. She put her hand to the knob and twisted. It opened easily. Feeling like she was trespassing, though he'd been so eager to get her here after work early Monday, she couldn't deny everything had changed since then.

The scene that greeted her in the living room shocked her. There were empty and half empty whiskey bottles on the floor, the coffee table. Suddenly his silence, not answering her call, made sense. The emotion that flooded her was an uneasy mix of worry, dread and shame, if her cut-and-run had in any capacity led to this. She found him lying on his stomach on the bed, unconscious. He wouldn't have heard his cell phone in this state. He was so inebriated, he was barely breathing.

Did he do this because I left? Because he thought it was over? Does he love me so much, he loses all hope when things are wrong or kaput between us? Or is this all about Roxanne? Since he quit booze cold turkey and came to work at Duff's, he's had no incentive to go back to it. The second something went wrong, he returned to it, like a pig to slop. And he drank himself into a stupor. Dammit, I promised myself I wouldn't get involved with a drunk ever again. I know where that road leads.

But it's too late. I love him.

She went to the kitchen and started a pot of strong coffee, then assessed the state of the cupboards and fridge. She found his booze stash--it looked like he'd unloaded a case of whiskey into the cupboard above the sink. While her instinct was to pour them all down the drain, she knew they needed to talk first.

He'd bought some groceries, as he'd said he did, so she could make him a good breakfast--the best thing for him despite that it was early afternoon. She would make something to sober him up, hydrate him and cleanse the alcohol from his body. Seeing that he didn't have dishes or much of anything by way of pots and pans, she had no choice but to get creative with what little she had to work with. After she'd cleaned up the empty or mostly-so whiskey bottles from the floor and coffee table and prepped for the meal, she poured coffee to get him started on his recovery.

He was awake, on his back, squinting at the light overhead she'd turned on in the otherwise dark room. "Thought I heard something," he muttered thickly. "What are you doing here?"

She offered him the coffee. He looked at the cup for a second like he might refuse, then he sat up and reached for it. He gulped it down like it wasn't boiling hot. "I told you I needed to think. I was upset."

"And?" he asked.

"And you were in love with her for most of your life. It can't be easy to get over something that was your whole life."

"Wasn't a *good* part of my life. Not something I care to even remember. Don't forget that."

"Okay. I just want you to know I'm not interested in promises in the dark that no longer apply in daylight. I'm not interested in being a transition."

"I already told you, you're neither. What more can I say? You won't believe me." He spoke as if he was reading a script he didn't give a damn about. Because he was still smashed and didn't have the energy to put into making her believe him?

"I do believe you," she said softly, not feeling even a little bit of confidence. Maybe she'd misread the whole situation. Maybe he didn't really care. He was wearing a mask that said either *Go away, bitch; I already got what I wanted* or *I won't let you hurt me*. His defenses were so strong, she couldn't convince herself he felt anything for her beyond wanting her to get out and never darken his doorstep again.

"What do you believe?" he asked grumpily, not vaguely interested, going in for more of the scalding coffee.

Those words came at her like grenades. She didn't possess the strength to do anything but her usual runner. As tears flooded her already scoured eyes, she heard the sound of the coffee mug hitting the dresser, then he snagged her around the waist and turned her to him. The stink of booze was coming right out of his pores, but the only thing she could see was the disarmed, ashamed expression he now wore. "Dammit, Sapphire, tell me you love me. Nothing else on this whole f@#in' earth matters to me but that."

She shuddered against the coarse demand. This was what she'd needed so badly and didn't want to stick around without another minute. Now she knew everything he'd done and said since she left the first time were because she hadn't given him those words. What else could she believe when he was looking at her like he might disintegrate before her very eyes if she didn't speak what he needed to hear that very second?

"I love you, damn you, but now I'm scared to love you. I'm afraid to let myself be hurt because I've been used before."

"Abused," he corrected.

"Yes. And willingly. I don't want it to be like that with you. I love you more than anyone else I've ever loved, or thought I loved. I think I loved you even before that bastard tried to rape me. I think I've loved you from the minute we met. That doesn't make any sense, but..."

He crushed her to him, murmuring, "Say it again."

"I love you, Deck."

"Thank God." He was crushing her without restraint, but she didn't care. She hugged him back, pressing her face against his shirt and willing herself not to cry again.

"I don't ever wanna lose you again, Sapphire. I don't give a damn about anything that came before you. What I may or may not have felt with somebody else. If I was hung up on her, it'll go away.

I've moved on and I don't want anything to do with that. It's history. I don't give a s@#t about what's wrong or right either, 'cause this is the truth, babe: There's not a damn thing you and I could do together that could be wrong. Not from where I'm standing. I want you any way I can get you. If you're not with me, there's not a g@#m reason for me to go on."

"Don't talk like that."

"I don't want you to be obligated to stay with me. I don't want responsibility or sympathy, but that's the way it is for me. I want...I want things with you I've..."

Sapphire gasped at the shudder that went through his whole body, as if he was electrocuted by his emotions. "You want my love."

"Yes. God, yes."

"You have it. I love you. It's not about obligation or responsibility or sympathy. I love you. You're a good man. You're the best man I've ever known. But...I can't be with a drunk, Deck. I can't take that risk, even to be with you."

"Okay," he said as if her request wasn't even a consideration.

"Okay?" she asked, easing back to look him in the eye.

"I couldn't handle it when you left and wouldn't talk to me, wouldn't answer my calls. I did what I always did before. But I'll do whatever you want now. I won't touch the s@#t again. You want me in AA? I'm there."

"Really?"

"Whatever you need."

She cradled his face in her hands, holding his gaze with her own. "You understand why I'm asking this of you, don't you?

Because you went back to the booze almost as if you never left it. It's how you handle pain, baby. You can see that for yourself, can't you?"

He nodded, offering, "You'd know best."

Though he was saying and doing everything she required, she couldn't help wondering if he didn't believe what he was committing himself to. Some part of him seemed detached from his actual behavior that had led him to getting him bombed-drunk so he'd passed out cold. Deep down, did he think he'd merely slipped, big deal, and now he was vowing without truly committing to it that he wouldn't again…until next time? The next time they fought or he was faced with some pain he couldn't handle on his own, couldn't handle *sober*, would he go right back to the booze, almost as if he'd never left it?

I should make AA a condition. For going forward. But how? He won't admit he has a problem he can't fix with his own current determination. He refuses to face that he loses his determination in the face of problems he only knows how to handle drunk on his ass.

"I won't do it again. I promise, Sapphire. I'm wishing I hadn't touched the stuff in the first place, you know? I'll get a sponsor. Okay?"

"And that stash in your kitchen cupboard?"

"Gone…if I didn't already drink it all last night."

Did he actually think he could have downed that much without killing himself? *Maybe he could. He used to drink more than any other person I've ever seen in my life and still act like he was sober.*

"Go shower. I'm going to make you breakfast."

He nodded, one arm still around her. "We don't have a lot of time left."

"I know." They had to go back to work tomorrow already. Instead of spending every second together, they'd been apart and more devastated than their last "weekend", when they'd both been longing to make their relationship more committed and permanent.

As he hugged her once more, kissing the top of her head, she couldn't help closing her eyes and thinking, *He'll be my downfall. One way or another. All I can do is let it happen.*

Chapter 14

Decker couldn't stop looking at the other toothbrush in the rack while he used his own. He'd noticed it at some point when he'd been guzzling the booze right from the bottle and he was fixated by the anomaly, wondered if it would have stood there for the rest of his life, even if she hadn't come back. He already knew the answer to that.

Stupid to fall off the damn wagon like that. As if she needed more reason to doubt me. She doesn't trust me anymore, and why would she? I went back to the s@#t without thinking twice. I reach for it without thinking almost every time. Though I've mostly been sober for the last two months, I still chug it here and there, go through a bottle a week. I can't do that anymore.

The full bottles he must have unloaded in their cupboard in the kitchen stood next to the sink when he went out, his hair still wet, wearing only jeans. His head was pounding. Though he could smell that she'd been cooking, about all he wanted were a half-dozen ibuprofen tablets with Iron-Man-strong coffee.

To get the issue off the table, he cracked all four of the bottles and dumped their contents down the sink. Just like that, Sapphire moved into his arms, and he kissed her the way he'd wanted to since she appeared like an angel in his bedroom doorway, holding coffee for him instead of an axe.

"I'm sorry," he muttered, wanting heaven again with her.

"I love you."

The words were like an instant jolt of Vitamin C. He felt healthier, stronger, taller, better, just hearing them. He kissed her again, his hands finding her incredible curves, but she slipped away in another second. "You need to eat, Deck. Get that poison out of your system."

He knew better than to argue, despite the fact that his stomach didn't feel up to digesting anything. She served him scrambled eggs, bacon and toast--all cooked on a hotplate--and orange juice that chased four ibuprofen he desperately needed. She said she'd eaten with her daughter at lunch, but he wanted her close and he drew her down on his lap with her coffee while he ate with gusto despite his lack of appetite. Surprisingly, he felt better after eating. "You're a damn good cook, babe. Never ate eggs that tasted better."

"I'm glad you like them. But you need pots and pans. Silverware and paper plates that aren't leftovers from restaurant takeout. I can cook a lot better when I have what I need."

"Okay. Tell me what you need. I'll get it."

"You need them for *yourself*, Deck," she laughed the words out in disbelief. "I don't know how you've lived this long without basic necessities."

"Until I met you, I didn't know what I needed."

She smiled, shaking her head with affection stealing her expression. He grabbed another kiss. He considered asking her to marry him--the one clear thing he remembered from his drunken derailment--but something held him back. He wanted to know everything was okay first. Maybe he'd have to use it as a last resort if she changed her mind. Maybe the proposal would make a difference if she started this rocky incline with doubts and the cautious intent to survey the landscape before she fully committed herself.

As soon as he finished the food, he captured her mouth over his and unbuttoned her blouse slowly, anticipating she might try to stop him and insist they needed to take things slow. Instead, she set aside her coffee and wrapped her arms around his head, holding him close. The sound of her breathing becoming more and more ragged made him crazy. Every button was like an individual, random Chinese puzzle. He fought the urge to tear them out of his way. *I need her so damn bad, I don't know what I would've done if she'd tried to hold out for any reason. DTs are mild compared to this addiction. But she knew I'd be like this.* Decker reeled at the memory of trying to tell her how he felt about her when he'd been so close to losing her. "I want you any way I can get you. If you're not with me, there's not a g@#m reason for me to go on."

"Don't talk like that."

"I don't want you to be obligated to stay with me. I don't want responsibility or sympathy, but that's the way it is for me. I want...I want things with you I've..."

"You want my love."

"Yes. God, yes."

He'd been shaken to his core, shattered, unhinged and insane with wanting her love--every single part of it, the kind of love he'd never had. *Wanted, but never like this. Nothing like this.*

A part of him felt fried by the shock of what was happening inside him as he lifted her, carried her to his bed, and couldn't get enough. Not even close. Then he was shaking violently until she seemed to realize how close to the edge he was. Whispering words that felt too incredible to accept as truth--and he equally couldn't deny to save his life--she turned so he was on his back under her with a view of pure fantasy that could make a grown man cry. Slowly, tenderly, she took the reins, kissing him, stroking him, making him all but explode out of his own skin. He had no idea how he held out, kept himself in check, except that he wanted to be inside her so bad, he wouldn't ruin that dying wish for anything in the world. Nothing had ever felt so good either. He'd never experienced love like this. Watching her react to her own pleasure told him something he never would have believed before. *She loves me. She really loves me. Maybe she even loves me enough to stay with me, forever, no matter how many times I fail her.*

"You're so beautiful," he said when they both let go and the world detonated with them barely intact. "Nobody compares. Nobody could. Love you so damn bad."

"Love you," she said without energy, not moving from where she'd collapsed on him. He didn't want her to either.

As if they'd lost consciousness, he woke when she shifted sleepily and he turned to wrap himself around her on his side.

"I'm a mess," she murmured.

"I don't care."

"I'm forgetting everything."

"What?"

"Birth control. I don't remember the last time…"

"I don't care."

Maybe when he was awake, he would, but he'd never been so content. They slept again, enveloped in each other, and he woke, feeling a power inside him at seeing her still with him, still loving him. When they kissed, she reminded him about birth control. He reached behind him to the nightstand drawer. After groping for a moment, he found a strip of condoms. "Use them a lot?" she asked jealously.

Decker laughed. "They're ancient. You wanna take another risk, using 'em?"

"Do you? Again?"

"We're together, babe. Nothing can touch us." He believed that and the certainty affected every part of their hours together. But the sense of invincibility dissolved when she reminded him the next afternoon they had to go to work in a few hours.

"Let's call in sick."

"Both of us?" she said with her finely arched eyebrows raised. "That won't look too suspicious."

"So everybody'll know about us. I don't care. I'm the happiest man on the planet. If they know, how does that hurt us? I'll consider myself lucky. None 'of 'em'll believe it. Guy like me, angel like you."

"Everybody loves and respects you."

He snorted, not really concerned. "My staff doesn't. I bust their asses every night 'cause they don't know the meaning of professional boundary lines."

"They deserve to be busted and they know it. They respect you for doing your job so well."

"Like hell they do. You mind if they all know about us?"

Sapphire pursed her lips. "I'm not crazy about the attention we'll get. But they'll find out sooner or later, I guess."

"That place--sooner rather than later."

"You think they haven't noticed anything in the last two months?"

He had to concede she had a point. He'd gotten questions, a hard time, and didn't doubt she must have, too, from waitresses and barbacks wanting to know why they kept staring at each, always closed down the bar together, the last two there. "I'm tired of trying to hide how I feel about you, Sapphire Stephenson."

"Good. I am, too. And maybe it'll make things easier."

Decker questioned how things could get simpler, but he didn't get the answer until many hours later, when Sapphire went on her first break. She gave him a long, meaningful look before she went into Duff's office while the barback took over for her for the next ten minutes. He waited a minute, a precious minute he already regretted losing, then followed her at a discreet distance. He'd barely locked the office door behind him before she was in his arms, muttering, "We should have called in sick."

"Told ya." He eased her top over her head and she helped him eagerly, reaching for his straining button-fly the second she was free. Her hot hand made him feel drunk with desire for her. He'd thought of almost nothing else since they got to work, when everyone had to comment on the fact that they'd come together in her car. That they hadn't bothered explaining had made the gossip spread like wildfire.

The incineration was over almost too quickly, and he didn't want to let her go, especially when her eyes got all misty. "I hate work. I hate anything that means we can't kiss and I can't be in your arms and we can't do this."

"So do I. Come home with me again." Maybe too soon to ask her, but she had to figure he would sooner or later.

"Yasmine is spending the night at Darlene and Jace's again. She called me not long ago to say Darlene is actually in labor now. It's not false this time. So she has to stay with the kids until they can bring the new baby home."

"How many days do we have?" he asked greedily.

"I don't know. One. Maybe two."

He swore in gratitude, kissing her so deeply she groaned her anguish because they had to get back to work--back to what would surely become relentless ragging now that they'd stolen this time together and everyone would have seen them come in here together. He didn't care. His mind ran miles ahead to the time when she'd be back in his arms again. *I'm gonna ask her. When we get back to my place. I'm gonna ask her to marry me and, if she agrees, we don't have to be apart ever again.*

Right now, it sounded almost too good to be true. With his experience, he expected a jinx one way or the other. But he vowed the only thing that could stop him from this single-minded course was Sapphire's outright rejection.

Chapter 15

"Marry me."

Sapphire had been halfway between deep thought and sleep. She quickly looked up at Deck lying beside her. They were wrapped possessively in each other's arms. They'd gotten off work a little over an hour ago and had already made love twice in his bed. She hadn't allowed herself to feel ashamed--something that was sure to strike her viciously once she saw her daughter. But they'd needed this freedom to reach for each other and the intimacy to express their love after things had almost gone south between them. There was no way back to the higher ground, she'd realized and accepted though not without a certain amount of nervousness. She didn't know how to love a man without this physical dimension driving the relationship. She'd never known any other way.

How often over the years had she considered that she and Lionel Cougar didn't have love, though he'd married her and proved he believed himself to be her owner when he pursued her even after their divorce? She'd let sex be the end-all, be-all between them because the dark mystery of the bad boy had intrigued her. They'd shared little or nothing else. She couldn't remember a single conversation that had anything to do with likes, dislikes, past or present emotions, hopes and fears. *I don't want what I have with Deck to be anything like that. I want to know him through and through, the good, the bad and the ugly. I want him know me the same way. Sometimes it seems like the passion between us is too intense though. It takes over everything. I need more, but I want this, too, as desperately as he does.*

Ironically, his marriage proposal mirrored her own thoughts. She'd wondered sleepily what would make their oversexed relationship right. He'd asked her to move in with him, but she wasn't sure how that erased the lack of 'moral example'. Sure, there was a commitment implied in living together, but there wasn't anything necessarily permanent about a situation like that. *We could break up just as easily that way. We wouldn't be forced to work out our problems because we'd built something stable together. Something solid, like a firm commitment...*

"Are you drunk?" she asked in shock that refuted the fact that she'd been thinking along the same lines. She realized what she'd said when he winced. "I'm sorry. I just meant...are you serious?"

"Never been more serious. We could get married soon. Not sure if there's a waiting period, but I doubt it's long even if there is."

"Deck...I--"

He shook his head, quieting her. "Ah, dammit, I was supposed to do something else here. Flowers, chocolate. A ring. I can get down on my knees--"

"Deck!" she said, laughing when he slid off the bed onto the floor to do just that. Buck naked, he knelt beside the side of the bed. "I don't need anything like that. I can't believe you're serious. It's only been a few months and marriage is...*huge*."

"Solves all our problems, doesn't it?"

Did it? She was too flustered to consider all the angles.

"I love you. You need something legal to make you feel like we can have sex anytime we want."

"But do you really want that? Marriage? Because it's not something I would do lightly or consider revocable if one of us gets tired or bored of the other."

"I've never asked a woman to marry me before, babe. Never. It's a damn big deal to me, too. I don't hand out proposals. You're the only woman who's made me wanna do it. It's right with you. Whatever shackles you to me for life, by law, works for me."

She'd noted the way he'd chosen to define "commitment" in the past--as a cage, now as a handcuff--both forms of imprisonment. Did he really see monogamy that way? And did he see those forms of captivity as *good* things? "You haven't met my daughter. My family. Friends. How can we even consider this?"

"So I'll meet your daughter. Your family and friends."

"What about yours?"

"You already know Duff and Bev. There's nobody else."

Sapphire silently remembered those who considered him a friend, namely her cousin's friends: Roxanne Hart and her whole group. Even if he didn't want to be included in that, they called him friend. "What about your mom?" she asked.

"Ah, hell, Sapphire, you don't wanna meet her. Trust me, you don't. I wouldn't do that to you 'cause sooner or later she'd be hitting you up for money for her next fix."

While that didn't sound pleasant, she couldn't help wondering if there was more to his refusal than that. Did he not want her to meet his mother for another reason?

"You want me to meet *your* mom?" he asked.

She inhaled, not exactly comfortable with that prospect either.

Her expression must have prompted him to decide to go back to the heart of the matter. "Why don't we hold off on all that, babe? I'll meet your daughter. That's the important thing."

"I still can't believe..." She shook her head.

"Would a legal marriage, the whole thing--license, ceremony, ring on your finger, combined assets, mutual place to live--make you feel right about us sleeping together and being together every second we can, like I want? Would you feel like your daughter couldn't call you a hypocrite anymore if we were married?"

Her cheeks blazed, though she remembered how Yasmine had insisted she wasn't judging her. Even now, she didn't quite believe that. "I'm not sure she'll ever respect me the way I need her to, or give me any credit, but...yes. I'd feel right about our relationship if we were married."

"Then what's stopping you from saying yes? Do you love me? Do you think you could be with a guy like me the rest of your life? Or does that not appeal to you at all?"

She felt soft inside and out as she drew herself closer to where he was still kneeling by the side of the bed. She pressed her forehead against his. "I love the idea of coming home together, sleeping together, making love whenever we want without guilt. I want that more than anything. I love you, Deck. It's just so fast."

"By whose standards? I'm thirty-five years old, babe. I've been alone long enough. But think about it. Take as long as you need. The offer's valid for life."

"You've never been married?" she asked stroking his rough jaw. "Never even been close?"

"You know I haven't. Never been anywhere near that galaxy. The idea of permanency..." He snorted. "...not been in my vocabulary up 'til you came along, you know? I don't want transitory. I don't want short-term. I don't want this to be something we drift in and out of. But I know you need time to consider whether you want a long-term commitment with a guy you're not entirely sure of, one who's been a drunk for most of his life, might always be. You've had abused by drunks. But I'd never hurt you. Not like that."

"I know you wouldn't."

"Do you?"

She kissed his mouth. "Yes, I do believe you wouldn't physically hurt me. But you can hurt me in other ways, honey. Emotionally. I love you. I've given you every part of myself. That makes me vulnerable to you, always. It means you can hurt me mortally, deeper than anyone else. You might do it unintentionally, but the people we love can potentially hurt us worse than the rest of the world *because* we love them."

"I'm sorry I made you doubt me."

"That's the problem," she said softly. "The fact is, no matter how much we feel for each other, how much of it is fueled by the chemistry we have, we don't really know each other very well. Past or present. We're not part of each other's lives yet, the way getting married requires."

"You think I might turn into Frankenstein at any minute?"

Sapphire swallowed, remembering despite how long ago it'd been that Coug had changed from the irresistible bad boy she couldn't get enough of into a monster she only wanted to escape. "It's not that, necessarily. Sure, from the point of view of what we actually know about each other in any given situation, you could, I could. But we don't really know each other outside of the bar. Our daily routines away from that place. Until we're daily fixtures for each other and know each other's habits, have brushed out teeth side-by-side, gone grocery shopping together, watched bad movies together, met the people closest to both of us, even gone on a single date, how can we skip to the finish line and get married?"

His expression didn't change when he asked, "So you're turning me down?"

"No," she rushed to say.

He blinked as if he'd missed something. "No? How was all that a yes?"

"It's not a 'no'. It's more of a 'yes', but first… Deck, I just don't want us to rush into anything we might regret."

"I'll never regret a second of my time with you," he said with the kind of conviction that would shame a saint.

As much as she wanted to return the sentiment without reserve, the past few days revealed proof of the opposite. Even still, she couldn't help wanting to accept his proposal and rush into a marriage that would eliminate the shame she felt for their highly sexual relationship. She wanted to be with him all the time and show her daughter that sex belonged in marriage, between two committed adults who respected each other and were willing to take the responsibility for anything that happened between them.

"I'm just being straight with you, baby."

He nodded. "Okay. That mean you wanna go home?"

She shook her head. "We need to sleep, but maybe we could go out together today, before work? Do something normal people in a relationship do?"

"Sure. You'll sleep here?"

She couldn't help smiling at the tension in his expression while he waited for her response. "I'll sleep here."

"Good." He relaxed instantly, sliding back into bed and pulling her into all the alcoves of his body. "You're crazy, lady, you know that, don't you?"

She laughed. "I'm fully aware. Thank you for putting up with me and loving me anyway."

"I'm not exactly Freud myself," he said, and they both laughed.

Chapter 16

Sapphire's cell phone woke them. She sleepily reached over the side of the bed, searching for her discarded clothes. Decker moved back to give her room and, when she finally answered, he could see immediately that she was alarmed. She sat up, strangely wide-awake awake as she listened intently. He guessed her daughter was the caller, based on her clear upset. When she did speak, she didn't make a lot of sense from his end. "He's there now? But Darlene and Jace have made it clear... Good. But what does he think he's doing?... No. It's fine. I'll be there in twenty minutes. Don't open the door until then. Call me if something else happens."

She hung up and jumped to her feet to get dressed when he demanded, "What's going on?"

"The twenty-one-year-old guy my daughter has been dating decided he wanted to see her, no ands ifs and buts, so he's at Jace and Darlene's. She babysits for them, like I told you, and you know

Darlene is in the hospital having her baby now. Obviously they don't want Yasmine's boyfriend there while she's supposed to be taking care of their other children. And she told him he had to leave. She's a responsible person. She doesn't take her job lightly. She didn't invite him over, but he's there. He won't budge. He's insisting she let him in, but she won't open the door. Nothing she says gets him to leave."

Decker guessed what Sapphire wasn't saying. She was stunned, touched, that her daughter had called her, her above anyone else, but Sapphire probably assumed it was because she had no one else to call. When her daughter called for help, she'd go in a heartbeat. She was already dressed.

Decker got up and started yanking his own clothes on fast. "I'm going with you. Guys that age are trouble."

For an instant, she looked like she might argue, but then she said, "That might be a good idea."

"Probably not the way you wanted us to meet," he said, yanking his boots on. "We'll plan something better later. Let's take care of this now."

In her car, Sapphire said, "I've seen you handle unruly customers. You use diplomacy first. You're good at that. I know that's why Duff relies on you. He did even before you took the job he offered you."

For years, Duff had been trying to get Decker to take over as head of security. Until Sapphire's trouble, he hadn't considered it. But he was good at defusing tense situations. He'd been a good bodyguard with a cool head and a lethal arm, too.

When they arrived at Jace and Darlene's two-story, Decker

saw a Kawasaki, then summed up the guy near it. Sapphire called her daughter on her cell phone so she'd open the door to her as soon as she got to it.

Once she was on her way, Decker headed straight for the trouble. The young guy lowered the phone he was all but yelling into--probably leaving a voicemail for Yasmine, who'd no doubt stopped answering long ago. The dude stood, looking ready for a fight, and Decker didn't let him get his intimidation on. "You need to leave. Now."

"Who's gonna make me? You, old man?"

"She's taking care of young kids. You're feeling lonely, but it's not a good time to be selfish, not unless you wanna burn your bridges with Yasmine."

"What do you know? Who the hell are you?"

"I protect the interests of Yasmine and her mother. Remember that for the future. It's all you need to know about me. Now leave. If and when Yasmine's ready, she'll call you. That's my last warning. Take it or leave it."

When the kid swung a fist at him, Decker caught it easily, whirled him around, twisting his arm around to his back and shoving it up until he yelped. With his head over his shoulder, Decker said in a low voice, "Get outta here. Now. While you still have the use of both your arms."

When he let him go, the bruiser had to give it one more try. A second later, Decker had him in the same position. He pushed the arm up a little higher, and the kid capitulated with a curse and scream, panting, "I'll go. Okay?"

Stepping back, Decker gave him just enough room to get on his bike and withdraw. Treating his sore arm gingerly, he did what he was told with a backwards glare that had no effect on Decker whatsoever. He stood his ground until the last flicker of the tail lights disappeared around the corner. Only then did he go up to the porch and take a seat on the step, planning to wait patiently until both Sapphire and Yasmine felt safe enough to believe the badass wouldn't be back as soon as the coast was clear.

A quarter of an hour passed before Sapphire came out, her daughter trailing her to the door with a little kid--the girl older than the boy--in each arm.

"You should tell Darlene and Jace about this," Sapphire said. "You did the right thing. They'll understand. They won't blame you for this."

"I already did. I told Darlene you were on your way. They're waiting for me to call back. But I have the feeling Jace might come home if I don't call soon."

"Should we wait a little longer? Make sure he's not coming back?"

Yasmine's gaze was on Decker, and he did his best not to quail under her scrutinizing assessment. "No. That's okay. I don't think Justice will come back. I'll lock the doors anyway. The backyard is fenced in, with a locked gate. Thanks for your help."

Sapphire turned to him, obviously at a loss about how to introduce them in a way that wouldn't be awkward. So Decker said, "William Decker."

Yasmine nodded. She was cool, composed, and he had a surprising feeling that she wasn't judging him prematurely. He had to conclude Sapphire had the measure of her daughter. She was a good kid, mature beyond her years. "My aunt Cherish has mentioned you. She said you were Roxanne Hart's bodyguard for a long time."

He nodded, wondering how much she'd heard about that. He'd had scant contact with Cherish Stephenson in his time, and the bad connotations he associated with her had nothing to do with her personally. Roxanne had foolishly tried to fix him up with the woman once upon a time, and he'd wanted nothing to do with her insulting pity and attempt to deflect his attentions onto another woman. "We can stick around as long as you need," he offered to Yasmine.

"No. Like I said, he won't come back. He wouldn't have left without your intervention, I'm sure, but he won't come back again. I can handle things from here."

"Will you be home later?" Sapphire asked.

"Probably not for a couple days, now that the new baby is here."

"Did she have a boy or a girl?"

"Another boy. They named him Jeffrey. Seven pounds. I'll send you a picture from my phone after I get these two down for their naps. Have fun, you two." She directed the two kids on her hips to wave "bye-bye", then closed and locked the front door behind them.

"You wanna wait around for a while anyway?" Decker asked, shifting his gaze to Sapphire.

"No. She'll call me back if she needs me to return. Let's go get something to eat. And I need to shower and change my clothes before work."

Back in her car, Decker said, "She looks just like you, babe. The two of you could be sisters." That was the honest truth. Her daughter seemed older than her years, Sapphire far younger than hers. "And you're right. She's a good kid. Mature. You did a damn good job with her. Anybody could see that."

"I'm sure she'd say she can take most of the credit for that herself. But...thanks. Thanks for thinking I had something to do with how well she's turning out. I'm proud of her."

"You should be." He put his hand on her thigh. "Have we done enough 'normal stuff people in a relationship people do' for the day?"

She turned to him, not inserting the key in the ignition. "Deck...maybe we could..." She swallowed, looking half terrified and putting the fear of God in him in the process. "Maybe we could get a marriage license today. I mean, in case there's a waiting period."

Decker stared at her, blown apart by the abrupt change. "What made you decide this?" He realized almost immediately, recalling the way her daughter had said, "Have fun, you two" teasingly as if implying they were a couple of kids going to the prom together--or skipping right to the hotel, and she knew it. "Your daughter knows we've been sleeping together after work, and we've been joined at the hip for the past how many days. Is that it? That what's got you marriage-minded?'

She sighed. "I won't deny that's part of it. But...seeing you from the house, taking care of Justice, however you managed to get him to leave, I realized that I do know you. I know the kind of man you are. I've known it for years. Maybe we haven't gone about our relationship in any way that could be considered 'by the book'. We've done it backwards and crazy, but we fell in love anyway. I know we'll have problems at some point and we'll have to deal with things that won't be easy, but nothing can change how I feel about you, that I want to build more than notches in a bedpost with you. We'll deal with it as it comes. We'll figure it out. In the meantime, I want to start our lives together. I want to be with you. I want to love you fully. Without guilt, self-ascribed or otherwise."

Looking into her eyes, he felt the kind of love he couldn't have imagined before if he'd had a thousand years to custom-design his own image of what that would look like. He pulled her mouth to his and kissed her. The gratitude saturating him was enough to choke him. Gutturally, he murmured, "I promise you won't regret this, babe. I'll do everything in my power to make you happy so you won't regret taking a chance on me."

Chapter 17

By the time they had to go to work at six, they'd eaten, applied for a marriage license and purchased simple, inexpensive wedding bands. She'd refused the sapphire engagement ring he wanted to buy her--which had led to a discussion about their financial situations. She had a decent savings, separate from the account she put a certain amount into every paycheck for Yasmine to go to college. She had enough to live on but never extravagantly. Deck spoke what she'd already suspected. He'd blown any money he'd made being the personal bodyguard of a supermodel and rock star on booze, bartender tips, fixing up his house and top-of-the-line vehicles. He had some savings left but nothing huge.

The marriage license required a twenty-four-hour waiting period. The plan was to get married on Monday at the Staten Island Borough Hall. They would have time off after for a very short honeymoon. Deck had no one he wanted to be there, though he mentioned Duff and Bev and quickly added that he wasn't sure he was ready to dispel the rumors at work just yet. She wanted Yasmine, Cherish and Ty to be there, of course. Calling them had been the hard part of the day.

Yasmine astonished her with her lack of surprise, reminding Sapphire vividly what had prompted her change of heart about that morning's 'maybe' to his marriage proposal. She and Yasmine had watched Deck outside with Justice from the window. At first Yasmine had asked questions like, "He wouldn't actually hurt him?" and then, the first time Deck effortlessly got the smartass kid into an arm wrench, she'd muttered under her breath over and over, "Don't hurt him; don't hurt him." But it couldn't have been more obvious the amount of restraint that went into Deck's actions. While it'd been clear even without being able to hear anything from where they stood inside the house that Deck had the upper hand in the situation, he'd used only enough force for to get Justice to do the right thing. Yasmine had concluded, "Wow. That was pretty good. Justice won't be happy, but he deserved that, showing up and being such a selfish jerk."

In a combination of pride at Deck's effective defusing of the situation and the strangely illuminating realization that no part of her feelings about being a role model had to do with shame about Deck specifically, Sapphire had made her decision to say yes to his proposal. She wasn't ashamed to be involved with him, not even with her daughter. He was a good man. She knew him, despite their lack of solid relationship beyond the last two months. She remembered asking her mother why she'd married Dan out of all the men she'd been with. She'd said because he alone took care of her, wanted to do that, and he stayed, always came back and loved her too much to let her go for good. She'd realized Deck had been doing that, maybe for longer than she'd ever been aware--given his violent reaction to the thug who'd tried to rape her. That incident had led to his sobriety and willingness to come to work at Knuckleheads officially to watch over her personally. Maybe he'd told Duff he was doing it to give him and Bev peace of mind, but Sapphire knew he'd done what he had because he couldn't do anything else. He didn't trust anyone other than himself to watch over her and take care of her.

"I was actually expecting it," Yasmine had said when Sapphire told her she was getting married.

"You were?"

"Of course. It makes perfect sense. I know how your mind works, Mom. So I'll talk to Darlene and Jace about Monday so I can be there. They should be back by then anyway."

"Thanks. We'll move into Deck's house. He says you can take your pick of the extra bedrooms. Is that okay?" Sapphire had braced for a fight.

"Sounds good. I better go. Stevie-Jade is upending the toy box in the middle of the living room."

Sapphire had called her cousin while Deck was in the shower. Cherish required a lot more explanation. She'd wanted to know everything from the beginning, and what could Sapphire tell her beyond it'd just happened and they'd realized they were in love and wanted to be together? Hence, marriage Monday. "We're planning to move into his house after the ceremony," Sapphire told her. "Would you and Ty mind helping us do that?"

"Of course not. I can make some arrangements at work. Ty doesn't have any photo shoots that day."

"Good. Thanks. Then I can get started packing on Sunday and hopefully have almost everything in boxes by the time I have to go to work that day. We'll get home from work early on Monday, get a few hours' sleep, and have the ceremony at one. Deck knows someone with a moving van. I don't know what's going on with Darlene and Jace, but could you watch over Yasmine for the two days of our honeymoon?" Two days was actually an optimistic view of their days off.

"Two days for a honeymoon? Why so little?"

"We have to go to work on Wednesday night. Duff practically requires a full review before he lets anyone take a vacation, even a single day. Besides, we haven't spent a lot of time planning this. Financially, I don't know that we can afford too much. We're talking about doing more later."

"You'll probably want that. You know, I think I understand now how you felt when I first got involved with Ty, so fast. One day he wasn't in my life, the next day he was my *whole* life. You must have thought I was giving up everything for someone I barely knew."

"Yes, I did feel like that. I worried, but it turned out. It'll work out for me and Deck, too."

Sapphire had heard her cousin take a deep breath, then she'd said carefully, "I don't want to bring this up and make you doubt, but you must have thought about it yourself, honey. Deck's feelings for Roxanne were pretty intense. Are you sure he's over her?"

"No," Sapphire had admitted quietly. "Not at all. But I know he's accepted that nothing will ever happen there. He can't be with her. I believe he loves me. So that's all I can hold onto."

"What do you think he'd do if Roxanne suddenly became available--I mean, that's as unlikely to happen as snow in the Bahamas, but do you think he'd...well--"

Sapphire had suddenly become aware she wasn't alone in the room. She wasn't entirely sure how long Deck had stood in the doorway but she'd realized when she turned to him that he'd heard Cherish's words, though she didn't have her phone on speakerphone. She'd swallowed guiltily.

"Sapphire, are you still there?" Cherish had asked at her silence.

"I need to go--" she'd started.

Deck had shaken his head. "No. She apparently needs to hear it, too. Put it on speakerphone."

Sapphire winced and said, "Cherish, I'm going to put you on speakerphone."

"What--?"

As soon as she'd changed the setting and held her cell phone out, Deck said, "You're the only woman I want, Sapphire. I loved Roxanne. She was in my life for a long time. Maybe I'll never stop caring about her. But I *love* you. You're my whole life. The only thing that can change whether we're together is you."

"I'll call you later, Sapphire," Cherish had said quickly in response, obviously chagrinned. "Congratulations, you two."

Sapphire had disconnected the call. "I'm sorry you heard that."

"I'm not. I don't want you to have any more doubts about me than you have to. And she's important to you. I want her to trust my intentions. Do you still doubt you're the one I wanna be with?"

"No. I don't."

"Good."

She'd made a quick dinner (she'd brought a few of her own pots and pans and dishware to his house), then they headed to work. Duff and Bev were there, they both saw with his van parked in the handicap spot near the front. The bar had been built wheelchair-accessible from the start. Duff sat huge in his chair, tall and, at one time, muscular but now mostly chub. Bev was a formidable woman herself at six feet tall, at least two hundred pounds. Immediately upon seeing them enter, Duff said in an offended tone, "So that's how I have to hear about it?"

"Hear about what?" Sapphire asked.

"You know what. About you two. Everybody's talkin' about it."

"I think it's great," Bev thrust in. "I always thought you two worked together."

"You seem upset," Deck noted of their boss. "Don't bother telling me that it's against company policy. The hookups around here are a dime a dozen."

"Yeah, and, if you two break up, where does that leave me? Out my two best."

"Selfish bastard," Deck said harshly. But he and Duff grinned.

To soften the blow, Sapphire said, "We're getting married. On Monday."

The look on the faces of their old friends was almost comical. Duff went from mad as hell to utterly elated in a way that was insane to say the least. Sapphire and Deck both refused the celebratory drink Duff wanted poured out. Luckily, their boss didn't push it, but Bev insisted to be in attendance for the ceremony, which was exactly what Sapphire had hoped, despite Deck's uncertainty because it'd be a hassle for Duff.

Duff looked around the room. At the moment, they had customers but nothing like they'd see in a few hours, when the bodies would be packed to the rafters. "The two of you don't belong in a place like this. You know it. If you get married, maybe have kids, then you can't stay in jobs like this forever. Neither of you."

"You firing us?" Deck asked.

"No. Hell, no. But..." He grunted in disgust. "This place ain't gonna move anybody up in the world."

Even as he urged them to think about it, Sapphire understood he didn't really want either of them to.

"What the hell was that?" Deck asked a little later, when she'd asked the bartender currently on duty what was running low and went down to the storeroom to stock up. Deck had followed her, not usual, on the offer to help her carry what was needed, but they endured relentless teasing from everyone who crossed their paths in that direction anyway. "One minute he was busting our chops for being together, potentially breaking up and quitting our jobs. Next thing, you mention marriage and suddenly everything's Cloud 9 and he's telling us to strike out elsewhere for greener pastures."

She raised an eyebrow. She'd rarely heard Duff wax philosophic. "I think he just didn't want to hear we were engaging in some bar hookup, something that'd never last."

Deck nodded. "Probably protective of you, getting involved with a bastard like me."

"You're not a bastard," she said simply, loading bottles into a crate. "I know 'bastard'. You're not it."

He sighed. "Can't wait to get that ring on your finger, babe. Have you in my house--our house. Our bed. Our life."

When he stalled her from reaching for another bottle, drew her close and kissed her, she wrapped her arms around him. So they got razzed for taking too long? She didn't care. She needed this to get through the next eight plus hours.

"Duff's right. I wanna get you away from this place, honey. I know what can happen in a dive like this."

"Not with you around, defusing situations and resolving conflicts."

He wasn't reassured. "The one minute I don't have my eye on you, somebody might hurt you. I failed once. I couldn't take it if I failed again."

"Deck, you make it sound like you've always been watching over me, even before you took the job Duff's been trying to give you for years. Were you really? When you came back that night…"

"I didn't see you get in your car and drive away, safe and sound. It bothered the hell out of me. What if I'd been too ripped to notice or remember? But, yeah, I always watched over you. I think you know I did. From the first. First time I met you. You can take care of yourself better than most women, but…I felt protective even then. Maybe you're tough, but you're also fragile." He slid his hands over her arms. "You think I haven't notice these bruises I left all over your arms, trying to get you not to leave me when things almost went south? I barely touched you, not like I could have, and you're all bruised."

"They don't hurt. You weren't trying to hurt me. I know you

weren't. I want you to take care of me, honey. I want to do the same for you."

He chuckled under his breath. "I may need it more than you."

"I'm not so sure. But I've thought about getting another job, Deck. Cherish has been trying to get me to work at her flower shop since I fled to New York City. She says she and Darlene will train me in any area--cash register, designer, mail order, delivery. Whatever I prefer and I'm good at. It'd be first shift. I could have a life. But I don't want that if you're here by yourself. I want you to have a better life, too."

"Why didn't you take her offer long ago?" Deck said, sounding almost mad that she hadn't.

"I don't know. I suppose because at first, I knew Coug could make some connection between the shop and her, and I didn't want to endanger her or her business. She was successful from the time she opened her doors, and she worked hard for that. I didn't want to be the cause of her empire toppling. And I also felt like I needed to do it on my own. I needed to take care of myself and Yasmine. I didn't want her to give me a job I was no good at just because we're cousins."

"Who says you wouldn't be good at it? You already know how to use a cash register. You're good with customers."

"What about you?"

"The only reason I'm here is you. That's been true from the beginning. But Jace offered me a job at the company he's president. Security job. Maybe he offered it 'cause Rox asked him to, but I could do that kind of job, and it might be first shift, too. Probably would be. I'd have to ask for sure."

"We should consider this."

"After we're married?"

She nodded. "I want you to get to know my cousin better. Her and her husband."

"They're important to you. I'm fine with that. I wanna be a part of your life. It's all I want."

"Good. We better get back to work."

During her shift, she considered that Duff would surely regret being the one to mention they should get away from this place sooner or later, if they took him up on it. Maybe eventually he'd wish them well, but he'd be hurting at first. Sapphire headed the bartending staff smoothly. No one had any problems with her, but she expected she'd be easy to replace. Knuckleheads was known for being rough. Security had been a problem because bouncers came and went, most not staying long when they found out it sometimes meant going home with bruises and scrapes, black eyes. Duff had been asking Deck to come on board officially since the first time he saw how well he handled trouble, heading it off many times before it ever started. Deck hadn't been interested in becoming an employee, let alone head of security, at first because he'd had a job with Roxanne and he was at her beck and call. When she cut him loose, he hadn't seemed to care about anything. Instead, he'd seemed content to piss away what money he had in booze. Sapphire had always assumed he'd refused Duff's job offer because of the off-chance Roxanne might need him sometime down the road and what she wanted was paramount in his life. He wanted to be unfettered if she called him back. Now she wasn't so sure.

A different life, a better one, safer, more settled, serving customers in a way that didn't shame her, working with people she could respect and not simply tell them what they wanted to hear, working with a staff who deserved the same...it sounded like a utopia. True that Sapphire had realized early in life that she didn't have big aspirations like her cousin, had no wish to own her own business or even be successful in something that could loftily be considered an actual career, but she did want a job she liked, one capable of paying her bills and could see herself doing indefinitely. All she'd ever really wanted was to be was a good mother, the best she could possibly be considering her limitaticns. *And my mom was absolutely right, even when I don't want to accept her archaic view of things: I want to be in love with a guy who loves me like the sun rises and sets of me, one who makes my life worth living. A guy I can take care of who takes care of me. That's my idea of the good life. With Deck, maybe I'll finally have that.*

Chapter 18

"Four-thirty's too long apart, and I can't even have you the way I want you then," Decker complained, not wanting to let her get in her car and drive way, forcing him to drive home alone and go straight out of his mind in the hours they couldn't be together.

"Pretty soon we won't have to be apart at all. And eventually, you probably will wish for some space." She smiled.

"Not gonna happen." He couldn't imagine a time when his entire life and thoughts weren't focused on her.

"It's a good time for you to start getting to know my daughter," she said softly.

Her plan was to go home, get a little sleep, spend some time with her daughter alone, talking, then he'd show up for dinner and the official meet and greet. He rarely remembered feeling nervous about anything, not like this. Standing up straight before Yasmine without flinching back at Jace and Darlene's house had been hard enough. He couldn't be more aware that her daughter knew they were sleeping together, he was corrupting her mother, maybe disrespecting her in Yasmine's estimation. *How the hell am I gonna come off like a good guy to her, someone worthy of her mother? But somehow I've gotta do that.*

Defending himself to Sapphire's cousin after she'd justifiably asked about his well-publicized fixation with Rox had been his first test. He'd been aware the only way to handle that situation was head-on. But he doubted he'd done much to win Cherish over. The experiences he'd had with her thus far had been beyond awkward. He'd wanted to kill Rox when she'd tried to play matchmaker, thrusting him into a circumstance where he'd had no choice but to tell Cherish he wasn't interested in being fixed up. The only consolation back then had been that she hadn't wanted anything to do with the fix-up either. Beyond that, he'd almost never given the woman a thought. Now he needed to make her see him as honest and true, worthy of Sapphire. If he didn't, she'd be whispering in her cousin's ears the rest of their lives about how he couldn't be trusted. The best way to get into Cherish's good graces was to meet her and her husband and do everything he could to become friends with both of them.

Resigned to the plans she'd made, Decker gave her one more kiss, watching her get in her car after he agreed he'd see her at four-thirty in the afternoon. Inside his house, he did a walk-through, wondering if the twenty some years he'd spent replacing and renovating just about every room had been worthwhile. Was this a good enough house for a family? For the first time, he realized with a jolt that he'd be something like a stepfather to

Yasmine. Hell, the idea was enough to make him feel nauseous. What did he know about that role? Nothing. Luckily, she was old enough not to expect too much, probably. He was hoping, foolishly he suspected, that the two of them would end up liking each other so their simple relationship would satisfy Sapphire.

As he walked through some of the bare rooms, the thought registered that he'd never considered someone else might live here with him. He'd fixed up what he had for the sole reason that the activity gave himself something to do when Rox didn't need him, when he wasn't wasted out of his head. Evaluating his own work made him feel uncomfortable because a part of him wanted to hear that Sapphire thought this house was more than simply a step up from her apartment, which it was--at least that. Did she think he'd done a good job? Would Yasmine like any of the rooms that currently had no decoration, little beyond a coat of paint that could easily be decorated any way she preferred?

I'm getting a wife and a teenager in one swoop. Never would've believed either could happen. But there's something else I've never conceived of happening to me. Sapphire's still young, certainly young enough to consider having more kids. God! With me. Me, a father? S@#t.

That thought made him stagger like he'd been shot in the head, and he actually found himself leaning against the door jamb in the room he was standing to keep his balance. They hadn't talked about that at all. He'd never imagined a life that he could have anything like that. He wouldn't have even thought he'd *want* something like that, and he wasn't sure now. He couldn't imagine what a father did. How to be a good one. He knew two extremes of mothers: The best and the worst. But a father? He'd never experienced a father. The foster families had either ignored him or yelled at him for one thing or another, even if he'd done nothing wrong. For the most part, he'd kept his distance. His childhood had been about hiding, withdrawing, finding a place where no one took notice of him. *I was lonely as hell. All my life. Until Rox. Even if she never meant it to be more than friendship, I guess after having no love, no concern, no softness whatsoever, there wasn't a stone's throw in hell I wasn't gonna fall for her, so far down, there was no way back up even when I'd had all the boundaries she erected memorized.*

Rox had loved him more than anyone else ever had. She'd been a mother to him, a best friend, his hangman when he realized almost from the start how self-destructive she was. He'd learned fierce protectiveness with her. He'd learned how to wrap her in a bubble that no one else could get through unless she allowed it. He'd wanted to keep Jamie Dubois out at every turn, especially when he became aware that, no matter how closed-mouthed she was about it, Rox had given that bastard her heart when they were both just kids. Nothing, even good commonsense, could talk her out of it either. *I wanted to kill him. I plotted his murder so often, it's a miracle in one of my drunken stupors I didn't go through with one of my jealous scenarios. The only thing that stopped me was the voice whispering that Rox would hate my guts if I hurt a single hair on his precious head. But there was nothing I wouldn't have done for her. Nothing. Even accept that I'd never have her, she'd never love me the way I wanted her to.*

Sapphire loves me that way. Everything I've felt for her for longer than I let myself admit, she feels for me, too. If I lose her...

His mind turned instantly to his downfall, what could be his snare. He walked down to the basement where the boxes were lying in full view. Two cases of whiskey: one untouched, another torn open with half the bottles missing. He'd poured the ones he brought upstairs down the drain because the symbolic gesture had been necessary to convince Sapphire he was done with the booze.

S@#t, I don't want her knowing all my money's tied up in whiskey. I paid a pretty penny to stock up. No way I'm gonna pour all that cash down the drain, just 'cause I know Sapphire'd have a fit if she found out these were here.

He decided he'd haul them over to Knuckleheads one day she had something else to do. Duff might even give him something for them.

Closing the open box the best he could, he shoved both as deep under his work bench as he could, piling empty whiskey boxes from past cases around them to keep them out of sight. *Precautionary. I'm getting rid of these soon. Not drinking anymore. So she doesn't need to see these. She doesn't need to know, doesn't need to doubt me yet again.*

Would she insist soon that they needed to attend an AA meeting together? Did she expect him to stand up and admit he was an alcoholic in front of a bunch of strangers? He liked the idea about as much as he did Aunt Clara's pink bunny pajama suit. But, if Sapphire needed him to do that, if it was the only way to get her to trust him again, he didn't have a choice. He'd wait for her to initiate that step though. He didn't need to convince himself of what he already knew. He didn't need booze. He could live without it. No public confession, sponsor or meeting were required to prove himself. As long as he had Sapphire, alcohol wasn't even a consideration in his life.

While he moved more things around under the workbench, he realized Sapphire would need empty boxes for their move to his house. He might as well get his motorcycle in the garage and use his car today, get the boxes he had down here into his trunk, ready for when he went over there today. *Also have to call about using the moving van on Monday.*

The mental list he was making himself would keep him from being nervous about having to meet her daughter. *I want her to like me, approve of me. If she doesn't, Sapphire's gonna have doubts. That's the bottom line.*

Decker remembered that sapphire ring, the bright blue color of Sapphire's eyes, in the jewelry store. He'd wanted to put that beauty on her finger, but she'd seen the price and wouldn't hear of spending their "future" on something so impractical. Maybe she didn't need it, maybe he couldn't even afford it, but he wanted to get it for her anyway. Their wedding would be so simple, no woman could consider the cut-and-dried ceremony the fantasy she'd been looking forward to since she was a little girl playing bride dress-up. Sapphire insisted she'd never been that kind of romantic girl, but deep down he suspected she was as much of a romantic as any other woman. She wanted flowers and fairy dust. Considering the plain, poor life he was capable of offering her, she deserved at least one romantic extravagance.

Chapter 19

After a few hours' sleep, Sapphire wanted a single thing--to go shopping. In truth, she'd been growing more and more distressed about what she was going to wear to her own wedding. She didn't have a lot of clothes, didn't need anything really considering her job was her life, and, though she and Yasmine sometimes went into each other's closets and "borrowed", even her fashion-trendy daughter had nothing appropriate for this albeit-informal wedding. Over and over, she'd told Deck she didn't want anything fancy, but she couldn't stop thinking that her first wedding had been undertaken in jeans at the town hall. They'd required the consent of her parents' and a judge's approval before they could get married because she was so young.

I want more than a shotgun wedding. I want to remember every detail of this one, even if it's not the wedding of the century. I want my dress to be special, memorable, something I'll recall for the rest of my life, something Deck will see me differently in. I want to be blow-him-away beautiful on our wedding day.

She knew just which dress shop she wanted to go, and she called her cousin so Cherish was already there when she arrived. Like she was, Cherish was usually tall for a woman with a figure that was svelte, especially in the ultra-feminine, tailored business suits and skirts she wore. She'd changed her hairstyle just before she met Ty and the long, blond strands framed her classically lovely face in a way that was much more attractive than the uptight chignon she'd worn forever before that.

After they hugged and caught up quickly, Sapphire said, "It needs to be informal. I don't want my dress to scream wedding. But I want something gorgeous."

"Definitely. I hope William's not too upset because of what I said on the phone. I didn't realize I was talking so loudly."

"He's fine about it."

"William? Is that what I'm supposed to call him? Roxanne always calls him that."

"I call him Deck."

Cherish nodded. "Better. Roxanne says she's spent years trying to get him into her group of friends, but he refused. I imagine he's going to be hard to befriend. He probably doesn't want to meet Ty, me--I mean, officially, as your cousin."

"And best friend. Actually, he does. He realizes how important you are to me. He says he wants to be a part of my life."

"He really said that? Without you suggesting it?"

"I asked him if he'd meet you, and he seemed to know on his own that the way to be a part of my life was to get to know you. So he suggested, after things aren't so busy, we should get together--couples' night, or day, out."

Cherish reached to hug her again with a happy smile on her face. "That would be great. I'd love it if we could see each other more often. But you both work at the bar, so we'll have to figure out how."

Sapphire nodded, not sure how to jump into talking to her cousin about a job at the flower shop. When they pulled apart, they started walking through the racks, looking at the dresses. "Cherish, I don't know when I'd have time to really do anything about this, but is your offer to work at the flower shop still good?"

"Are you kidding?"

Sapphire glanced over the rack at her. "No. I'm just so tired of that bar. Deck thinks it's dangerous there."

"Especially after what happened a couple months ago?" Cherish's beautiful face wore the same worry it'd been immersed in when Sapphire told her what had happened back then.

"Yes, especially that. But Deck and I both want to get away from it. We don't have a life. That job is our whole life, working night shift, sleeping all day and barely having a few hours to do anything else before we have to go back."

"So you'd want to work the first shift?"

"Yes, unless it's a big problem for you, or if Deck can't find a job that's also first shift."

"It's not a problem at all. I expanded into mail order, as you know, and that's an area I really need to hire people. I can't seem to get enough people to cover the amount of orders we get from the internet and other sources. But I'd like to get you trained in all areas of the shop first so we can see where you excel. It helps to have employees who can fill in on different positions, especially during certain parts of the year, since the flower business has a lot to do with holidays. Just tell me when you're ready. I would hire you at any moment. I know you'll do well wherever I put you."

"Thanks, Cherish. You're being too kind. I don't have a lot of experience in anything beyond--"

Her cousin broke in. "What is bartending if not customer service? And you excel at that."

"I do my job," Sapphire agreed.

"I think you do more than that. You've told me about the tips you bring home in a night. If you weren't amazing at what you do, you wouldn't be bringing that much in."

"You do understand these people usually get drunk out of their skulls? And I'm not exactly chopped liver? That's when money is no object and one kind word can get you a hundred dollar bill."

Cherish laughed. "Okay. So what does W... Deck? Decker...?"

"Either."

"Okay, well, what does he have in mind for a different job?"

"Security is what he knows. Jace apparently offered him a job at Bandoleer Babies in security. If he can get a first shift position, it'll be perfect."

"It would be. But I could also use delivery truck drivers, if he can't get something else right away."

"Really? You'd do that?"

"Of course."

"I'll bring it up to him later."

They both moved to another rack. Nothing Sapphire pulled out thrilled her, not when she put it in context with City Hall.

"Are you going to Roxanne and Jamie's wedding?" Cherish asked abruptly. "She told me she sent you an invitation, but now that she knows you and Decker are together, she'll want both of you there more than ever."

Sapphire sighed, the stress inside her increasing with the volatile question. Cherish was a very close friend of Roxanne's and she'd been trying to bring Sapphire into her circle of friends for years, too. Sapphire's job hadn't allowed any real bonding to occur there. Personally, she'd wondered why Roxanne invited her to her wedding, beyond that she was friends with Cherish. The two of them didn't know each other well. "Deck doesn't seem to want to go," she offered, trying not to sound like it bothered her either way.

"That upsets Roxanne so much. She loves Decker. He was there for her when no one else was. The fact that he doesn't seem to want anything to do with her anymore hurts her deeply."

"Surely she can understand why he might need to pull back?" Sapphire suggested carefully.

"Yes. But Roxanne..." Cherish grinned. "She never understands why people can't just be friends and love each other. She's always been bothered by the 'contention'--to be polite--between Jamie and Deck. Especially now that she's in remission, she wants all the people she loves in one place at her wedding."

Sapphire pursed her lips before saying, "I'm glad she's going to be okay. I think it goes without saying that, even if Roxanne has never and will never be in love with Deck, only felt friendship-love for him, she must know that at one point in his life he saw that inferior love as an insult, a slight and a cruelty, rather than something kind and beautiful, the way maybe she intended it."

"I guess that makes sense." Cherish shoved a dress back onto the rack, looking over at her. "I have to ask this because we've never talked about this before, Sapphire, and I barely know Decker. The two of you weren't together until recently, though Roxanne knew both of you for a long time."

"Okay."

"Well, you're not jealous of Roxanne, are you, honey? I mean, is he unwilling to go to her wedding because he knows you wouldn't like it?"

Sapphire remembered how she'd reacted, hearing Deck talk to Roxanne outside his front door. She'd been floored by the absolute certainty in that moment that he wasn't over her, that he might never be. *Would going to her wedding prove the truth, one way or another?* While she didn't like seeing this side of herself, Sapphire couldn't deny if they attended Roxanne's wedding and Deck seemed removed, unaffected by the event, she would feel a hundred percent more reassurance that his heart belonged to her. She couldn't decide for sure if it was wrong for her need that, but the affirmation would relieve so many of her fears. *But if he isn't removed, if he's* troubled *seeing her get married...*

To give herself time, Sapphire said in a light voice that didn't match the feelings warring inside her, "She was a supermodel. Who can compete?"

"You."

She glanced at her cousin after Cherish spoke without hesitation, with total confidence.

"I love that you don't seem to realize it, Sapphire, but you could easily be a supermodel, too. You're one of the most beautiful women I've ever known. And don't you dare suggest I'm biased because we're related. You are. I know for a fact that isn't the first time you've heard that either."

Sapphire had realized her effect on males--and females, who wanted to hate her because of the way she looked--for most of her life. But she'd never felt the kind of conceited confidence beautiful women displayed. Men were too fickle to allow her anything like that. Maybe they wanted her at first, but she'd found their ardor cooled almost as quickly as it took for the sweat to dry.

"I have no problem with both of us attending Roxanne's wedding," Sapphire said in a level tone. "We'd have to get off work for it, though, if we're still working at Knuckleheads then."

"Well, I hope you do. You've been working too much. Sometimes it feels like you're a vampire that only comes out at night."

Sapphire laughed, feeling like she fit the assessment a little too well. "Well, I'm out today in daylight and I'm not disintegrating into ash in the sun."

Cherish had pulled a dress off the rack, and she was staring at it in awe. "This is it, Sapphire. You would look incredible in this."

The knee-length satin was champagne-colored, not ivory--a very critical difference--strapless and gathered in an hourglass shape at the waist with gorgeous, soft, sapphire blue pearls dotted over the material of the skirt. Sapphire fell in love at first sight, but immediately she knew it was inappropriate. She shook her head. "It's strapless. We're going to the Borough Hall! It's too much for such a lack of grandeur."

"Who cares? You would look amazing in this, Sapphire. This dress was made for your figure."

Even as her mind insisted she had to reject the dress, she let her cousin talk her into at least trying it on. The second she slipped into it and saw her reflection in the mirror, her decision was all but sealed.

Cherish was staring in the wide, full-length mirror with tears in her eyes. "Oh, Sapphire, you're going to stop his heart. You're so beautiful. You have to get this one. It's your wedding. Whatever you want is appropriate. The bride is boss."

Sapphire turned to look behind her in the mirror. The dress was backless, dipping to a widow's peak, the zipper covered with more sapphire pearl appliques. Her shape was a perfect hourglass in the beautiful satin. Though her breasts were easily full enough to hold up the sleekly pleated mermaid bodice, there was nothing sleazy about the neckline. She felt like a princess in the sheath, and she could already imagine how she'd gather her hair at the back, giving it a little lift and drama at the top, while the rest spilled over her shoulders like a waterfall. Even pulled up a little at the top, her hair would cover most of her bare back so it wouldn't be too scandalous for a town hall wedding.

Deck won't remember his own name. That's what I want. I want to knock him senseless when he sees me, and his only goal will be to get me to the judge as fast as possible. This dress will be the only part of my wedding that will be spectacular. I can have one thing, can't I?

Her eyes met her cousin's in the mirror. She let herself be talked into buying the highly inappropriate and expensive dress, but all the way home she felt absolutely certain she couldn't possibly wear it. She'd been seduced by the thing. It was much too fancy for such an informal wedding. She hadn't spent any time considering that she didn't have the shoes or jewelry to go with it either.

She carried the dress up to her floor, telling herself sadly that she'd just have to bring it back to the store at some point and get her money returned. But now she was right where she'd started. She had nothing to wear to her own wedding.

Yasmine met her at the door when she entered the apartment. "Did you get your wedding dress?" she asked when she saw the dress bag.

Sapphire felt her face reflecting her internal pain. "Yes, but I can't possibly wear it. Cherish talked me into buy it, but it's over the top for a simple courthouse wedding."

"Let's see."

Even as she shook her head definitively, her daughter was drawing her into her bedroom, taking the bag and unzipping it. *I'll just put it on one more time. What will that hurt?* While Sapphire undressed, Yasmine unveiled the wedding attire. "This is perfect, Mom," she exclaimed--always animated when it came to fashion and beautiful things. "Cherish has good taste. Did you already get shoes and jewelry?"

"No. I forgot." The dress had blinded her to all else.

"I think I have a clip you can wear in your hair... I'll be right back. You put the dress on. I have everything else you need."

Yasmine rushed out into the hall, to her room, and Sapphire slipped back into the heavenly satin. A moment later, her daughter returned with the perfect pair of sandals, a faux diamond clip for her hair, and long, faux sapphire-studded earrings with a matching bracelet.

Setting everything down, Yasmine zipped her up, then turned her so she could look. "It's perfect," her daughter sighed. "You're stunning. This dress was made for your figure."

Tears stung Sapphire's eyes, accumulating as Yasmine excitedly went to work getting her decked out in the jewelry, hair clip and the two-inch sandals she'd wear without nylons. It'd been so long since they'd shared anything like this. When Yasmine turned her back to the full-length mirror, she nodded decisively. "Perfect. Are you happy?"

"Yes," she murmured, too close to tears to be effusive.

Yasmine fussed over the hem for an instant, murmuring, "Hard to believe just a few days ago you thought it was over with him. Now you're marrying him." She straightened, standing beside her in front of the mirror. Sapphire couldn't have failed to see what so many others had before--she and Yasmine did look like twins, sisters, not much age difference between them. "Is there some reason you're rushing into this, by the way? And don't tell me because you want to be a good role model for me. You know you don't have to feel guilty just because of me, Mom, if that's why you agreed to this--if it's the only reason."

"I love him. I want to be with him. And he loves me. That's why we're getting married. But I don't deny that the timetable might have been speeded up because...I don't want you to think I'm a hypocrite, Yasmine. He's a good man, and I've never loved anyone the way I love him."

Yasmine nodded. "From first appearances, he does seem like a good guy. Not that I really know him. But I saw the way he looked at you."

Sapphire couldn't say Yasmine and Deck had hit it off famously. After all, there hadn't been a lot of time for getting to know each other after Deck defused the situation with Justice. There'd been plenty of awkwardness, but both had obviously been willing to put forth the effort to be open to each other in these early stages.

"How does he look at me?" she asked in a whisper, wanting to believe her daughter approved.

"He looks like he wants to consume you, wrap you in cotton. I can tell he feels a lot for you. He can't hide it when he looks at you. And he's protective of you. You need that."

She saw a lot in those few minutes we stood on Jace and Darlene's porch. "He's coming over later. I was hoping--"

Yasmine smiled at her irresistibly. "I'd play nice? I will, Mom. He's going to be your husband. Of course I want to get to know him, but we'll see how it goes."

"Are you really okay with all this, honey?"

Yasmine shrugged. "It's not really up to me."

"Maybe not. But I do want you to be all right about it. I would never let anyone I'm involved with hurt you."

"No. I know you wouldn't, Mom. But you could be a bit nicer to Justice."

Sapphire's mouth fell open, and she tried to cover her shock hastily. "I...I thought for sure you'd break up with him after what happened at Jace and Darlene's."

The shrewd look Yasmine gave her clearly stated that she

knew Sapphire had *hoped* that was the case. "Why would we break up over that? He just needed to respect my boundaries, especially when I'm babysitting. My priority has to be to Stevie-Jade and Ty, and, later when they're ready to go out in public again and need me to take care of the kids, the new baby Jeffrey. Justice promised he wouldn't do anything stupid like that again."

Even as Sapphire felt obscene pride at her daughter's maturity and sense of responsibility, she couldn't help wishing that relationship was nothing more than the done deal she'd been pushing for from the first time the womanizer had ogled her without knowing she was Yasmine's mother. 'All right. I'll try to be nicer and not so disapproving of him. I really am proud of you, honey. You handled that so well. You didn't lose your cool when you easily could have. Are Darlene and Jace all right about it?"

"Yes. They appreciated how I handled it, too."

The doorbell rang, and Sapphire sent a stunned gaze at the clock, seeing it was four-thirty already. "That's Deck! I lost track of time. I haven't even started dinner."

"I did. I had the feeling you'd want him to come over so we could get to know each other better, and you were dress shopping. You change. I'll get the door and entertain him until you're ready."

"Are you sure?"

"Of course. That's the point of this meeting, right?"

Unable to help herself, Sapphire reached out and her daughter returned a tight hug. She couldn't help smiling tearfully when her bedroom door closed behind Yasmine. Knowing they wouldn't have a lot of time here before they had to go to work, she put on her work uniform--jeans and the Knuckleheads staff tank top--then rushed out so she wouldn't force Yasmine and Deck to have too much alone-time together already. Before she reached the living room, she caught Deck's voice and the sight and sound of a blue velvet jewelry box snapping open. "What do you think?" he asked Yasmine in an irresistibly unsure tone. "You think she'll like it?"

Sapphire drew back behind the wall. She didn't have any doubt what was inside that box. Deck had fought her when she'd resisted him getting her an engagement ring. They weren't in the financial position to afford something that cost thousands of dollars and she really didn't need an engagement ring anyway. She'd tried to convince him she'd be just as happy with the simple, inexpensive wedding bands they'd purchased. But she remembered the one from the jewelry store vividly because Deck had said the center stone matched her eyes. The ring had been white gold, an oval sapphire surrounded with diamonds. She'd loved it as soon as he'd picked it out for her. He hadn't seemed convinced when she shot down all argument either. *Because he planned to go back and get it for me later, when I couldn't protest?*

"It's gorgeous. Perfect for her. Even if she insists it's too much, she'll love it," Yasmine, who loved jewelry, said enthusiastically.

If Deck had been intent on winning her daughter's heart, he'd done it in spades with his romantic gesture and the genuine humility he'd employed in asking Yasmine's opinion of the gift. "That's what I'm hoping. But I'm afraid she'll tell me to take it back if I give it to her now, like she did when I tried to buy it for her in the store."

Yasmine laughed. "That does sound like something she'd do. But not this time. You went on your own, over her financial objections, and bought it. I can't imagine she'll refuse it. And wait'll you see her in her wedding dress. That ring will go perfectly."

"Wedding dress?" he repeated, sounding flabbergasted. "We're getting married at City Hall."

"Of course wedding dress! You do understand how important a woman's wedding attire is, don't you? It doesn't matter if she's tying the knot in a dark cave. Every woman wants to be wearing something that'll make her groom faint dead away at her feet."

"Ahh…" Deck groaned like the wedding had been upgraded to a serious event and his discomfort did the same.

Again teary but smiling at what she felt slightly bad for overhearing, Sapphire crept to the kitchen and took over finishing dinner. She'd started teaching Yasmine how to cook when she was a little girl, so she knew the chicken enchiladas would be delicious.

Hearing her being noisier than she needed to be to cover up for her eavesdropping, the two of them came into the kitchen. She'd never understood what it meant to have her eyes devour anything, but her gaze was ravenous for him, and, when he came over to her, she couldn't feel any discomfort when he hugged and kissed her right in front of her daughter. "Missed you, babe," he murmured under his breath, for her ears only, when the kiss ended, damnably short and unsatisfying.

She agreed, her face lifted to his. She could see exactly what he wanted in his burning eyes and didn't dare do anything more than put her head against his chest until she could recover from her mutual desire. "Me, too," she said softly. "Are you hungry?"

"Starved."

"I'll set the table in the dining room," Yasmine said.

Sapphire drew back. "That might be nice for a change."

The apartment had a dining room, and she'd bought an inexpensive table for it after they settled here. She'd liked the idea of the two of them having formal meals together. Unfortunately, it hadn't worked out that way. They rarely used the dining room unless they had guests, which was almost never.

As soon as Yasmine left the room, Deck kissed her again, this time long and deep, and she couldn't help remembering what her daughter had said about the way he looked at her as if he wanted to consume her. Her cheeks flushed as she breathed, "Can't wait for Monday."

"You can't want it to come faster than I do," he muttered huskily.

I can't imagine I'll ever regret this, she thought in bliss just before Deck pulled out the ring box. Her eyes overflowed with premeditated tears. "You shouldn't have…"

"Don't you dare try to get me to take this back," he said as he opened the lid to reveal what she'd rejected purely out of commonsense.

She looked at the beautiful ring that couldn't have been more perfectly chosen for her. Instead of speaking, she held out her hand. Deck slid the ring onto her slim finger. "It's so beautiful. Thank you."

"You're beautiful. It's perfect for you."

She kissed him passionately until he warned in a rough, hushed voice that they needed to back off. He cradled her face in his hand, probably seeing how pink her cheeks were. She was so happy, dinner with her daughter, the start of an official relationship between her and Deck strong, only solidified how balanced her life felt. *Nothing can go wrong now.*

"Let's go to my place first, drop off the bike, so we can go to the bar together," Deck suggested on the way to the parking lot.

She agreed. At his place, he got into the passenger's seat of her blue Chevrolet Aveo and immediately reached for her. When they both needed to take a breath, she said, "It went so well. Thank you."

"Your daughter? She reminds me of you. Outgoing. Charming. Hard not to be impressed with her."

"I agree. But we're not alike. She's so cool and calm and collected all the time. I'm never that way."

"Really? 'Cause I doubt a single person who comes through Knuckleheads would say anything different about you."

"Well, I don't feel that way inside."

"You hide your lack of confidence well then."

"Thank you, Deck. For being so willing to get to know her. And Cherish and her husband soon. I want us to share our lives completely." She took a deep breath. "I was thinking…maybe we should go to Roxanne's wedding. Together."

His expression altered to the point of being almost unrecognizable. She watched him sit back in the seat, withdrawing physically but also mentally and emotionally. He turned to look out the passenger window, then he shook his head, turning back to face her. The expression on his face made her wonder if he was taking her suggestion as some kind of blow. But he said coolly, "I don't see any reason to go. Are you really close to either of them? I know you're not. So what's the point?"

"She asked both of us."

"Trust me, she doesn't want me there. She doesn't expect me to go anyway."

Sapphire swallowed. For a long minute, she wondered if she should just drop it. But then the thought that this *shouldn't* bother him--if Roxanne meant nothing to him, that was; if he wasn't still in love with her--convinced her otherwise. "Deck, maybe you need to prove to yourself and to her and Jamie that you really have moved on with your life."

"You mean, prove to *you*?" He didn't turn from staring straight ahead. His tone was neutral.

"I just think it'd be good for you."

He turned to the passenger window again. "Look, if you wanna go, fine. If you want me to go with you, I'll go. But there's not a single other thing that'll convince me to set foot at that wedding. I don't have anything to prove."

Were his teeth clenched?

"It's up to you," Sapphire insisted, feeling like she'd done damage, but she couldn't understand why he was acting like this. If he was truly over Roxanne, why would it matter in the least? *If he loves me, it's no big deal.* They could go, and he should be unaffected by seeing the woman he'd once loved like a drug marry another man.

"No. It's up to *you*."

Now she knew his teeth were clenched around his words. The harshness was bone-deep.

Sapphire stared out the windshield ahead, finitely aware that if they attended the wedding and he proved he was still in love with Roxanne while there, it would be too late. They'd already be married--a week before Roxanne's wedding. *Too late for anything but a lifetime of regrets.*

Chapter 20

The shift was the longest Decker had ever endured, made worse by the bombshell Sapphire had unexpectedly dropped before they arrived at the bar and knowing they couldn't be together after their shift was over. She needed to sleep and start packing and Yasmine had mentioned wanting a new dress for the wedding, too, and she wanted her mom to go with her. He'd also heard from Duff, who came in just before they shut down at almost four in the morning. Sapphire had requested the week off, including their regular days, after their wedding--along with the actual weekend...the same weekend of Rox and Doobs' wedding, when the bar was busiest. *Instead of a damn honeymoon, she expects me to attend somebody else's wedding, a wedding I'd rather die than go to. But I have to go along with it, or she's gonna believe the worst.*

How the hell am I gonna get through that fiasco in one piece? Maybe she needs proof, but all I need is distance--as in, never see either of them again, ever, end of story...for me anyway.

Duff granted their time off, Bev scolding her 'old man' every time he groused about it, insisting he knew they were both thinking about leaving him--not just their jobs, but *him* personally. Decker didn't have the fortitude to be reassuring. All he cared to think about was that in two days, Sapphire would be his wife and she'd belong to him, he would belong to her, and to hell with the rest of the world. If they could just get to that point, he'd work the rest out somehow.

The days and nights were agony until that point. He didn't think about his own wedding attire until Monday, once they got off shift and agreed to meet at the Staten Island Borough Hall at 12:30, after a couple hours' sleep, apart. He didn't have a lot of dress clothes. While he'd been a bodyguard in a glitzy world, he was expected to dress nicely, but he'd never been over the top, never bothered with suits or full-on tuxedos. He owned a few pairs of mildly dressy black, tapered slacks, white button-down shirts, and a pair of shiny Italian loafers he hated but figured they fit and so he wore them anyway. He'd never put on a tie in his life, and his leather biker jacket was his nicest.

He barely slept, barely tried. He was ready in twenty minutes flat and got in the twelve-foot moving truck he'd borrowed so they could pack up her apartment after the wedding and headed to the Borough Hall. Although he couldn't imagine when they would have had time, he wished they'd done the moving the weekend before, despite the fact that they'd had to work and there wasn't much time for sleep, let alone moving from her apartment to his house between their shifts.

His phone rang, and he pressed the speakerphone button as soon as he saw Sapphire's number.

"Did you get any sleep?" she asked.

"Eh."

She laughed. "I didn't either. So I got started packing. Hopefully it won't take too long to get everything in the truck and over to your house after the wedding."

"Should've hired a crew to do that part while we go to a hotel. I just wanna be with you."

"We have all day after the moving is done," she offered quietly. "All night. Tomorrow. The whole week and part of next."

"It's not enough. You know as well as I do that Duff's gonna be calling by Wednesday, insisting both of us work 'cause nobody else can possibly do it."

"I know. But Bev'll keep him in check."

"We could ignore our phones," Decker suggested.

"Then he'd come over."

He couldn't help laughing, feeling like it was the first time he had since Sapphire mentioned going to Rox's wedding. "Probably would at that. I want a honeymoon with you, baby. I want two weeks without a single, damn interruption. I want you wearing my ring and not a damn other thing. We never have to leave bed for anything but food. Even then…"

"We'll have that, honey. When we can afford it better," she said in a hushed, longing tone. "I can't wait to sleep in your arms. Even if we have to go to work in a few hours when we wake up, that'll make everything worth it."

He wanted that, too. But more than anything, he wanted to

take her far away from this place, far from Rox's wedding when the time came, not giving that part of his life another thought because all that mattered was being with Sapphire, the only place he'd ever been happy.

Chapter 21

Sapphire and her daughter had almost reached the Staten Island Borough Hall when her phone rang. She glanced at Yasmine behind the wheel, feeling the blush creeping up her neck again. She'd called Deck a little while ago, just before they left home. Yasmine had said she'd wait in her car while Sapphire called him in the foyer of the apartment building. Apparently, she'd taken too long and Yasmine had come back in without making a sound and overheard the last part of the conversation. Naturally, her calm, composed daughter hadn't been in the least embarrassed. She'd acted like she hadn't heard anything private and deeply personal.

On her phone screen, she saw her mother's phone number, and said to Yasmine, "It's my mom. Why in the world would she be calling? *Now?*" Point of fact, her mother almost never called her and never in the middle of the day, since she knew Sapphire worked the night shift.

"About that," Yasmine started, not sounding anything but her cool, confident self, "I called and told her you're getting married today. She needed to know."

"Yasmine, you didn't! How could you?"

"Because you might never have told her."

"That's my choice." She sighed anxiously and, before she could fully consider what she was doing, turned off her phone. "I really wish you hadn't done that, honey."

"Okay. But Mom, how long will you punish her, and then try so hard not to be like her, when you're obviously *just* like her?"

Sapphire turned to look at her daughter, feeling like she'd been slapped silly. "How can you say that? And what is it you think I'm punishing her for?"

"She didn't help you when you divorced my dad and then he came after you. Us."

Heat flooded Sapphire at this assessment. Even sixteen years later, she had trouble forgetting how helpless she'd felt. She'd been so young and all her mother could say was that she had to make the best of the mess she'd made. Never mind that Coug had beat her black and blue whenever he got drunk and desperately jealous because some other guy had looked at her the wrong way, never mind the potential he had in hurting her baby someday when she couldn't stop him. And, when her ex-husband proved that his violence was criminal, her mother's husband had thrown Sapphire and Yasmine out of his house in an effort to protect his wife. He'd told her the name and address of her real father--whether for good or evil--and fleeing there had been her only recourse. There, she'd met another weak, bad man who didn't care about anyone but himself. For a while, he'd put her up, helped her, but Sapphire had realized he didn't consider her in any way his responsibility. Coug had been on her heels then--she'd never know how, but she'd suspected her step-father had had tried to protect his wife when Coug cornered and threatened her, essentially throwing Sapphire and Yasmine to the dogs. Her ex-husband had found her and beaten her within an inch of her life. But it wasn't until he'd busted up her real father's expensive toys as a threat if he didn't give Sapphire up, that her dad had told her about his estrangement from his sister, that she'd had a daughter, and therefore Sapphire had a cousin who was about her age living in New York City. She'd gone to meet Cherish, who'd been horrified at the sight of her so bruised with a black eye, and finally she'd met a decent person she was related to. Her mother had been the first bad domino to set off a chain-effect.

"If I was punishing her," Sapphire said under her breath, "she would deserve it."

"I know, Mom." For the first time in longer than Sapphire could remember, there was compassion in her daughter's voice.

"You know?"

"Of course I know. You have every reason to feel the way you do, but you'll never heal if you hold onto your bitterness the way you do. You're only hurting yourself. I know Grandma as well as you do, even if I've never met her. She doesn't think about anything but herself. It's just the way she's wired. So, yes, you really are just hurting yourself. So either cut all ties with her or find a way to forgive her even if there's no reason to. Doesn't Aunt Cherish always say forgiveness is old, deep magic? Forgiving someone, especially someone who doesn't deserve it, heals the person who gives that blessing even more than the person receiving it."

Sapphire pressed a cold hand against her burning cheek. "Yes. But I'm nothing like my mother, Yasmine. Nothing."

"I know you take that as an insult, Mom, but I don't mean it that way. You've raised me to be completely different from her because I think you always wanted to be different. But your mom taught you that all there was in life for a woman was to get by until she found a good man who'd take care of her. Who cares about a career, personal fulfillment? Once your knight in shining armor showed up, you'd take care of him and his house and kids in exchange for not having to work. Am I right?"

"I don't want that for you. Is that so wrong, Yasmine? I want you to have a good life. A career and personal fulfillment. I want you to be independent and strong so you can make something of your life without depending on a man. I wanted you to feel free to make choices of your own, not to simply have things happen to you that you have no control over. I want every part of your life to be *your* decision."

"*You* succeeded, Mom."

Feeling shattered, Sapphire blinked at her daughter, unable to speak.

Yasmine spoke softly without looking away from the road. "I am strong, Mom. I'm independent, and I fully intend to make something of myself. My choices are my own. I'm not judging you, Mom, or anything you had to do. Sure, you did make a choice in the first place. After that, I think things just happened and you did the best you could with the fallout. You went on and made a safe, comfortable life of your own for me and you even when my dad was chasing you, stalking you, threatening everything you built for us. If that's not strong and independent, I don't know what is."

Sapphire had never realized her daughter understood the sacrifices she'd made, the fear she'd lived in of having everything she'd built so carefully torn down and destroyed. She'd lived countless years of her life in abject terror, always ready to run. But, in all that time, she'd been aware that, even if her own mother had been a terrible example for her, she herself had made the initial decisions that led to her eventual downfall. *Yes, I made the stupid choice to drink, smoke, have sex with worthless guys who could only take me down bad paths. I chose to believe I fell in love with Coug, a guy six years older than me. I let him get me pregnant. I wasn't smart enough to care about school one way or the other. Even when the danger Coug posed in my life was past, I didn't care to go back to school and make something of myself. It already felt too late for me. But I wanted Yasmine to have the opportunities denied me, in part by my own actions. I wanted her to have the opposite of what I got in my own mother: someone who didn't bother giving me guidance and acted like I wasn't supposed to learn something from her foolish, short-sighted way of life. I wanted to show Yasmine she was worth more than that. That she could do anything, have anything, be anything she wanted.*

"You *succeeded*, Mom. If what you were isn't strong and independent, I don't know what is."

Sapphire choked on a sob, and her daughter reached over to squeeze her hand quickly before putting it back on the steering wheel. "Don't cry, Mom. You'll wreck your makeup. You've given me every opportunity, and you helped me to see I can do anything if I'm smart enough to make the right choices for myself. But I think a part of you thinks it's weak and somehow wrong to fall in love, to need to be loved and taken care of. It's not."

"It's not," Sapphire repeated on a gasp, not sure if she was questioning or simply incapable of doing anything but reiterating words.

"It's not wrong to fall in love. I made the choice to love Justice. I don't like it when you tell me I can't see him just because you have problems with him. You don't really know him. What does his age matter? I know wrong from right. I'll make the right choices even if he's older than me, even if he wants me to make choices I'm not ready for. I'm not doing anything I don't feel a hundred percent comfortable with. You raised me right."

"You can't trust..."

"This isn't about me. You're a good person, Mom, a good mother. You deserve love. You deserve to be taken care of. You've taken care of me to the exclusion of all else all these years, but you don't have to keep doing it. I'm not going to throw my life away carelessly. I promise."

"You're only sixteen. I'm not ready to let go."

"Okay. But I meant, let go of your belief that you can't have love, that it's wrong for you to be loved and taken care of, to give love to anyone but me."

Frantically, Sapphire took long breaths, trying not to give in to her urge to cry.

"And maybe you can also realize that I want to be loved and to love someone else, too."

"Justice?" Sapphire said through her teeth. *A man six years older than you who may not have the same intentions for your relationship as you do...*

"For starters. You're not always going to approve of my boyfriends, Mom, but I know what I'm doing. I'm making good choices. You taught me well. Trust yourself if you can't trust me."

She almost laughed out loud at the thought. "I don't know how far my understanding will stretch," she admitted. "You're too young for a serious relationship."

Yasmine let out a defeated exhale. "Well, I had the feeling that last part was pushing it. We'll figure it out. Today's your wedding day, though, Mom. Can you just be happy? Let yourself be happy? And, by the way, after we get everything packed up and over to Decker's house, I'm going to stay with Cherish and Ty for the week you have off."

"You don't... But don't you want to get your new bedroom in shape?" She hadn't wanted to suggest any such thing, though she'd already talked to Cherish about the same thing and she suspected it'd been Deck's first thought. She'd never been away from her baby for a whole day let alone a week.

"I will. And he said he'd paint and decorate it whatever way I want. But we have plenty of time. School doesn't start for almost a month. If you're not going on a honeymoon, at least the two of you need to be alone for a while. No arguments, Mom. Aunt Cherish and I have already decided. I'll call you every day, okay? Or you call me so I don't interr--"

"Yasmine!"

When she laughed, Sapphire couldn't help laughing, too, her face and neck so hot, she felt permanently scarred by the scorching.

She pulled down the passenger mirror, glad to see she hadn't wrecked anything with her overload. She caught a glimpse of the sweetheart neckline of her dress. Though there was nothing sleazy about it, she felt so exposed. "I can't wear this, Yasmine. Do we have time to turn back? This is way too much. It's more appropriate for a formal church wedding. I don't know what I was thinking."

"Yes, you do. You're stunning. That's all anyone's going to think about when they see you in this. Deck will forget his own name, I guarantee it."

Sapphire had seen him dressed up a scarce handful of times in the years she'd known him. Sometimes he'd come into the bar in dress slacks and shiny shoes that he seemed to want to kick off, a nice, white, button-down shirt that emphasized his muscular torso. He'd said something about the glitzy world Roxanne lived in, having to dress the part, though his goal was never to be noticed, simply to blend in so he could be on the alert if anyone crossed the boundaries he'd set around his charge.

As Yasmine pulled into the parking lot at Borough Hall, Sapphire saw a moving van already parked there and Deck standing near the stairs of the building with Cherish and Ty. He had on clothes similar to the ones he'd worn to be Roxanne Hart's well-dressed bodyguard. Though he definitely looked more comfortable in his usual worn jeans, biker boots, t-shirts or tank tops and leather jacket, she couldn't help thinking he was gorgeous--and wondering if she could really go through with this. She was so overdressed. He and Cherish, Yasmine and Ty, were dressed appropriately for a city hall wedding.

Yasmine got out and came around to the passenger's side, all but refusing to let her hide in the car, the way she instinctively wanted to. Sapphire couldn't remember ever feeling so nervous. After rearranging and smoothing her dress after she got out, her daughter decisively led her toward the group waiting for them. Instantly, she saw the change in everyone's expression. Cherish was positivity glowing with pride at the sight of her. Ty grinned approvingly. But it was Deck's face that floored her. He looked like he might keel right over from a heart attack.

"I know. It's way, way too much--" she started.

"My God, you're not of this world," he muttered. "I'm not worthy." Though everyone except him laughed, he didn't seem to hear anything, see anything but her.

They reached for each other, but Yasmine protested. "None of that," she insisted, putting a hand between them, the level-headed chaperone. "Soon enough."

Cherish handed Sapphire one of her handmade Chantilly lace bouquets draped around the stems of blue hydrangeas and champagne-colored roses. Surrounding the base, a blue satin ribbon threaded with sprays of pearls had been expertly tied into a bow. "It's so beautiful, Cherish. Did you make it just for me?"

"Of course. They're so popular now, I had to vamp-up production, so I was able to finish this in a few days instead of the six months it used to take to make one. Now you have something old--the concept of Chantilly lace is vintage anyway, though this is newly made."

"And it's blue," Sapphire said, lifting the flowers to her nose, still feeling Deck's gaze on her. The bouquet was so large she could have hidden her whole head behind it if she'd wanted to.

"Sapphire, like your eyes," he said softly.

She could read in his expression his blatant desire to kiss her. She couldn't help blushing. "You look nice, too.'

"Ty made me take the jacket off."

"Your leather?" she guessed. He wanted to hide, too, or at least be wearing something that would feel comfortable.

They chuckled again. This time he joined them in the laughter. Inside, they filled out forms, waited in a long, seemingly unmoving line that Duff and Bev joined them in eventually for a ceremony that seemed comparatively, shockingly quick. For part of it, Sapphire remembered almost too vividly what it'd been like to stand in front of a judge, pledging her life to Coug, a guy she'd been abruptly asking herself how well she knew He'd been bored, couldn't wait for it to be over so they could celebrate by getting wasted. Their wedding night had been...*disgusting*, if truth be told. She'd refused to drink--not while she was pregnant. She'd already decided at that point she never wanted to drink again. Children and alcohol didn't mix at any time.

Deck's eyes were devouring every inch of her, as if he wasn't listening to a word the clerk was saying, but he didn't miss any cues, and, before long, they were posing for pictures that felt a bit silly in front of the grand building overlooking the ferry terminal and harbor. Though the ceremony itself hadn't been much different than her first, she knew the difference was Deck, a good man, the best, and she easily let herself believe they would have a wonderful life together.

Duff and Bev hugged and kissed Sapphire, Duff reiterating the exact day he wanted to see them back at work, with Bev tempering his insistence with her encouragement that they should enjoy themselves thoroughly. After they left, the rest of them agreed to meet up again at Sapphire's apartment building to start the move--after they changed their clothes.

Not surprisingly, Deck pulled her into his arms as soon as they reached the passenger's door of the moving van, which he opened. "You're so beautiful. I've never seen anyone so beautiful in my entire life. Why the hell did we decide to do the move right after?"

"Because we wanted to move in together right away, didn't we?" She smiled teasingly, hedging despite that she understood exactly what he was thinking.

"Yes. But *now*? All I wanna do is touch you." He pressed his forehead against hers, his hands sliding over her silken sides. "How did I get so lucky? You're an angel, baby. Spotless. I feel like all I can do is get you dirty."

She laughed, shaking her head. "It was totally the wrong dress."

"Totally the right." He pressed his mouth against hers for another long, deep moment. "You know how bad I want you, honey? I wanna take this dress off you." He kissed her and she moaned, feeling her body tighten at the husky sound of his voice, the way his hands were getting so close to dangerous ground, the feel of his lips, so close yet not kissing her the way she wanted him to. "Put it back on and start all over again."

"Deck?" she murmured, gasping because this was too much in the wrong, very public place.

He growled, increasing the heat flowing like lava through her veins. Glancing down, his eyes seemed to flame up like twin infernos as he devoured her body yet again with the hunger in his gaze. "How long will it take?"

She shook her head. "I didn't finish packing, though I fully intended to, so I thought us girls could do that while you big, strong men carry down furniture and what we did manage to get in boxes."

"I hope you're not tired. Even if I'm dropping dead from exhaustion tonight, I'm gonna want you, babe."

Unable to help herself, she laughed, her cheeks warm. But he looked utterly serious again.

"Yasmine is going to help us move, but she's going home with her aunt and uncle for the time we have off work. So we can be alone together at least that long."

"Hell, I couldn't ask for a better gift."

She giggled. He put his hands firmly on her waist, then lifted her and set her on the high passenger's seat of the moving van. More than once during the drive, he glanced over at her as if he was going through withdrawal from not having her in his constant sight. Strangely enough, they were the first ones at the apartment, and, once they went to her bedroom to change, Sapphire said, "I have the feeling they stopped off to get some pizza for later."

"You mean, to give us time to--"

"A little time--"

The words were barely out before he reached for her and the kiss outside the Borough Hall continued almost as if it hadn't ended. While Deck had been eager to take the dress off her, he had trouble with the zipper and, not surprising, he obviously just wanted the inconvenience gone after he figured it out. They made love swiftly, barely making up for the time they'd been apart in anticipation of their wedding. Deck took her hand in his afterward, bringing the beautiful sapphire ring and wedding band to his lips to kiss. "I'm the happiest man alive, honey. Thank you for marrying me."

"*Thank you*?" she asked languidly. "Are those the usual words after the wedding night begins?"

"I'm not anywhere near your league. That you looked at me even once is a miracle."

"You're a good man. I'm lucky to have you. You're everything I ever wanted."

"Low standards?" he asked on a grin. But then he kissed her again. "I love you, Sapphire."

"I love you, too."

"Are you really happy, babe?"

"Yes. I'm so glad you asked me to marry you."

They both heard the door, and Yasmine calling pre-emptively to warn them they were no longer alone.

"We better get dressed and get to work," she said, even when all she wanted to do was sleep in his arms and wake up there when they were both ready for more loving.

He grumbled unhappily. Sapphire got up to put on ragged jeans shorts and t-shirt she'd left unpacked so she'd have something to wear after the wedding. Surprising her, Deck came up behind her and pulled her back against him, proving he was already aroused again. "God, and I thought you were sexy in that dress."

"They're just old shorts."

"On you, they're every man's fantasy."

She laughed, shaking her head as she turned to him. "I'll tell everyone you're still getting changed."

"Yeah, they'll believe that. But whatever gets you with me twenty-four hours a day, I say 'Godspeed' to."

Chapter 22

Smiling, Sapphire gave him one last kiss and left her bedroom, closing the door so he couldn't see her anymore. Even in memory, her beauty and sexiness made him ache. It took longer than was appropriate for a certain part of his body to calm down. He kept seeing her appear before him at the Borough Hall, wearing that angelic concoction that fit her incredible body curve for sinful curve, her long, sexy hair cascading over her sun-kissed shoulders and back, her gorgeous face filled with love and an adorable blush. She hadn't looked real enough to touch. More than once during the endless wait to their marriage ceremony, he'd wondered if he'd always feel this way for her. No matter what she gave him, it was never enough but so much more than he could ask for. Damn straight he wasn't worthy of a woman as amazing as she was.

I can't believe I'm married to her. That she agreed to this crazy scheme. How soon before she regrets it? Hell, what I wouldn't do to stall that as long as possible. But how can I stop being me? Stop screwing up? How long before she no longer thinks she can keep loving me?

Not surprisingly, his mind supplied the exact date: The following Saturday. He'd screw his whole life up because she had to see him react to Rox marrying some other bastard. If he could convince her to skip the wedding, maybe he still had a chance of getting through all this unscathed.

When he went out of the room, he found her family had gotten a mini feast of Chinese food, since it would be dinnertime once they finished packing and loading the van. He didn't want to take more time out of this day to eat. He wanted to get the move over with so he and Sapphire could be alone together, preferably naked. He suspected Ty understood that better than anyone because, when Decker excused himself to go open the van so they could start hauling instead of partaking, Ty nodded and said he'd figure out what was the heaviest furniture, since they'd want that to go in first. Sapphire had said she wanted to keep her furniture, even if they had to put it in storage. He suspected they'd be able to use most of it. He'd only ever gotten the bare essentials and, frankly, he'd never cared about furnishing or decorating most of his house.

He got the van open, the loading ramp extended and set up. A Kawasaki motorcycle pulled into the parking lot, and Decker recognized it instantly as the one belonging to Yasmine's boyfriend. After a mutual look of recognition, Decker went up to Sapphire's apartment and pulled her aside to tell her quietly, "Your daughter's boyfriend decided to put in an appearance."

"Justice is here?" she asked in surprise. "Now?"

"You want me to get rid of him?"

She sighed. "No. Yasmine probably invited him, asked him to help her move. And it will go faster if he helps."

"Okay. Your call."

But he went with her to the open door of the apartment after she called for her daughter then went to greet the guy she'd suddenly decided to trust. The instant Sapphire was in his sights, the kid's gaze made a leisurely stroll down every inch of her body. If looks were actions, Decker knew his wife would have been stripped naked, the victim of a flyby with the scorching heat in the walking hormone's eyes.

Before Sapphire had a chance to say a word, Yasmine appeared at her mother's side. After only a moment, she stormed past Sapphire and grabbed Justice's arm. While she dragged him off, Decker swore under this breath. Sapphire glanced up at him. "What's going on? I didn't say anything. I tried not to look upset by his presence. I swear I was going to be nice--"

"Babe, guy like that ain't interested in nice when it comes to a hot body like yours."

Sapphire went rigid, her eyes wide open in shock as she realized what he was suggesting. "What are you talking about? Yasmine was upset, probably because she assumed I was going to throw him out--"

"The SOB just undressed you with his eyes. She saw it. Undressed *her mother*. Yeah, she's upset. But not about what you're assuming."

Sapphire's eyes widened a second time, as if she could be a stranger to a guy any age checking her out. The same thing happened on a nightly basis at work. But he suspected it would never occur to her that a guy that age, not much older than her daughter, would look at her like that when he had her daughter to ogle. "I--" she started. She glanced down at her sexy shorts and worn t-shirt guiltily.

"It's not your fault."

"I wasn't trying--"

From the end of the hall, they heard Yasmine's voice growing louder. "I've put up with this long enough, but now my mother? Actually, I should say, *again* my mother. Right? Who could forget how you checked her out the day I was going to introduce you to her as my boyfriend?"

"Hey, babe, not my fault your old lady's hot. How's that my fault? And she's dressed like that."

"You don't have to look! You don't have to look at every single girl on the planet like that. What a disgusting display. Do you think *any* girl wants you to look at her like that?"

"Doesn't mean anything," he defended without the slightest remorse in his tone.

"I told myself all this time that you were right, that it didn't mean anything, because I wanted it to be the truth. But this is the last straw, Justice. I'm sure now that nothing could ever keep you from straying for long. I deserve better. It's over. Leave."

"You're makin' too much out of this, babe."

"I'm making just enough of it. Don't come back. I'm done." A second later, Yasmine said, "Let me go."

Decker didn't hesitate any longer than Sapphire did. They darted into the hall, and Decker raised his voice to an authoritative shout across the distance still left between them, "Let her go now. And don't let me see you around her again if Yasmine doesn't give you an explicit pass."

At the sight of them, Justice let go of Yasmine, looking frustrated. He turned on his heel and walked away, past them and down the stairs, muttering, "To hell with this."

While Yasmine ran to her mother, Decker followed to make sure the creep actually left. Fortunately, he didn't have to deal with anything. The roving-eye Romeo got on his motorcycle and took off without a backward glance. When Decker returned, Sapphire was hugging her sobbing daughter, telling her she did the right thing and apologizing in the same breath.

"Why are *you* sorry?" Yasmine asked, hiccupping slightly.

"I shouldn't have...dressed like...this--"

"Oh, Mom, how could it be your fault that he's a pig? Maybe those shorts are sexy, but it's not the first time he's commented on your 'hotness'. Far from it."

"Yasmine..." Sapphire looked mortified.

"You can't help the way you look any more than I can. But he really didn't have to look at you like *that*." Swiping at her wet cheeks, Yasmine turned to look at Decker. "I'm surprised you didn't hit him for it."

Decker couldn't help raising an eyebrow. "Was that an option? Believe me, I thought about it."

The teenager drew in a heavy exhale. "Well, that's over. I knew it couldn't last."

"I'm guessing he looked at a lot of other girls," Sapphire said softly. "Idiot. You're more beautiful than any of them. I'm sorry, honey. I know you really liked him."

"*Despite.*"

"You gonna be okay?" Decker asked.

Yasmine nodded. "Let's just get everything moved. I have a lot to look forward to. Staying with Aunt Cherish will be fun. And I can figure out what I want for my new room in that time, right?"

"Sure. Whatever you want," Decker agreed, more than a little grateful that he was getting time alone with his new wife for the next week. But, odd for him because he'd never had kids and didn't really know how to act around them, he felt strangely worried about the teenager and wondered if she'd need her mother during this time. "But don't feel you can't call, or come over, if you need to talk to your mom."

"I know I can anytime. But I'll try not to. I'm going to finish packing my room."

She rushed away, and Sapphire looked after her, obviously worried and a little ashamed again. "I had no idea," she said under her breath. "I mean, I did notice the first time we met, how he looked at me… But it sounds like he did that with every female."

"Dudes that age, they're looking. Every female is in their radar, from sweet sixteen to hot mama."

"Deck," she cringed.

"Just saying." He ran his hand over her backside and she spun away from him, turning back to point an adorably scolding finger at him. "Get to work, mister."

"Whatever you say, beautiful," he said, trying not to laugh as he held up his hands in surrender.

Chapter 23

Just before Cherish and Ty left Deck's house and the emptied moving van, saying they'd develop the wedding pictures (Ty was a professional freelance photographer) at their place, Yasmine told them she wanted to pick out her new bedroom and pack a bag, then she'd head that way. Yasmine's phone rang while the three of them stood in one of the potential rooms, talking about the possibilities. She dug the device out, saw who was calling and held it up so Sapphire could see. She groaned, and Deck asked, "What?"

"It's my mom. Apparently, Yasmine told her I was getting married today."

The look on his face wasn't exactly happy. She knew he wanted only to get everyone out of the house so they could be alone. But he said, "Okay."

"Mom, if you want to get this over this, just talk to her," Yasmine advised, holding her phone out to her. Sapphire didn't take it.

She remembered the emotional conversation they'd had in the car on the way to the Borough Hall. Since then, she'd considered that for the past year she and Yasmine's relationship had been rocky--much the same as Sapphire and her mother's had been for most of her life. From the time she was a teenager, the rockiness in her own relationship with her mom had been a given, one she was sure they blamed on each other, not on themselves. Sapphire couldn't deny there was an element of unforgiveness between them, and neither was willing to be the one to crack. But, despite how her mother couldn't be bothered to visit them even once since Sapphire fled from home, she'd kept up the communication just as Sapphire had.

I don't want to have my daughter go out on her own and never look back, never contact me, never come to see me, never make any effort to salvage what was once the most important part of both of our lives. For that reason alone, maybe, I'm going to forgive and try to stop punishing my mom, even if I can't help feeling she deserves it. Maybe someday I'll deserve Yasmine's punishment--but would I want her to dole it out constantly? No. I would want her to forgive me, even if I didn't deserve it. Cherish does say often that we forgive the ones who have wronged us if for no other reason than so we can be forgiven by the ones we've wronged.

"I'm sorry, Deck. I know this day hasn't gone the way you wanted it to, but there's only one way to make the best of this. We're going to have to initiate a video call."

"Good idea," Yasmine said approvingly. She thrust her phone at Sapphire, forcing her to take it. "Answer that. I'll go get my laptop and start up the program up in the living room."

"We're gonna have *what*?" Deck asked.

"Video call. Trust me, once my mom sees you, she'll be all for this marriage."

"*See?*"

He looked completely taken aback, but Sapphire was already answering the call, and, an instant later, they were in the living room where Yasmine had set up her laptop on the coffee table, saying, "I'm logging in."

"Mom, why don't we have a video chat so you can meet your new son-in-law?" Sapphire suggested when she answered her mother's call.

Though her mother seemed uncertain, she agreed and Sapphire, Yasmine and Deck sat in front of the laptop camera on the sofa so the introductions could be made. Her mother had called her husband into the room, so Dan was with her, too.

"I was going to say this is all so sudden, Sapphire, but I can guess now why it had to be." If anyone had the audacity to flirt with a man quite a bit her junior, it was Sapphire's mother. "You wouldn't want to let this one get away, would you?"

Sapphire completely ignored the assumed dig in her mother's words. She conceded her mom was driven by good looks in a male, and it'd been a big factor in why she'd been so charmed by Coug-- before he proved himself to be a homicidal manic and threatened to hurt her if she didn't tell him where Sapphire was. If Sapphire's mother hadn't seen Deck with her own two eyes, she would have been negative about the marriage, assuming the worst because he worked at the same bar Sapphire did. Instead, she did everything short of open her blouse and flash him. Maybe that wouldn't have elicited disgust since her mother had aged extremely well and she was still beautiful, her face completely free of wrinkles, with the same killer body she'd had as a twenty-year-old. Deck was mildly charming and polite without laying anything on too thick. For his part, Dan was used to his wife's overt flirtations and barely reacted to any part of the conversation except to ask, "You got married today? Is this your honeymoon?"

Sapphire felt herself grow warm and wondered if Deck was experiencing the same discomfort.

"I'm staying at Aunt Cherish's for a week so they can be alone. They took a mini-vacation from work," Yasmine answered for them.

"You're not going anywhere for your honeymoon, Sapphire?" her mother asked in surprise. "You're not doing anything special?"

"We moved into Deck's house today. That's where we are now. I'll have to give you my new address, Mom."

"You moved in? As in a thousand boxes, furniture, and moving van? After your wedding? What in the world were you thinking, Sapphire? Oh, you poor thing, Deck. But I guess you already know how practical and unromantic my daughter is."

"I wouldn't go that far. But her practicality is part of why I love her," Deck said smoothly, winning himself extra points even if he didn't realize he was doing that.

"Well, you're a good man for appreciating those qualities. But I'm glad you understand who my daughter is upfront. That would be an unpleasant cold shower if you were only just learning about this now."

"I don't know about that," Yasmine said with the kind of light coolness that was neither cold nor heated but somewhere in-between. "I'd rather have a practical deliberator in my bunker than someone who's swept away by impulsive, romantic gestures."

"I'm gonna have to agree with Yasmine on this," Deck said.

Sapphire realized she'd done what she intended in keeping the lines of communication open with her mother, refraining from active punishment in the things she said and did, and now it was time to get on her with her new life. Trying not to smile at her daughter's unexpected defense of her and Deck's unofficial 'amen', she wrapped things up.

"Well, if you don't mind, I want to take a look another look at all the open rooms, maybe make a decision on one, before I pack and get going," Yasmine said, looking satisfied once she closed her laptop.

When Sapphire smiled at her, she left them alone.

"Sorry if that was bad," Sapphire said to Deck.

"Not bad. And it's over with anyway. You look like your mom."

"She's hot?" Sapphire guessed.

Deck laughed. "Beyond looks, you two are opposites. And that's a good thing."

"Well, I doubt you'll ever meet her in person. She's not much for travel, though Dan has the money. She acts like I should be the one going to her, as if she's decrepit and can't leave the house. Anyway...what about your mother? Are you sure we shouldn't meet?"

"I'm sure. You realize that's got nothing to do with you? I just know what she'll do the second she's aware you exist. She'll be hitting you up day and night for money. I'm not gonna let her."

"When's the last time you saw her?"

He shrugged. "Few months. It was the same as always. She acts like she cares, then she proves she's only seeing me for one reason. I refuse. Done. She calls to apologize occasionally. I listen to the voicemails, but it's always the same."

Sapphire wondered why he bothered, why he didn't cut all ties, but she suspected she already knew the answer. As she didn't want to have regrets with her mother, he didn't with his. He'd done all he could without compromising his integrity and self-respect. He deliberately attempted not to invest himself in the relationship so he'd never have to feel the pain he'd probably buried so deep, he might not recognize it if it surfaced for a razor-glimpse here and there.

"Why don't you go see if Yasmine has chosen a room yet? I want to unpack my dishes so I can cook you breakfast tomorrow."

"You're not too tired?" he asked, snagging her around the waist and pulling her against him. "We did a lot in one day, babe."

"No. Not at all."

He grinned and kissed her. "Good. I'll be back. Don't do too much."

Sapphire started in the kitchen. Since almost all the cupboards were bare, she easily unpacked all the dishes, pots and pans, in hardly any time at all. The lack of decoration and "filling" in the house was shocking, and the room felt warmer and more lived in when she finished unloading all the kitchen boxes.

After breaking them down and laying them flat, she carried a stack down the basement. She'd never been in the wide open space before, but now discovered laundry facilities. The lower level of the house was sectioned out as if Deck had planned to create some rooms sooner or later, but mostly the space was empty. In the middle was a huge work bench, shelves, with tool cabinets and carts, bins neatly organized--everything a carpenter would need to renovate a house.

Below the work bench was a stack of flattened cardboard boxes. She assumed he kept them here until recycling day, but, when she pulled them out to access what she assumed was his recycling system, she saw a couple boxes beneath the bench that didn't look anything like recycling bins. One of them was opened. Setting her boxes aside, she knelt down to draw the opened box out from the bench. Inside she saw full bottles of whiskey, his favorite brand. She knew the second, unopened box held the same. He'd dumped the unopened ones out that'd been in his cupboard, but these... Did he forget they were here? Or...

Was he fully aware that these were down here and he wasn't completely out? What are they doing here? Hiding under his workbench with empty boxes blocking them from line of sight? Was he actually trying to conceal them? From me?

At the same time Sapphire couldn't shake the feeling that this wasn't her house, didn't feel like hers at all yet, and she'd essentially been snooping when she came down here, she knew she couldn't let this go. She didn't want to ruin their "honeymoon" either. *I can't imagine he really believed he could hide these from me. I need to know his intention--in hiding these, his intentions in the future when it comes to alcohol. He said he'd join AA, he'd do whatever I wanted him to. But he hasn't done anything about it. I know he hasn't.*

Back upstairs, she found that Yasmine had chosen her bedroom--not surprisingly, the one furthest from her and Deck's. She planned to choose a color in the next week and wanted to help Deck paint the room before they put her furniture in. She'd packed a small bag for her week away and assured Sapphire she'd be fine and available when she called.

"Thanks for everything today, honey," Sapphire said when she hugged her. "You're wise beyond your years, and I'm proud of the person you are. I love you so much. Call me, even if you just need to talk." The implication 'about the breakup with Justice' was clear without the words.

"I'll be perfectly fine, Mom. I love you, too.'

Yasmine turned and hugged Deck. He seemed a little surprised but willing. "Welcome to the family," she said to him. "Treat my mom well. She deserves it."

"I know she does. I intend to do everything I can to make sure she's happy."

"I think you will. See you two in a week. Have fun!"

She headed out. Sapphire was embarrassed, only too aware that everyone knew what the next week would be like for them. Deck waved, but he was already reaching for her when Yasmine pulled the front door closed behind her.

"Deck, we need to talk," she said because she couldn't put this off. "I found the boxes in the basement."

He went stark still. His expression told her he knew exactly which boxes she meant. "The booze?"

She nodded, not speaking beyond that.

"Looked like I was hiding them, I guess."

"Were you?"

"I'm planning to take them to Knuckleheads. There's no reason to waste 'em. Duff'll take 'em and put 'em to use. I just haven't had any time to deliver the boxes to the bar."

"Really?" she asked, feeling a little relief but not completely assured.

"I told you, I'm not gonna drink again. We'll take 'em with us when we go to work next Wednesday. Okay?"

"All right."

"I won't forget."

"Okay. Are you still going to AA with me?"

His face had been firm and open--clearly wanting her to believe he had nothing to hide. A veil seemed to slip over it now. Yet he said easily, "If you insist."

"Don't you think you should?" *You were telling me what I wanted to hear before--never expecting me to enforce it. Weren't you?*

"I'll go if *you* think I should. I agreed to that. But I can do this on my own, Sapphire. It's the way I do everything. Always have."

"Other people have said the same thing," she said softly. "But it's not as easy as you make it look most of the time. Sometimes you need help. Yes, even you."

"You said it yourself, babe. I'm not like most people. I slipped once. I'm sorry about that. But it won't happen again. I told you I'd go if you want me to. What do you expect when we get there? Do you want me to give a speech? Check off a list of apologies for my grievances?"

While his tone wasn't sarcastic, it didn't need to be for her to be aware he meant the words in that vein. *Why do I feel like he deceived me? That he gave me lip service with all this and nothing more? He's telling me what I want to hear, but deep down he doesn't believe he has a problem that he may need help with, a problem he'll return to the second he has to deal with anything like conflict.*

Her expression must have spoken a thousand words about her tense uncertainty because he softened, holding her a little tighter against him. "I will, babe. I'll do whatever you want."

And that's the whole reason he's doing this. Not because he believes he has a problem, that he's an alcoholic who'll fall off the wagon as soon as a situation arises that he needs the numbing effects of booze, but because I asked him to. For that reason and that reason alone.

"Do we have to do this today, Sapphire? For f@#k's sake, we've been through this before. Nothing's changed except you found those g@#m bottles. None of 'em are open. You noticed that, didn't you? The seals are all intact."

"Yes," she said hesitantly with the sting and incinerating heat of tears raging behind her eyes.

"I'm getting rid of 'em as soon as possible. So what's changed?"

Even as she heard her mother's cruel words in her head (*"What in the world were you thinking, Sapphire? How practical and unromantic you are."*), she knew she had to resolve this issue and not keep putting it off because the issue was unpleasant and she'd rather have the fairytale over reality. "Deck, do you realize you're an alcoholic? Do you know you have a drinking problem?"

Oh, how she wanted to read his mind as he stared at her in

disbelief over the next, excruciatingly long minute. "Lady, you joined AA 'cause you thought you might *someday* have a drinking problem. You don't have a f@#g drinking problem. You never have. You never will. Yet you're in a group for alcoholics, whether or not you attend every meeting. And you think that solves the problem. And, hell, maybe it does for you 'cause you got iron will, baby. But so do I. And you know that about me, don't you? I don't need to be accountable to somebody else, anybody but you. You're the one I care about. So why don't you give me a chance to prove I can do this without help? I promise you that's all I need."

Sapphire recognized he was saying so much more than the words he actually spoke. She knew he thought he made a mistake the last time. He believed he could rectify that mistake by following the protocol she'd set for him--the one that would make *her* feel better about trusting him. But she didn't have a single doubt that the next time some emotion left him in pieces on the floor, he'd return to the booze to numb his pain. He'd work hard to hide his lapse from her--that was a given. But, one way or another, he wouldn't be able to camouflage his slip from her completely. She'd be mad, he'd make any and all promises she needed to hear. Ultimately, he'd only see that he'd stumbled, nothing worth worrying about because he truly believed himself when he said he wouldn't do it again.

He *would* do it again. She'd heard promises before, and not just from him.

"You don't believe you have a problem, Deck. You think I'm acting crazy, asking too much when you have it all under control. But what happens when you do fall off the wagon again? You say you'll be accountable to me, but will you just try to hide what you're doing from me instead, so you won't have to admit the truth to yourself? Or will you own up to it and listen to me then?"

His expression shuttered, pushing her out emotionally so there was no way she could discern what he was thinking. "If I fall off the wagon again, no matter what, I'll tell you. I'll do whatever you want." The words were emotionless, hard, slightly bitter.

"You'll admit you're an alcoholic and can't deal with the problem yourself?"

"Yeah. I'll admit it. I'll get active in AA. All right?" His jaw like granite, he turned away from her. "I'm calling Duff. I'm gonna put the boxes out on the front step and he can come by and get it whenever he wants."

She started to protest but couldn't. She'd never seen him look so forbidding. When he walked away from her, down the basement, to do what he said, she sank to the sofa and huddled there, unable to stop her shell-shocked tears. She heard him banging around, slamming doors, muttering to himself. The last thing a bride should wonder on her wedding day was if she'd just made the biggest mistake of her life. She thought seriously about getting in her car, but where would she go? She had nowhere to run now.

Deck delivered the boxes to the porch, came back in and locked the door. She felt so exposed, but she knew she couldn't hide. He swore under his breath at the sight of her. "Why do we have to do this s@#t today?" he spit from between his teeth.

Sliding down to the floor, the sofa at her back, she laid her head in her arms on the coffee table. *I don't want to make another mistake, another big one like falling in love with violent bastard with the face of Adonis, one who can't see his own flaws, can't admit he has any, would rather continue on the stubborn course he's always traversed--*

"I'm sorry, Sapphire. You're right. I'll do whatever you want, okay?" He sounded sincere, softened by her collapse. He kneeled at her side.

She lifted her head, not bothering to wipe away the tears streaming down her cheeks. "Deck, maybe you don't realize this yourself, but you can't handle pain. I've seen how you handle it, okay? When you're hurt, you drink. You've never done it any other way. You don't know anything else. But...I love you. When you're in pain, I want you to come to me. Okay?"

She understood she was asking him to do the opposite of what he had his whole life, but at least he had some experience in how to turn to her. Shifting her body, she reached for him, hiding her face against his neck as he clasped her tightly against him.

He'll be tested. His resolve in this area will be tested sooner rather than later. I already sent the RSVP for Roxanne and Jamie's wedding and included Deck's name with mine on it. Maybe it'll be nothing. Maybe he'll wish them well and prove in every way he loves me and he's over her...

"Okay. I'm sorry I was so rough." He kissed her wet cheeks. "I made you cry again. I'm sorry. I love you."

When his mouth sought hers, she was on overload and the need felt just as charged.

His hands cradling her face, he asked in tone that was obviously an attempt to defuse the tension and get back their eager wedding mood, "Can we get naked now, babe?"

She laughed giddily through her tears.

Chapter 24

They did little the whole week beyond make love, unpack boxes, get furniture into place, and enjoy short, spontaneously scheduled visits from Yasmine on the pretense of trying a variety of color swatches against the white walls of the room she'd chosen for herself. Friday, she stayed for dinner with urging from both of them, then insisted on leaving right after they finished the dishes together. Decker hung back in the kitchen to wipe down surfaces. Even from there, he overheard the two of them in the living room near the door. Yasmine asked her mother if they were going to Roxanne and Jamie's wedding the next day. He was glad he was a room away when Sapphire said they were and would see her there.

"Okay. But I'm just staying for the ceremony. I want to get started on clothes shopping for school, so I'm not going to the reception. Michelle and I are going to Macy's in the afternoon--here in town."

Sapphire came into the kitchen smiling, as if a bomb hadn't been dropped over his world. "I can't get myself to believe my daughter misses me, but that's the third time this week she's dropped by. It's like something was broken and it's fixing itself now between us. I think it's because of you."

"Me? What do I have to do with it?"

He tossed the washcloth over the edge of the sink, and they went into the living room, sinking to the sofa as one.

"I think you--and, inadvertently, Justice--created a way for us to bond again." Sapphire snuggled against him. "Yasmine really likes you. I can tell."

Even though the teenager was far from outspoken in that regard, Decker had sensed it, too, and felt the same. "She's a hell of a kid."

"She really is."

His mind wasn't on the visit or the weird but potentially wonderful stepfather role he'd stepped into. He was still thinking about the next day. "Let's go somewhere, babe," he said, hugging her tighter, his mouth against her ear.

"What? Now? Where would we go? We have to go back to work soon."

"I mean, let's pack a bag and just go anywhere else. Call in sick all next week. Duff'll understand." *Hell, I'd be agreeable to going wherever her mom and stepdad live--Atlantic City, I think she said. Anything to get outta New York, far from that damn wedding tomorrow. Break every bone in my body and have to be hospitalized, be drafted into the service--either sounds better than going to that wedding.*

Whether she presented it that way or not, Decker sensed Sapphire saw this as some kind of a test. Proof about whether he was still hung up on something that was never going to happen. He didn't have a single problem accepting Roxanne wasn't part of his life anymore. Hell, he'd accepted she'd never be his twenty years ago, pretty much the second she introduced him to Dubois. He'd even acknowledged that the dude would be in her life for the long haul. But none of that made him interested in watching the f@#g marriage take place in flesh-and-blood or in playing nicey-nicey as lifetime friends with them.

"What about a cabin on a lake? Just you and me? We could leave tonight. It doesn't have to be fancy or expensive. Just private."

"We can do that, Deck. But we decided it's better to do that later. Maybe next year, after we've saved for a while for it. Or another idea I was thinking about: Maybe we could do it after we quit our jobs at Knuckleheads, right before we start our new jobs. I already talked to Cherish and she's willing to give me a full-time position whenever I want to start. You could also work there. She said her mail order has expanded so she's never got enough staff to keep it going, and she always needs drivers for deliveries. Or maybe you can talk to Jace about that security job when we're at the wedding reception tomorrow."

Reception? He'd hoped she'd be satisfied with just the wedding ceremony. He'd be spending the whole damn day wishing he was somewhere else, or dead. He didn't kid himself though. She refused to budge on the issue of whether or not they were attending all of it. Something about the way she spoke told him her heels were dug so far into the soil, she wouldn't be uprooted for anything. They were going if she had to drag him kicking and screaming. His point in bringing it up had been to talk her out of going altogether, give her an incentive not to go. Instead, she'd given them more reason to attend.

I'm not getting out of this. Accepting reality and watching the freak show... How the hell am I gonna get through it? I'll be bouncing off the walls, waiting for my chance to escape, get away, drown out what I don't care if I ever think about or see again.

He turned her face up to his. "I love *you*. You're my whole life, babe. I don't give a damn about anything else. That's true no matter what." *No matter what happens tomorrow, that'll be the only reality I wanna face. But I have the feeling already it's gonna go wrong, go straight down to the burning flames of hell. In the process, I may end up destroying everyone and everything instead of holding onto what matters. I'm not sure I'm capable of doing anything else. Why does it always end this way?*

Chapter 25

Sapphire cried more than she would have liked the next day. Deck almost made them late for the wedding when he seduced her--deliberately, she knew, hoping to talk her out of going to the wedding at all--and his tenderness, his love, the words he spoke about never fitting in anywhere, with any group of friends...but wanting to fit into her world with those she loved--had filled her with emotions she hadn't expected. She'd anticipated disappointment, even blows to her heart, today. But Deck had been almost non-communicative at the wedding. He'd put his arm around her, rarely leaving her side for longer than a few minutes, and not really paying attention to the main event. Whenever she looked at him pointedly, he said nothing, performed whatever appropriate action she silently compelled him to for a moment, then went back to ignoring the ceremony as if by withdrawing mentally he wouldn't be there in any other way outside his physical body.

The wedding was a celebration of life and love, and she couldn't help crying at how much Roxanne and Jamie obviously loved each other, all the obstacles they'd overcome to be together "until death do us part". In the reception line following the elaborate ceremony in one side of the wedding venue, Roxanne hugged them both tight enough to leave bruises, congratulating them on their own recent marriage and going on and on about how thrilled she was for both of them, how she'd longed for William to find love like she'd found with Jamie. She had tears in her eyes the whole time she engaged them as if they were the only ones there. Deck barely responded, simply went through the motions, saying and doing what was expected of him and not a blessed other thing. No one spoke of his distance, but Sapphire knew the bride and groom felt it like an Artic breeze just as she did. Neither were willing to ruin their own wedding to point out the obvious.

Jamie looked so deeply, quietly overjoyed, so involved with the love of his life, his wife at long last, he would have agreed to a private trip to the moon if she'd suggested it. Instead, she told them that after the reception, they wanted their closest friends to come back to Jamie's cruise yacht with them and spend the night in their own private cabin.

Sapphire was stunned by the invitation she didn't believe she warranted, not even as the wife of a person Roxanne believed was one of her closest friends in the world. She couldn't speak, and Deck didn't need to. As if she wanted to believe all was perfect in paradise, Roxanne laughed and said that they could decide later. Cherish knew all the details.

Deck shunted them unceremoniously out of line for the next well-wishers. As they followed the crowd to the ballroom of the wedding location, he kept his arm around her in a possessive way that made Sapphire wonder whether he was being protective of her or himself.

"Do you want to talk to Jace?" she said, hating the awkwardness of their mingling as the room filled with guests that Sapphire didn't really know well. Yasmine had already left, saying she was heading back to Staten Island to picking up her friend so they could shop at the mall. She said she'd also been invited to spend the night on the cruise yacht, but she hadn't decided yet whether she wanted to. Cherish had given her the key to her apartment, so she could either go back there, go to the yacht, or spend the night at Deck's--her new home.

Deck agreed in a grunt to Sapphire's suggestion then moved back toward the couple they'd talked to before meeting up with Yasmine. Feeling a bit of relief to be alone for the moment, Sapphire went to the restroom. Surprisingly, it was empty, and she was grateful for the silence that allowed some of her stress to melt away. Deck would want to leave soon, if not immediately after she returned to the hall.

Will a part of him wonder if he's done his duty, if he's proven himself to me? I honestly don't know what he's proven to me today, beyond that he's as socially awkward as he claims to be--but is this normal for him? Or is he acting so "automaton" because of Roxanne and Jamie? I can't imagine he's always this unfriendly in a crowd. He's warmer to Knucklehead patrons than he's been to anybody he's come in contact with today.

As soon as she emerged from the bathroom, Deck was right there, waiting for her. "Did you talk to Jace?" she asked, her throat sore from the tight way she'd been holding it.

"He says they have openings and I should come in, fill out an application, interview. Can we leave now?"

"We'll have to say goodbye to everyone."

He swore under his breath, then nodded. "Whatever."

Sapphire moved close to him, intending to tease him about his social gracelessness, but when his gaze met hers, her heart stopped at what she saw in his eyes. She'd seen Deck sober, drunk, hammered out of his skull. In the latter two instances, she recognized the graduation as his pupils became increasingly more dilated and unfocused. She gasped as though punched in the gut. "Deck, you're wasted. How--? When--?" There was a free bar in the reception hall, but he'd barely left her side since they came into the ballroom... *Unless he started drinking before that today...? But when? Before we ever left the house? Where did he get booze? It is possible he kept a bottle of the whiskey before putting the rest in boxes out on the porch for Duff to pick up?*

"Don't start."

She gaped at him as the pieces fell into place. She understood his levels of booze consumption intimately. He talked a lot during the "drunk" phase, but once he gotten into the full-on hammered state, the pain he was in was so great, he drank more and more to numb every part of himself. That kind of agony didn't allow for words. He withdrew inside himself so far, no one could reach him. Sapphire had never been able to either. No one could. *And that's where he is now. He's hammered. He's long gone from this scene. He's* inside himself, where he's comfortably numb.

What does this mean? What else can it mean except that seeing Roxanne, the woman he's been miserably, hopelessly, unceasingly, foolishly in love with for most of his life marrying the man he's hated beyond reason simply because Roxanne loved him instead is killing him and he can't cope? His promises to me mean nothing in light of that.

"You're still in love with her," Sapphire said so quietly, she wasn't sure he heard her over the loud music. "And you've had enough whiskey to knock a normal person on their ass. When did you start? Before breakfast? After we--?"

"I told you I didn't wanna come here. Why the f@#k would I wanna witness any of this? Even if hated her g@#m guts or just didn't feel a thing for her, why would you think I'd wanna watch that or participate in anything afterward?"

"You're in love with her."

"No. I'm not in love with her. I loved her. Maybe I always will, but it's...been deactivated. And, sure, I wanna hate him. I don't. Not anymore. But none of it matters. I don't wanna see either of them. I never wanted to, not since she agreed to get treatment and they got together for good. It's not part of my life anymore. I don't wanna involve myself there. But you insisted. You had to see for yourself...see what? That I'm unaffected? How'm I doing? What the hell did you think was gonna happen?"

Sapphire swallowed as a massive sob worked its way up her throat. She acknowledged now that she'd wanted to somehow discover through their attendance that he was so over Roxanne he could actually be happy for her today. *What the hell did you think would happen?* Of course her purpose in coming had been to affirm her belief that he was over Roxanne and ready to commit himself fully to their life together. "You could have said no," she murmured, feeling faint.

"Really? I could've told you, no, I don't wanna come to this f@#g thing and you would've accepted it instead of assuming the fact that I didn't wanna go must mean I'm still hung up on her? You're assuming that s@#t right now. I know you are. But you're wrong."

"What else could all this mean, Deck? You're hammered. If you weren't affected by her, by her marriage to Jamie, you wouldn't have needed to get this drunk just to cope with your pain."

"I'm in love with *you*." His voice had risen to a decibel that was competing with the blaring music. Quickly, she grabbed his arm and dragged him toward the nearest empty hall. He hadn't stopped shouting, though he compiled with her movement. "You're the only woman I want. How many times do I need to say it? I'll do whatever the hell you want."

"I want--" She couldn't finish. Gasping against the force of the sob rising like a tsunami inside her throat, she tried again a few seconds later. "I don't want...you...*chained*...to me." Tears flooded over her cheeks without restraint.

"What?"

She could see how much he hated seeing her cry. He had that devastated look on his face, as if he wanted to reach for her but knew she wouldn't let him right now.

Sapphire drew in a deep breath, trying to calm herself. "When you first told me you loved me, you said we're all in cages. We start building them out of the womb. When you asked me to marry you, you said you wanted to be shackled to me. Legally. But that's the problem. I want to be *free* to love you. I want you to know you're free with me, too, that we chose each other, not out of obligation or bondage. That no one else would do for either of us. But you're not free, Deck. You're not free of anything. You won't let yourself be unshackled by all the pain you've ever felt in your entire life. It's all still inside you, and you push it down deep, over and over, burying it, drowning it in booze, but it never goes away because you're chained to it. You believe you don't deserve what other people have as if they're entitled to it, but somehow you're exempt from the same basic human rights. I know who made you feel that way, too. Your mother made you think that only a cage and chains would help you keep what you want more than anything."

"Ask yourself what else is holding you to me, babe. Ask yourself that. You married me. Legally."

"I love you," she said in a whisper, cruelly stunned that he could doubt how much she loved him--that she loved him freely, of her own will, without his damn cage or chains, even the legality of their wedding ceremony.

Feeling faint, she spun back out into the ballroom, searching the cavernous, shadowy space for her cousin. When she found and approached her, she'd wiped the traces of tears from her face, hoping the dark room would hide the rest. "Could you please tell everyone we had to go? I'm sorry I can't."

"Sapphire--"

Ignoring Cherish's shocked expression, she turned and rushed out of the reception hall. She found her car in the parking lot and, a heartbeat after she was inside, Deck slipped into the passenger's seat, startling her. "Don't walk out. Dammit, Sapphire, don't do that. I f@#d up, again, but it could've been avoided if we didn't come here. Why didn't you listen to me?"

"Because I knew this would happen, that..."

"Don't believe anything you're telling yourself. Believe you're all there is for me 'cause that's what matters in this. Not a damn other thing."

She started the car and drove, forcing back tears that could easily have choked and blinded her to everything. *Did I bring this on myself? Because I needed marriage--legal grounds for morality--so I could have sex with him without guilt? But I love him. I married him because I want to be with him. I wanted to love him freely. But he never saw it that way, did he? He's acting like he expected me to stop loving him, to walk out, all along. At the same time, he did everything to ensure I would, too. He knew he wouldn't be able to stop drinking, knew his way of dealing with pain is by saturating himself until he's numb, realized I couldn't be with a drunk who's relying on nothing but his own willpower to stay on the wagon.*

And I can't do this again.

Deck allowed her silence on the drive, but as soon as she pulled into his driveway he said, "Let's go inside. Let's talk. Let me prove myself to you."

"I need to be alone. A minute."

He looked at her--she felt his stare but didn't face him as the tears slid one by one down her face. After an agonizing instant, he got out, probably knowing exactly what she'd do when he did. She backed out of the driveway and raced away, glancing back to see the lack of surprise as he watched her flee.

Not aware where she was going, she somehow found herself at the Staten Island Mall, pulling into the empty slot next to her daughter's car. Only then did she shock herself with the realization that she'd done what she had a hundred times before, back when she was on the run from her ex-husband and her first thought when she even vaguely suspected he'd caught up to her had been to find her daughter, make sure she was safe. Yasmine had always been her lifeline, her main concern, the one she ran to when all her defenses were up. Falling back into her old habits jolted her. She'd almost forgotten in these safe years what her life had been like back then, terrified that someday her ex- would find them, what he would do to punish her, what would happen to her daughter if she couldn't protect her anymore. While it'd taken a long time to relax after she'd heard Coug was dead, it'd been years since this pure survival mode had kicked in.

Shaking violently, she gave herself over to the onslaught, hating how familiar the ugly emotions felt, that the situation with Deck could be anything like the trauma in that life-and-death one she'd endured for so many years.

She gasped when the passenger door opened and Yasmine slid in. "I thought this was your car. Mom, what in the world is going on?" she asked. "How long have you been here?"

For the first time, Sapphire noticed the time. It'd been more than an hour. She'd barely felt the time go by she'd been so caught up in her grief. Tears had come and gone, but something inside her told her that a protective barrier had gone up and encased every part of her being.

"You look terrible. What happened?" Yasmine demanded, urgently shaking her when Sapphire turned to her, unconsciously reaching out to her to make sure she was safe.

When she couldn't speak, Yasmine guessed, "Something happened with Deck. What?"

"He still loves her. He'll always love her. He did nothing but drink today to get through it." Sapphire took a deep breath to calm herself. "I'm sorry I came here. I don't even know why I did, honey. Just...I was on automatic. I'm fine. I'll be fine. Don't worry. I'll call you tomorrow at Cherish's. Okay? You should spend the night in her apartment. You'll be safe there. There's a doorman and..."

"Mom..."

"Go. I'm okay."

Yasmine obviously didn't want to, but she got out and moved around to stand with her friend, Michelle, who was obviously asking what was going on. Although she had no idea where she was going, Sapphire pulled out of the mall parking lot a moment later, scolding herself for having come, for scaring her daughter. Any danger in this situation was restricted to her own treacherous heart.

Chapter 26

Decker looked down at his phone, wishing he'd see on the screen that it was Sapphire calling him but instinctively knowing it wouldn't be. Instead, Yasmine's phone number was there. After Sapphire took off, he'd acknowledged that he didn't have the strength to go into the house without her, wait her out. He needed to distract himself. A part of him had thought about drinking himself blind at Knuckleheads once he arrived there. He was already halfway there today as it was.

Instead, he'd thrown his empty flask in a corner of the garage before he'd gotten in his car at the house. Since Sapphire had caught on that he'd been filling the thing with his secret booze stash in the garage--out of sight, out of the front of his mind anyway--from the time they got out of the shower that morning, he hadn't had a sip. But he'd already gone through almost a full bottle by that point, every time he was away from her. If their boss found out the truth, Duff would kick his ass. Decker expected that he'd be at the bar, like he usually was on a Saturday night. Bev would follow the ass-kicking with a head-cuff to make sure he woke up.

Upon arriving and greeting them, he'd said he was there to work and he walked away without elaborating. No surprise, the staff hadn't stopped looking at him strangely from the moment he went behind the bar and poured himself strong, hot coffee. He'd made his rounds, draining the coffee and getting another cup when his phone had started vibrating in his pocket.

"Where are you?" Yasmine demanded without any preface when he answered her call because he couldn't *not* answer. A part of him was afraid something had happened to Sapphire. She shouldn't have been driving in her state. *I'm such an a@#hole. I wasn't thinking, haven't been at all today, and that's the whole reason for everything.*

"Knuckleheads--" he started.

She didn't give him the chance to ask about her mother. "Stay there." She hung up.

Twenty minutes later, Yasmine walked in the bar and every SOB in the place seemed to stop whatever he was doing and stare. If any female didn't belong in a rough biker bar, it was Sapphire's daughter. She was young and sweet and looked like she belonged on the red carpet or the cover of *Teen Vogue*, not a place where drunks would only lust after her as little more than a hot piece of jailbait tail.

Decker hustled her into Duff's office. "What's going on?" he asked.

"What did you do to my mother?" she demanded, looking

furious--another thing that didn't fit her. She put her hands on her hips.

"What do you mean? Did you see her?"

"Yes. Just like when we were on the run from my dad. She always comes to me first."

Decker stared at her without comprehension. Though he'd sobered up some, he didn't feel capable of understanding what she was hinting at none too subtly.

"My dad?" she said pointedly, as if her meaning was obvious. "We were on the run from him for the first how many years of my life? Surely Mom told you. And, whenever she felt like he was getting close, she'd run to me. She'd come to me first. She's on automatic now, just like she was then. And that's bad. She hasn't been like that for years. She was almost healed from it. So what did you do? I know you did something because she says you're still in love with Roxanne Hart and you've spent the whole day getting smashed."

Without consciously thinking about the movement, Decker sank heavily on the sofa he and Sapphire had made love on for months before they admitted out loud what they wanted was more than a nightly tryst. After he set down the coffee mug, he ran his hands through his hair.

"Do you still love her? Roxanne?" Yasmine repeated with determination, intent on getting her answer.

"No. I... Hell, okay, I love her. I wish I didn't. But...it's not valid it anymore. It's not what I want. It was never..." He was confusing himself, and he didn't want Sapphire's daughter to be confused about his feelings for her mother. "No. I love your mom. She's all I want. She's everything I ever wanted and more. More than I would've let myself hope for."

For a long moment, Yasmine stared at him as if she had a built-in lie detector and she was using it full-force on him. Then she eased back slightly. "Honestly?"

"Honestly. Look, I just didn't wanna go to that damn wedding. You say your mom's on instinct. Well, whenever I get too close to...the past...I get the same way. Instinct kicks in and...I can't control how I handle it. But I know I have to deal with that. I can't keep doing this. Not if I wanna hold on to your mom."

"So you knew this would happen? Why did you go along to the wedding then?"

"Because if I didn't, I knew Sapphire would assume the worse. Assume exactly what she did."

Yasmine let out a deep sigh of frustration. "Only now she's utterly convinced of it."

"Something like that."

She came over and sat next to him on the sofa. "All right. I believe you. I think you do love her. It's just not easy to get over the things we've felt in the past, even when we genuinely want to."

"You believe me?"

She glanced at him, nodding her head with a very small smile. "If I didn't, you'd be in big trouble."

Decker couldn't help laughing. "Didn't foresee you going into 'protective of Mom' mode."

"Because I give her grief?" Yasmine shrugged. "I'm a teenager. It's my job. She really is way too protective of me. She'd have me locked in a play yard still if I didn't stand up for myself. But...she's my mom. She's been through a lot, and her biggest problem is she has no confidence at all. She always second-guesses herself. She's tough as nails and fragile as glass. As mad as that makes me sometimes…it's kind of beautiful, too."

Decker sighed. "That sums her up. You're a lot like her, kiddo." He slumped onto the back of the couch. "What the hell am I gonna do?"

"You already know," Yasmine said in that cool, collected tone that displayed the kind of self-assuredness Sapphire didn't possess. "Find her. Love her. Put her first. Don't lie to her just because you think the truth isn't what she wants to hear. Especially, don't cover up the fact that you have a drinking problem, Deck. You're not fooling anyone. You know?"

Even as he felt exposed and embarrassed, defensive, he knew he had to stop denying the obvious truth he'd let himself believe no one would ever realize if he didn't want them to.

"You sure can't fool her when it comes to that. She's the queen of knowing when someone's drunk."

Decker snorted. "I don't think I was trying to fool her. Or even hide it. I just didn't…don't…" He glanced at her, mortification washing over him. "…wanna admit it to myself."

He'd seen the truth about himself today when Sapphire had hurled that *"When did you start? Before breakfast?"* missile at him. When he'd made a show of putting those boxes out on the porch for Duff to haul away, he'd been fully aware he should tell Sapphire about the unopened bottles in his garage. But he hadn't. He hadn't wanted to think about them, not until this morning when he'd gone in there while Sapphire was getting ready for the wedding. He'd filled his flask almost subconsciously--also guzzled a quarter of the brand new bottle straight from the tap. He'd been in some kind of trance. Covered up the stink with plenty of coffee he'd chased the booze with. Before he and Sapphire had even left for the wedding and he'd seduced her--half-bombed--telling her all the things he wanted her to know before the s@#t hit the fan, just like he'd known it would, he'd been drunk out of his skull, most of that bottle in the garage drained, the second calling out to him like a beacon.

When Sapphire said those words to him in the reception hall, he'd seen things about himself he hadn't let himself face before. For the past two months, since Sapphire had almost been raped by a Knuckleheads client and he'd vowed to be the one to keep her safe from that moment on, he'd gone cold turkey for the most part. But he was still sneaking, hiding, never letting himself really think about what he was doing when he stole swills from the bottle in his cupboard by the sink, putting it out of his head the instant the dirty deed was done. He was good at concealing his own secret sins so he didn't have to consider them deeply.

I'm an alcoholic, a drunk. Sapphire said it straight, the plain and ugly, today. I know it. And I sure as hell can't handle this problem on my own anymore. I never could.

The office door opened, and Duff rolled in. Even as Yasmine got up to hug him, he was gently demanding to know what she was doing there. The bar was no place for a young, pretty girl like her. "And while we're on the subject of what's not right, why the hell you here, Decker? You're s'pposed to be on your honeymoon. If you're bored already, you can't be doin' her right. Where's Sapphire? Maybe she'd be smart to, but I can't believe she's come to her senses over you so quick."

"Where did you last see her?" Decker asked Yasmine.

"The mall. Hold on." She took out her phone and dialed her mother. Sapphire would answer her daughter's call and question about where she was without a fight. While Yasmine did that, Decker turned to Duff. "You need to start looking for replacements."

An ugly look crossed the old man's grizzled, hair-covered face. But, a second later, he grimaced and nodded. "Saw that comin'."

Even if Decker couldn't talk Sapphire out of staying with him, he'd try to talk her into going to work for her cousin immediately. She needed to get out of this place and give herself the chance to have a normal life.

I want the same for myself.

"She went to your house," Yasmine said when she'd hung up.

Decker looked at her quizzically. "Seriously?" He hadn't expected that move. "Is she okay?"

"I don't know. But she's safe. Maybe you should go to her now."

Duff waved him away as soon as Decker started to make excuses about not working tonight after all. Decker led Yasmine out of the bar and made sure she got into her car safely. "I'll have your mom call you. Where you gonna be?"

"Aunt Cherish and Uncle Ty are staying on Jamie's yacht. So I have their apartment all to myself."

"Is that safe?"

"There's a doorman. I'll be safer than at our old apartment."

He waited until she left the parking lot before getting into his own car and going home. The front door was open with the screen door in place, and Sapphire didn't immediately tell him to get out when he entered the living room. Thank God she wasn't crying, though she looked pale, utterly delicate, her eyes scoured red. Without waiting, knowing it was the only shot he had, he knelt in front of her and said the words she needed to hear because they were truth: "I'm an alcoholic. I know it. I know I need help. I can't do it myself. Never could."

"Are you just saying what I want to hear?"

"No. You were right. You have been all along. I didn't wanna admit I couldn't handle the problem on my own. But I realized the truth about myself when you looked into my eyes in the reception hall and knew in a second I was wasted. I faced hard facts then."

"Somehow downing all but the dregs of a whole bottle of whiskey today didn't tell you that? I found it, and the brand new one, in the garage. I dumped them both out." Nothing like an apology entered her expression.

"Good. My flask?"

"Empty and in the garbage."

He deserved blows instead of cut-and-dried statements. "I can't do anything to convince you I'm being honest this time. But I know you're right about everything. I'm one seriously f@#d-up bastard. But even if I love Rox and I probably always will, I'm not *in* love with her anymore. That's the God's honest truth, Sapphire. You're the one person in my life that's ever been real. I've never wanted to be with anybody the way I do you. I wish I could be a good man for you. I wish I could be who you deserve."

She sat up, leaning toward him. "You *can*. You *are*. I love you,

Deck. I've never loved another man the way I do you. I'm stupid over you. I see it myself, but I can't help it. Why can't you let me love you instead of deliberately making me afraid to love you, afraid you're like my ex-husband and will someday turn on me?"

"I'll never do that. God...listen to me. I promise I won't. I want your love more than anything. You're not my personal property. You're the love of my life, the most precious part of my life. I would never hurt you. I'd kill myself before I did. Believe me."

She swallowed but offered him the balm of reassurance he needed even if he didn't deserve it. "I believe you, Deck."

He took her hand and pressed it to his mouth. "I don't know why I can't let myself take what I want. But...don't give up on me, babe. I can't live without you."

"You aren't making it easy not to just give up."

"I know. I probably never will make it easy on you. But I'll go to the AA meetings. If you wanna come along to make sure I do go...I want you to 'cause I don't trust myself. I'll talk to you and a sponsor if I feel like drinking again. From now on, I'll try my damndest not to be an a@#hole you doubt and can't trust."

When she leaned forward again almost helplessly, her expression soft, he took a chance and reached for her. He put his arms around her waist and laid his head on her lap. "I love you."

"Do you really, Deck?" she asked shakily. "Do you love me most? Can you?"

He looked up at her. "If this isn't real love, then it doesn't exist. It's all a cosmic joke I don't want any part of 'cause this one would be on me, me personally."

"How can I ever know for sure?" she asked, her hands cradling his head. "How can I know anything's changed until it happens again? How can I trust it won't happen again?"

"You shouldn't. But I'm asking you to anyway--not contingent on you loving me, babe, 'cause you've already given me more chances than any man deserves. It's not proof, and I know you won't take it like that, but living without Rox...that was a given. I always accepted someday I'd have to. And I got by. Drank myself into a hole, yeah. But I didn't think about ending it all 'cause I told myself I never had her in the first place so nothing had changed, you know? But losing you...I couldn't survive it. I wouldn't want to. There's nothing for me without you. I don't wanna use that to keep you with me, 'cause you're afraid I'll kill myself if you do what you gotta do and walk away from me. I won't. But any part of me that was alive won't exist anymore if you go. I never loved anybody like that before. I want you to know there's a difference."

"Promise you won't hurt yourself if we ever break up."

"All right. I promise."

"You know I don't like it when you talk like that. Your mother made you feel like you weren't worth anything. And maybe, without intending to at all, Roxanne also made you feel that way. But you are worthy, Deck. Even if we're not together, you're worth something and I do believe you're a good man. I just think you've spent too many years of your life trying to cope in all the wrong ways, trying to handle everything yourself. But you can't help yourself in these areas. You need someone else to help you. You need to let someone else step in and help you."

"You?"

"If you'll let me, but you may need more help than I can give you. I love you, even if I'm scared about the future. I'd be miserable without you, too."

Decker couldn't help smiling. She loved him, maybe stupidly, but it was all he'd ever need. He had the feeling she could heal him when nothing and no one else could.

Dragging himself up beside her on the couch, he kissed her gently, seeking her permission. She wrapped her arms around him, holding him so tightly, he ran out of air in a second. He closed his eyes and breathed, letting her guide him so their heartbeats and breathing synched.

"Speaking of miserable, let's quit our jobs," he spoke in a low voice. "Let's find some semblance a better life. Anything's gotta be better than working in a bar."

She smiled, clearly onboard with his suggestion. "Poor Duff. But deep down I think he'll be glad, too."

Promises in the Dark by Karen Wiesner

Chapter 27

A month and a half later, she and Deck were set up in their new jobs and gradually adjusting to an entirely new schedule. After decades of being night owls, working the night shift, neither of them had fared well at first and things had been more than a little crazy and exhausting while they're bodies rebelled. She'd been grateful for how her cousin eased her into the variety of jobs she'd be doing at the flower shop, not forcing her to overtax her already strained brain those first few weeks of getting used to an alien lifestyle that she eventually found she preferred. Deck also liked his job at Bandoleer Babies as head of security a lot better, though she knew he was bored a lot. He rarely had anything tougher to handle than scheduling the weekly shifts for his team. "Better class of people, good benefits, and a normal life," he said often. She knew he shared her deepest contentment--now that their lives didn't revolve around their jobs, they could focus on what they were both living for: family, Yasmine, each other.

Life was nearly perfect, she reflected on a Wednesday afternoon. Wednesdays were the days of the week that all of Cherish's girlfriends came to the flower shop for lunch--Darlene (who worked there and brought her new baby to work with her each day), Diane Lund, Savvy Foxx, and Roxanne Dubois. Getting used to Roxanne's frequent presence had been part of the life alteration Sapphire had gone through. Instinctively, she'd fought anything that put her in contact with the woman who'd been in competition for Deck's affection, but her cousin's friendship with the former supermodel had made exposure a certainty. Against her will, she'd discovered Roxanne was the kind of person she couldn't hate, even on principle. She liked her too much, even admired her considering the battle she'd fought against cancer and won, and Deck seemed to be getting used to the frequent contact because Cherish and Ty and their closest friends got together often and she and Deck were now invited as a rule. She started to accept that she and Deck couldn't have stumbled upon better companions in life. They were embraced and treated so well by their new friends, she could only feel grateful to be included in such a loving group.

Cherish knocked on the employee bathroom door at the flower shop during the extra-long Wednesday lunch break and called, "Are you all right, honey? You've been in there a long time."

Sapphire opened the door to let her in, then she turned back to the timer and pregnancy test set up on the sink. Her cousin glanced from the stick to her and said, "Whoa."

Sapphire laughed at the efficient summary. "Yeah."

"Were you two trying?"

Unable to help herself, she laughed again. "No. The past month and a half has been crazy. Trying to change our schedules from night to day has literally been a night and day operation. In the process, I forgot birth control more often than I remembered. And we've been...well, pretty much like we were when we first got together. Can't keep our hands off each other."

"How do you think he'll react?" Cherish asked, just as the timer went off.

They both moved forward. Sapphire felt no surprise at all about the outcome. She'd known she was pregnant, and not simply because she'd missed her period. She remembered what her body had been like when she was pregnant with Yasmine.

"Everything's been so perfect between us. I don't want anything to upset the balance, shake up the glass globe." *I don't want to believe we've been biding our time, afraid of the world and any conflict that could separate us again. Are we strong enough to handle the heavy stuff? Maybe we haven't wanted to find out for sure.*

They'd attended AA meetings together on Wednesday nights ever since he promised to get help for his alcoholism. He'd also gotten a sponsor, Ted. Though he was older than Deck by a good twenty years and had a busy life, he made time to come over to the house every Friday night for dinner so he and Deck could 'connect'. Deck hadn't said the words per se--probably because he'd never experience the like--but she believed he saw Ted as a father figure. He respected and trusted him and a part of him was even coming to rely on him. Ted seemed to encourage that, and Sapphire had seen the pride in the older man's eyes when he looked at Deck. That, most of all, she suspected was something he'd need all his life and couldn't refuse no matter how he'd kept himself from being vulnerable to anyone in the past.

"Do you think Decker might not want this?" Cherish asked gently.

"I honestly don't know. And I don't know what I feel about it either. My daughter is almost all grown up. And now I'm starting over."

"You're young, honey. There's not a reason in the world you can't have more children. Deck's good with Yasmine. Maybe he's awkward with smaller children..."

Sapphire had seen him with the babies and toddlers belonging to their new group of friends. The kids crawled all over him like he was a tree. He didn't mind, but, as Cherish had said, he wasn't natural around children. His own... "He'll be a good father," she said softly.

"And you're an amazing mother."

"Thank you."

Cherish hugged her. "I wasn't going to say anything. Ty and I are keeping it a secret until we've passed the first trimester, but we're pregnant, too. We might end up with new babies around the same time, depending on how far along you are."

Sapphire felt tears of joy in her eyes. "Is Ty handling it all right? He hasn't had an easy life either."

"No, he hasn't. But he's determined not to be anything like his own father. We're both happy. We're ready for this."

"I'm thrilled for you. You deserve every happiness."

"So do you."

After another long hug, Sapphire cleaned up the pregnancy

test and the sink, washed her hands, then she went out so Roxanne could show them the photographs she and Jamie had gotten of the baby they were adopting from a Third World country. Because of her cancer, she couldn't have children of her own, but she'd wanted a baby for as long as she could remember.

Feeling emotional and uncertain of herself, Sapphire got back to work, ringing up orders at one of the cash registers. Before Deck picked her up at five-thirty, as he did almost every day, Yasmine called and said she and Lawrence were staying late at school for a Mensa meeting, then having dinner with the group after that. Lawrence was in Yasmine's class and his family had moved to Staten Island over the summer. He was by far the geekiest guy her daughter had ever dated, but Sapphire had loved him from the first meeting. He was so clumsy and sweet and shy, and he couldn't seem to get over the fact that a gorgeous, popular girl like Yasmine had even noticed him. Despite that he wasn't football-star gorgeous, he was as adorable as Yasmine gushed that he was on practically a daily basis.

"That's fine. Don't be too late though."

"I won't."

"Yasmine?" Sapphire hadn't realized she planned to say anything until the words were out. "I'm pregnant."

"What? Whoa, Mom."

"I'm sorry. I shouldn't have said it like that. My head hasn't exactly been clear for the last few weeks."

"I guess now we know why. You're sure?"

"Yes. I'm sure, honey. What do you think?"

"Did you tell Deck yet?"

"No. I... Maybe I should have told him first."

"I don't know about that. He'll be floored. You probably guessed I'd recover quicker."

Sapphire chuckled. "He will be. So you're okay about this?"

"It's weird, but you're still young, Mom. Why shouldn't you have another baby while you still can? I love babies."

"You'll be the best big sister."

"I will, won't I?"

Sapphire laughed.

"Are you telling Deck tonight?"

"I suppose I should."

"Good. Just do it. It'll be harder the longer you wait. You can hold off on telling Grandma for a while though. I give you permission."

Sapphire laughed out loud again. "You're a wise woman, Yasmine. I'll see you tonight."

She'd seen Deck come through the front door of the floor shop and hung up before he reached her and pulled her in for a long kiss and an even longer hug. She could tell immediately something was up. "What is it?" she asked while they walked to the car.

"Got a call while I was at work today. My mom is dead. ODed. No surprise. I had to leave work, ID the body."

Sapphire gasped, turning to clutch at him. "Oh, Deck, how horrible. That couldn't have been easy."

"There are things that need to be done."

While his voice wasn't cold, it was almost too calm. He opened the passenger door and she slid inside. *The thing I was waiting for--the catalyst to upset the balance--it's here. This could be it. If he does what he always has and pushes me out, tries to deal with his pain on his own, in his old way, we'll be right back where we started.*

"Deck, let me help you, baby. Let me be there for you," she begged once he was behind the steering wheel.

He shrugged. "I can handle it. There's not a lot to do--"

She swallowed as tears filled her eyes. "Let me share this with you."

He looked at her as if surprised by her reaction.

"Please, Deck."

He took a deep breath. She saw the acknowledgement of what they both knew in his expression. This was where he'd gone wrong in the past. Letting someone help him, even when he desperately needed it, was a foreign concept to him. But he nodded. "Okay." He hugged her when she initiated, clasping her tighter when she tried to back up an inch.

"Talk to me. Let me be with you through everything. Don't try to be strong so you don't have to admit you feel anything."

She couldn't breathe when his hold on her became like a vice grip. "I need you, Sapphire. I don't know what the hell I'd do without you."

"You don't ever need to find out. Was it...awful...at the mortuary?"

"Hell, yeah. Didn't...expect that. But I wasn't surprised either. Couldn't be."

"I wish you'd called me."

He didn't like the idea. He didn't need to say that for her to realize it. But he kissed her gratefully. "Come on, let's go home."

The moment for telling him about the pregnancy didn't seem

right, given what'd happened. At home, she made dinner, and Ted came though it wasn't his usual night. Unbelievably, Deck had called him while she was cooking and told him about his mother's death. Either Deck had asked him or Ted realized this was a hard situation he'd need help staying away from his old painkillers in.

Yasmine got home at nine, breezing through to say hi to everyone and saying she had to get to her homework right away. The look in her eyes when she faced Sapphire was obvious. She wanted to know if she'd talked to Deck about her condition. Very subtly, she shook her head and Yasmine gave her a pointed jab of her finger with a raised eyebrow.

As usual on nights Ted was there, Sapphire went to bed early. She now knew why she'd started being tired all the time all over again lately. But she always liked to give Ted and Deck time to talk one-on-one. Tonight, maybe even more. This would be so hard for her husband--to talk about what he was feeling, to not let the pain drive him toward alcohol.

Also per usual, Deck came in much later and woke her with his hands all over her. They made love slowly, and the knowledge that she was pregnant made her even more clingy and desperate to show him how much he meant to her.

"Love you," he murmured. "You're so incredible, babe."

"I love you," she returned, hearing his sleepiness, but somehow she was wide awake now. Her moment had come. "Deck, I need to tell you something and I'm not sure how you'll feel about it. Especially today. Too much happened today."

"Just say it," he said, sounding instantly wary. In the low lamplight she kept on so the room wouldn't be dark when he came in and he left on because he wanted to look at her while they made love, he also appeared uncertain about what she might say to him.

"I'm pregnant. We can't be too surprised about that, given how many times I forgot to take my birth control in the last month and a half. But..." She swallowed as the look of panic started to replace his wariness with a swiftness that made her even more worried. "I took a home pregnancy test at work today, and it came up positive, like I knew it would."

"You didn't have your period this month," he realized as if for the first time.

They both noticed when she had it, since they had to refrain for almost a week to accommodate the cycle.

"Tell me what you're thinking, Deck. Are you sad, mad...happy? I know you'll be a good father. Even if you think you won't be, I know you will with our baby."

"Hell, babe, I'm scared as crap. Me? A father? Easy to accept *you* as a mother..."

"I was so scared when I found out I was pregnant with Yasmine. I was only fifteen. And I knew Coug would be a horrible father. But I could feel her coming to life inside me, and it was the most incredible experience I ever had. The whole pregnancy, I was amazed. I was in love with her long before she was born. She was the best thing that ever happened to me until I met you."

"I don't have a clue how to be a father. A parent."

"No one does," she said on a light laugh. "I certainly didn't. It's not something you can prepare for--the lack of knowledge about how or how much you're going to love that tiny life you created, well, there's no way to study up for that or comprehend it. I'm happy, Deck. I want to have your baby. I want to do this together."

Surprising her, tenderness filled his expression. "If anything happened to you, Sapphire, I couldn't handle it."

"Nothing will. I'm healthy. We'll have a healthy baby."

He kissed her, turning her on her back, and asked, "You're happy? Really?"

"Yes. Are you?"

He looked down at her body, then he put a gentle hand on her flat stomach. There was a fascination in the way he stroked what might have been right above a baby's head. When he glanced up at her, she gasped at the sight of tears in his eyes. Hope swelled inside her at what she could only believe was the best possible future for them.

Epilogue

Eight months later

They'd had a long night. Sapphire's water had broken in the early hours of morning, a Saturday, and, eight hours later, they were both so tired, Decker had no idea how they'd get through the rest of labor. She'd barely started. The contractions the doctor had insisted would begin rapidly once she applied something called "prostaglandin gel" (Decker had no clue what that was) didn't do anything. The contractions weren't coming, but the baby couldn't stay inside her forever, safely, without the protection of the amniotic fluid that'd poured all over the floor at Sapphire's feet hours before breakfast.

At one point or another, all of their friends had come for a short time, including Cherish, but she was at the end of her own pregnancy (apparently Sapphire had been further along in hers) and she tired quickly. Sapphire had been the one who insisted she go home and get some rest. She could come back once Sapphire and Decker's baby was born.

Decker had vowed he wasn't going to gravitate toward Roxanne and Dubois even though they'd become a part of the overall group in the last nine months, but he supposed there'd been no way to prevent it. Sapphire's cousin and her husband were important to her, grew important to him and not simply to make his wife happy, and their friends had become his and Sapphire's. Rox was still in remission and they had their baby, adopted from Nepal, joining everyone else in the group with their ever-growing passel of kids. Another of the couples (Mikey and Diane) had moved to Staten Island, into a little house only a few blocks away from Sapphire and Decker, and they were preparing their new home for a second child.

Almost in the back of his mind, Decker had come to terms with the fact that he'd probably always love Rox, but it didn't feel the same anymore. How could it? Sapphire was his whole life. Sometimes he felt like his love for her would eclipse the sun. Nothing could compare with it. Crazy as it was, he felt friendship love for Rox now--all it ever was or should have been--and lately he even felt that for Dubois. Ty's friends had become his. Friends and brothers. Jace, Brett, Mikey--yes, Rox's husband. All was as it felt it should be...until Sapphire's water broke that morning. Nothing felt right after that.

Yasmine had been with them the whole time, and, between the three of them, they'd had almost no sleep. When the gel failed to produce the results her doctor expected, Sapphire had been given a medication through her IV to induce labor. Barely twenty minutes after that, contractions had started, so hard, she all but passed out between them. Decker felt sick, watching her in so much pain without the rest she needed to handle it.

The months he'd had to get used to the idea of being a father had prepared him for this, supposedly. They'd gone to classes, and he realized now he'd believed everything would go smoothly, by the book. Sapphire seemed convinced of the same. She'd said she had no trouble giving birth to Yasmine. And she made everything look so easy, he guessed he'd wanted to believe the best because it was easiest, less worrisome. What he'd most gotten used to and what made him feel so tender and vulnerable was the idea of the woman he loved carrying and holding their child. In ways, he'd wanted this baby *through* her, rather than for himself. In the insane hours that passed, he acknowledged that was just another of his defense mechanisms, keeping himself from investing too much in all he wanted. He'd marveled at her strength for months, aware he didn't possess the same. She and the baby had been so healthy during this time. *She's been my strength since I met her more than a decade ago. She got me through so much in this time, including my mom's death. How did I ever live without her?*

Although he'd never been close to his mother, her memorial had been hard for him. Almost no one else came other than Decker and Sapphire's friends, Ted, Duff and Bev. They'd all said they were there for him--they didn't know his mom personally, and frankly what they knew of her wasn't a compelling reason for them to attend. They did it for him. That meant something to him. They and Sapphire had, quite simply, gotten him through something he would have boozed his way through in the past--and put himself into a coma over.

He'd asked himself a million times why it was so hard for him. Ted had asked him but told him he didn't have to say the words out loud. All he had to do was find the answer inside himself. Decker didn't know where to look for something that elusive. He'd never had anything even vaguely resembling affection for the woman-- and she'd barely acknowledged his existence other than when she needed something from him, money for drugs, which he'd never once given her. He'd never been given anything that could be twisted and mangled into a believable form of love from her either.

At the sparsely attended memorial, a woman who looked as strung out as his mother always had been came to him after viewing the casket for a long time. She'd asked if he was William and, without waiting for his answer, said, "She had eyes like yours. Or she did when she was healthy."

"She was never healthy."

"No, you never saw her healthy, did you?"

Wordlessly, she'd handed him an envelope addressed to him. "She wrote this years ago and asked me to make sure you got it if anything ever happened to her. I was her best friend. Maybe her only."

When Decker, much later, had the courage to open it with Sapphire sitting right next to him, he'd found a short letter that said only "I'm sorry, William." He'd never be entirely sure what she'd been sorry for, sorry enough to compel her to write this years before her death and make sure was placed into his hands if something happened to her, but Sapphire half convinced him his old lady was sorry she hadn't been a better mother to him. She must have known she'd never be one either. He remembered all the times she'd want to see him, end up begging him to give her money for her next fix during the visit, he refused. A few hours later, she'd call. He wouldn't answer. She'd leave the same message every time in his voicemail box. "I'm sorry, William."

That was when Decker figured out why his mother's death was so hard on him. He'd never wanted her to be sorry. He'd wanted her to love him. Maybe she had in the only way she could, but it'd never been enough. Couldn't be. And now she was gone. His quest for what he couldn't have and always wanted from his mother also had to end. But not neatly. Raggedly. Bloodily. He'd remembered an old song that he'd listened to the night of her funeral. *Mama will make your nightmares come true, put her fears into you. Hush little baby, don't you cry...*

Gently wiping Sapphire's sweaty face with a cool cloth, he leaned down to kiss her forehead, murmuring how good she was doing. But then another contraction gripped her and everything they'd learned about how to handle this situation flew from his mind. Tears leaked out of her eyes as she fought the force that seemed intent on ripping her in two. By the time she collapsed back, she had no energy whatsoever and Decker wanted to tell the medical staff to stop this, help her, do something. Instead, the doctor said to the nurse, "The uterus is contracting too quickly. The baby is stressed. I don't see any point in prolonging this further. Let's prep for a C-section."

Decker and Yasmine looked at each other in shock. "What's going on?" he demanded.

The explanation that followed didn't make a lot of sense to two people who weren't in the medical field, and, not surprisingly, Yasmine rushed to her mother's side, looking as protective as she had been of her all through her pregnancy. Their relationship had changed during the time--for the better. Yasmine seemed to see her mother as fragile, and Decker couldn't deny she was, despite her core strength. He'd been grateful for Yasmine, and they'd bonded during the time. Maybe he didn't understand what a "stepfather" was supposed to be like, what to do, but they'd become friends, close. He liked her as much as she liked him, and they'd even spent time together when Sapphire didn't join them (Lawrence usually in company, too) and enjoyed the interactions.

During one of their Friday night connections, Ted had told him about his regrets as a father. He'd been a drinker on the way to becoming a drunk when his kids were small. By the time they were in high school, they hated him, their mother had thrown him out, and he'd lost everything that mattered to him when the booze ran out and he found himself on the street, sober for the first time in decades and hurting. Even years later, when Ted cleaned up his act, became a hard worker, respectable, stringent teetotaler, and he'd remarried and started another family, his first kids wouldn't give him the time of day. He didn't blame them. He insisted he didn't deserve a second chance--he'd had far more than two; had gotten his limit. "That's what I regret most. Losing the only people who'd loved me even when I was a drunk, until they couldn't love me anymore and respect themselves. Cherish your family, Decker, your beautiful wife, her daughter, that baby on the way. Those are your treasures. Nothing else matters, especially the worst motherf@#r of all--the booze. When that matters more, matters at all, you might as well chuck this life altogether."

Decker had asked himself after that night if he loved Yasmine like a daughter and he had no basis to answer the question. What did he know about being a parent? Of even *having* parents? Nothing. The closest thing he'd had to a father was Ted, who'd insisted he'd make a "helluva" dad, just being the man he was. But the visceral answer was yes. He loved Yasmine. He even loved Lawrence. He'd just been too afraid to love the baby Sapphire was carrying all these months because that was an investment, a big one, one that might steal the person who meant the most to him away.

Watching the flurry of activity that soon didn't include either of them, Yasmine drifted over to him and put herself in his arms. He was surprised at the hug they shared--this wasn't something they'd done before, for longer than a few seconds. "She ll be okay, right?" the teenager asked tearfully.

"She'll be okay," Decker said, not even sure himself and worried to the point of feeling like he might go insane before all this was over.

Finally, they rolled Sapphire out of the room. She wasn't conscious enough to respond to either of their words and last kisses. Not long later, the nurse returned and handed Decker scrubs.

"I can go in with her?"

"Yes, of course. You can get ready while she's prepped for the C-Section."

He rushed into the bathroom and changed in seconds. When

he emerged, Yasmine begged, "Take care of my mom."

He assured her without confidence that he could do anything of the kind. The rest went so fast, he hardly processed the events before the baby was in his arms, a boy so tiny that he might have been a doll made for a little girl to play with. Decker could hold his head and part of his body in the palm of one hand. He stared at the shockingly content baby, swaddled in a thin blanket, feeling tears scald his overtired eyes. *I have a son. Sapphire and I made a baby together, and he's beautiful. He's perfect.* "How'm I gonna take care of you, buddy?" he asked in a whisper.

Sapphire turned to look at them, her face lined, dark with fatigue, but she was smiling, too. She reached to hold their baby's tiny hand. "We'll love him. We'll make sure he knows every day of his life how much he's loved and wanted. We'll never have to be sorry for anything because we'll do it right. No regrets."

The very things I never knew, could never count on, until Sapphire changed everything with her beautiful magic and unconditional love. She transformed my whole love and gave me everything good, more than I could have ever asked for. And, because of her, I can give this baby, my son, everything I never had and always wanted and needed. He'll never lack for anything. No regrets.

"Shay David," Sapphire whispered. They'd chosen the names because they meant "gift, beloved".

Kissing their two small hands, he said, "I love you, baby."

"I love you." Her eyes were closing as if she couldn't stay awake for another second.

"Will she be okay?" Decker asked a few minutes later, accompanying the nurse as they rolled the baby in a plastic crib back to Sapphire's room.

The nurse smiled reassuringly. "She'll be fine. She'll be back with you in no time."

Yasmine wasn't relieved until the nurse assured her of the same thing and, not long later, Decker was sitting in a chair holding his son again and Yasmine was crying as she looked down at them. "He's so perfect. Welcome to the world, Shay. I'm your big sister, and I already love you."

He'd never seen such a content baby. He hadn't heard Shay cry at all, beyond a tiny sound after he'd been out of Sapphire. He was told his son was in absolutely perfect health. All the love he'd been holding back, just in case, out of stupid fear came flooding over him as he looked down at his baby and cradled him against him. The unbidden thought came: *If, after I was born, my mom had been allowed to hold me like this...would everything have been different? She might have loved me instead of been sorry. My whole life might have been radically changed from just that...*

"Can I hold him?" Yasmine asked, pulling a chair up beside him. Very carefully, they made the exchange, both marveling with tears in their eyes over the mini fingers and toes, the thick black hair sticking up from his head. The full mouth that went through about fifty unlikely shapes in the minutes that followed as Shay moved, slowly stretching out and getting used to this new world. Getting comfortable with them, entrusting them with his safety.

When Sapphire was returned to them, she wanted to hold her baby no matter how exhausted she was. They waited until the nurse had her all set up, then got up as one and moved over to her bed with the newborn.

"He looks just like you," Sapphire said softly, looking up at Decker as she cradled the baby that, in her arms most of all, looked right at home. *This is the welcome Shay needs to feel that he's okay, he's wanted and loved, and all is right in this new, bright world as result.* He kissed her forehead, then his son's.

When he drew back, Sapphire glanced as Yasmine reaching for her hand. "You're tired, honey. Why don't you go home for a little while? Get some sleep. We could all use that."

"Are you sure?"

"Yes. Of course. You can come back later, after you've slept and recovered from the long day we had."

Yasmine agreed with this plan but hugged and kissed all of them multiple times before she could be persuaded to actually leave. The nurse came to take the baby for inspections, and Decker moved a chair next to Sapphire's bed. "You could go with Yasmine, honey. You look wiped out," she said.

He shook his head. "I'm not leaving this room until you and Shay are ready to leave, too."

She smiled, shaking her head, obviously knowing she couldn't convince him.

"I was scared I was gonna lose you, both of you," he admitted. "I'm sorry. I shouldn't have…" *Been afraid to love him. Love him as much as I already do. And this is just the beginning.*

"We're healthy. Everything is fine. We have a beautiful, healthy, perfect baby."

Decker's eyes filled. She made everything seem so easy. For her, love *was* that simple. "Thank you, baby. For all you went through. For giving me everything I've ever wanted, all I'll ever need."

"I love you. We're in this together," she reminded him. "We did this together."

Though he was exhausted, he couldn't keep his eyes off his son when he was brought back in the room and Sapphire nursed him for the first time. *This is a miracle, the kind of blessing I couldn't have imagined for myself on my best day. I should've known Sapphire would be the one to give me the ultimate gift.*

When Sapphire had nursed Shay thoroughly, her eyes were closing again helplessly. "I want to hold him while I sleep, but...I don't want to hurt him if I drop him. Will you take him?"

"Go to sleep, honey. You've earned it and then some."

Decker lifted their son in his hands, marveling at how natural his small body felt against him when he fell asleep soundlessly against his chest, his face as peaceful as a kitten full of milk. *He's comfortable, the way I don't think I've been my whole life until Sapphire. Like he belongs here and knows it. Like he's known it since before he was conceived.*

The next morning, Decker was still exhausted, but he'd slept a little, waking with a fierce ache to see Sapphire and their son. He'd never seen her so tired, but she was awake and smiled at him. The nurse had brought Shay, and Decker had waited impatiently until Sapphire had nursed him so, finally, he could hold the adorable elfin form against him again. He couldn't stop looking into the adorable face.

"I love watching you with him," Sapphire murmured, her face soft with obvious peace and joy. Her eyes slipped closed again.

Decker looked down again, watching Shay desperately try to

open his eyes and look around. Though the lights were as low as they could get, the little guy just blinked over and over, his sweet little mouth moving and moving as if he was trying that out, too. Decker couldn't help laughing quietly with tears in his eyes as he watched him.

The door opened slightly, and Roxanne's head popped in. Their eyes met. Decker stood, moving across the room and out into the hall where Jamie was waiting, his own son asleep in a slung against his chest.

"How's Sapphire?" Rox asked.

"Exhausted."

Proudly, Decker lifted Shay, holding him out within the protective cradle of his hand, and introduced them proudly to his son. Rox wept at the sight of him, murmuring, "He's beautiful. Oh, William. You and Sapphire have a son together."

His wet, joyful gaze met Jamie's, and he was reminded how this unlikely friend of his had admitted recently that Rox still worried about him sometimes like an overprotective mother--not as much as she used to, because any fool could see Sapphire was Decker's whole life, he loved her completely, and she loved him so well, he lacked for nothing.

Decker glanced at Rox and he saw exactly what he suspected was mirrored in his own eyes: Relief and an acknowledgement that they would both be all right. The worst had already happened and, if it came around again, at least they could fall back on their own up-close-and-personal knowledge that love wasn't a mere promise in the dark that would leave them shattered and broken, stumbling along on a purposeless journey filled with life-long regrets at every shadowy turn. They'd found truth and light, the kind of perfect love that drove out all fear and sorrow and would last forever.

No regrets.

Angelfire Series

Falling Star, Book 1
First Love, Book 2
Forever Man, Book 3
Only the Lonely, Book 4
Midnight Angel, Book 5
Shadows of the Night, Book 6
Promises in the Dark, Book 7

You can find ALL our books on our website at:
http://www.writers-exchange.com

You can find ALL Karen's books at:
http://www.writers-exchange.com/Karen-Wiesner/

Romance:
http://www.writers-exchange.com/category/genres/romance/

Series:
http://www.writers-exchange.com/category/genres/series/

About the Author

In addition to having been a popular writing reference instructor and writer, professional blurbologist and freelance editor, Karen Wiesner is the accomplished author of 156 titles published, which have been nominated/won for over a hundred and thirty awards. Karen's books cover such genres as women's fiction, romance, mystery/police procedural/cozy, suspense, thriller, paranormal, supernatural, futuristic, fantasy, science fiction, gothic, inspirational/Christian, horror, chick-lit, and action/adventure. She also writes children's books, poetry, and writing reference titles which have been repackaged in the 3D Fiction Fundamentals Collection. Karen will begin illustrating children's books starting in 2025.

Visit Karen's website and blog at https://karenwiesner.weebly.com/. Check out her Facebook author page here: http://www.facebook.com/KarenWiesnerAuthor.

If you enjoyed this author's book, then please place a review up at the site of purchase and any social media sites you frequent!

Promises in the Dark by Karen Wiesner

Wounded Warriors Series by Karen Wiesner
Women's Fiction/Contemporary Romance Novels

Publisher Book Page:
http://www.writers-exchange.com/wounded-warriors-series/

Women who have faced pain, loss and heartache.
They know the score and never back down.
Women who aren't afraid to love with all their passion and all their strength,
who risk everything for their own little piece of heaven...
Men who live their lives on the blade's edge. Knights in black armor.
The only thing more dangerous than crossing these men is loving them...

RELUCTANT HEARTS, Book 1
What's a man to do when he's seen too much of life's dark side and suddenly finds himself believing in flesh-and-blood angels who can heal with a single touch? What's a girl to do when she believes in true love but can't trust the eyes of her own heart? Fall in love...reluctantly?

WAITING FOR AN ECLIPSE, Book 2
Steve Thomas has a self-destructive wife, three kids, more guilt than one man can handle...and a chance at true love for the first time in his life—if only he can allow himself to take it.

MIRROR MIRROR, Book 3
Twenty-five years ago, Gwen Nicholson-Nelson was in a car accident that left behind a strange gift. She can see the future, and death, before it comes to pass. She also has a disturbing connection with another psychic like her who not only sees into others but manipulates and destroys. When her nemesis targets the man she loves, Gwen must act—before her vision of Dylan's death comes to pass.

WAYWARD ANGELS, Book 4
What do you get with a former wild man who's committed his path to the Lord and a woman who has absolutely nothing to lose? It's either a match made in heaven...or a sure-fire heartache.

UNTIL IT'S GONE, Book 5
You don't know what you've got...until it's gone. Mitch has been playing a dangerous game. The lines between black and white, good and evil, saint and sinner are all blurred. Just when he thinks the stakes can't get any higher, in steps the only woman who could ever hurt him and the only one who can heal him. In the space of a skipped heartbeat, he can't imagine having more to

gain...and more to lose.

WHITE RAINBOW, Book 6
Jessie Nelson has been telling herself she doesn't deserve or believe in second chances, especially when it comes to love...until her white rainbow appears in a corporate pirate who conquers her, heart and soul.

www.ingramcontent.com/pod-product-compliance
Ingram Content Group UK Ltd.
Pitfield, Milton Keynes, MK11 3LW, UK
UKHW030632130325
456214UK00005B/162